Santa In His Own Words

Santa In His Own Words

Matt Spaulding

Alfheim
Press

For believers everywhere

Preface

I suppose many of you reading this will wonder how I, someone who, until now, was of no public note, came to edit Santa Claus's memoir. I was just as surprised to find myself taking on the task as opposed to someone much more well-known and widely read. But who am I to question Santa's wisdom? Helping him with this task has been one of the greatest joys of my life.

Interestingly, I came to this project through the United States Postal Service. I am, in my daily life, a mail carrier. I have always loved Christmas since childhood. A great thing about my job is that I get to collect letters children send to Santa every year. Every day, the office receives letters and sets them aside, away from the rest of the outgoing mail. This always puzzled me because the pile would be gone from the night before. But Christmas at the Post Office is hectic, so I never had time to give it much thought. However, one night, when I was working late, I plopped down the Santa letters I had gathered during the day on the top of the pile and then walked away to finish up the rest of my tasks for the day. As I did, I discovered another Santa letter in my mailbag and turned around to bring it back to the pile, only to find a stranger in the building. I was pretty startled. Customers aren't allowed in the employee section, after all. I was even more surprised to find that this person was dressed oddly. He had on a long green overcoat, which was unbuttoned, under which he had on a silver shirt, green vest, and maroon pants. He wore a green trapper-style hat, ear flaps and all, on his head. He was also fairly short, somewhere around four feet.

"Uh," I said, taken aback and looking around for the other employees that I knew were still on the clock, "can I help you? You aren't supposed to be back here. Unless someone let you in? Are you here to pick up a package?"

"Oh, no," the man replied, "I'm here for these." He waved the Santa letters with a bright, cheerful smile, which caught my attention.

"Why are you here for the Santa letters?"

"To make sure they get to him, of course." This struck me as odd. As I mentioned earlier, I'm a big Christmas lover. Santa is my main man. But I'm also interested in science and truth. I was sure that, as much as I loved the idea of Santa, there was certainly no such person.

"To get them to...Santa?" I said, making sure I had heard him right.

"Well, no one else is going to get them there," the man said. If it were up to the Postal Service, they would go right to the Dead Letter Office for recycling! We can't have that."

"Uh, look, I don't know who you are, sir, but you really can't be here," I said.

"Oh," he exclaimed, sticking out his hand for a shake, "where are my manners? I'm Lars."

I stared at him momentarily, trying to figure out what to do. He gazed back, the smile never leaving his face. Finally, hoping to keep the situation as tension-free as possible, I shook his hand.

"I'm Matt," I told him.

"I know! Matt Spaulding, right? One of your earliest gifts from Santa was a Play Skool basketball hoop."

I dropped his hand and stepped back, thunderstruck. I'm sure I looked like a cartoon character. My eyes were wide, and my mouth was hanging open.

"How...how..." I stammered.

"Don't look so surprised," he said. "I forget people eventually, but you're still in your thirties, so you're a long way from us forgetting you completely. Plus, you're one of our True Believers, which means you hold an extra special place in our hearts and minds."

I sat on a nearby chair hard enough that my teeth clacked. I shook my head back and forth, trying to make sure I wasn't asleep. Like I said, I'm interested in truth and science and, despite all I thought I knew about the world, it seemed I was having a conversation with an actual elf—one of *Santa's* elves. I couldn't believe it. As if I spoke my thought aloud, Lars reached up and turned up the earflaps on his hat to reveal pointed ears. My mouth dropped back open, and before I even knew I was going to do it, I hopped up, took one ear in each hand, and tugged at them.

"OUCH!" he hollered and swatted my hands aside before placing his own over his ears and rubbing them. Then he laughed and said, "I guess that's my fault. I really should have seen that coming. I am dropping a lot on you all at once. Oh, sure, we still think of you as a True Believer because you love Christmas and Santa and do so much to spread love and joy, but you have become a rather rational person in your adulthood."

I looked around. I knew there were other people still on the clock. The supervisor's car was still outside the building. Other carriers hadn't come back to the office yet. There had to be a clerk here to sort the outgoing mail and make sure it made it on the last truck of the night. Where *was* everyone? How could I possibly be the only one seeing this?

Again, Lars spoke as if I had spoken my thoughts aloud or maybe just had them written in bold print on my face.

"No one else is going to notice. You weren't even supposed to notice. You got caught in a bubble. Not even ten seconds have passed out there." he gestured just beyond my back.

"A bubble?"

"Look," he said, "I don't mean to be rude, but I really have to get going. I wish I could take the time to explain, but we're on a tight schedule this time of year, even with all our abilities. But," here he took a pause, tilted his head to the left and stared into the distance. He fiddled with the point of his left ear. "Yeah," he mumbled after a few seconds, "yeah, I'll tell you what: I have a thought. Santa has been looking for someone to help him with something very special and you might be the person. You went to school for creative writing, right?" I nodded at him, confused. "Great! I'll talk to Santa and see what he thinks. Write your phone number for me, please," he thrust a pen and paper into my hand.

Still confused, I jotted my number on the paper and handed it back to him. He glanced at it, stuffed it into his coat pocket, and said, "Perfect. If he agrees, sometime after January 6, I'll call you, and we can talk about the details. Great to meet you in person, Matt! Gotta run!" With that, he became a blur of color and motion and was gone.

I frantically swiveled my head back and forth, looking for him, even though I had just watched him vanish. I rubbed said eyes vigorously, blinked, and spun in a circle. I was looking under the supervisor's desk when she walked in and asked what I was looking for. Startled, I jumped up and bumped my head on the underside of the desk. Not knowing what else to say, I told her something about thinking I had dropped a quarter for a postage-due letter under there but must not have and went back to finish up my work for the day.

For the rest of the night, I went over and over the encounter, trying to rationalize what had occurred. I had met an elf—one of Santa Claus's actual helpers. Santa was real! The more I thought about the matter, the more excited I became! Like I said before, I'm a Santa super fan! The next day, and all the days after, I couldn't help but wonder what on Earth Lars had meant by Santa needing help with a special project that involved my degree in creative writing.

Then, after weeks of pondering that question, on the tenth of January, my phone rang with one of those "unknown caller" numbers. Like countless times before, when that popped up on my screen, I went to hit the "ignore" button. But then I remembered Lars, answered the call, and tentatively said hello.

"Matt!" an excited voice on the other end of the line said. "Hey, Matt, this is Lars! Remember? From the post office?"

"Lars, how could I possibly forget?" I said, a grin splitting my face. This was it. This was the moment I had been hoping for. Before he even said it, I already knew the most spectacular thing was about to happen to me.

"He agreed!" Lars whooped gleefully. "He agreed you are the *perfect* person to help him with his project!"

Barely able to contain myself, I asked, "What project?"

"He'll tell you all about himself. Are you free this Saturday?"

"For Santa Claus?" I said, as if he had just asked me the dumbest question in the world. "Of course!"

"Great! I'll pick you up at your place at, oh, say, ten in the morning."

Right about now, I imagine you are eager to get to Santa's actual story, and rightfully so. I apologize for going on this long. I'll speed up a bit at this point.

Lars picked me up and took me to the North Pole, and when we arrived, he took me right to Santa's office without haste. I won't lie to you: I almost cried from the excitement. Santa is exactly the person you hope and dream he is: warm, kind, funny, and jolly. He sat me down in a very comfortable chair across his desk from him and explained why I was there.

"Matt," he said, knitting his fingers together and placing his hands on his desk, "for many years now, I have been considering writing a memoir. I know many facts about my life are already public knowledge, and you and I can discuss how much of that does and doesn't make it into the final product. But there are a lot of myths out there, too. There are things I would like to clear up. Like the whole 'naughty or nice' business, for example. Plus, I think people would be interested in getting the answers to questions they've only been able to guess at before: 'How do reindeer fly?', 'why do I live at the North Pole?', 'how do I deliver toys all over the world in one night?', that sort of thing. And while I am over seventeen hundred years old and have read countless books and written even more letters in my time, I don't consider myself a *creative* writer. I want someone who has been truly educated on the subject to help me out. Check my grammar and spelling, and make the story more fun to read than an ol' gift-giver like me can accomplish. I have considered many very well-known writers over the years to help me. I've even met several of them. But, in the end, none of them ever struck me as having just the right spirit for the job. Now, I know you haven't ever had anything published, and you've been less creative lately than you used to be in your younger years, but I want you to know I have total faith in you. I *believe* in you the same way you've always believed in me, even when you had convinced yourself that I was a wonderful idea rather than an actual person. Oh, don't look ashamed, I understand. We live in a very scientific world these days! Heck, I think a lot of stuff we do here at the Pole *is* science, just science no one understands yet. What's that old saying: 'any sufficiently advanced science would be indistinguishable from magic'? I think that's it. Close enough, anyway. The point is, you've always been full of the Christmas Spirit, and I have always been very much alive in your heart, if not always in your mind. That's why I would very much like you to help me. Will you?"

Since you're reading this now, you know I agreed. With a bit of help from Santa (he's *very* connected!), I got an extended leave from my job at the Post Office and embarked on a magical journey that took me from The North Pole to Turkey, Lapland to England, and so many other places I thought I would never see. I made friends with Santa, Mrs. Claus, almost all the elves (it would have been impossible to meet and befriend them all in the time I had among them, there are over fifteen-hundred of them living at The Pole) and got to work on the most satisfying project of my life: the book you hold in your hands.

So, that's how it happened. A short version of it, anyway. Thank you for allowing me to tell you that little story, given that's not really what you're here for. I'll stop here and let Santa take over now.
Merry Christmas!
— **Matt Spaulding**

My Earliest Days

Beginning a story that is as long and wonderful as mine is hard. Conventional wisdom would be to start at the beginning. But the earlier parts of my life are pretty well-known in the history books, so I thought it might be a boring place to start. However, my collaborator has informed me that, despite anyone in the world being able to hop on to Wikipedia and search out the actual historical parts of my life on their own, people might be interested to hear at least part of it as I remember it. Since I don't fancy myself a writer, I will not question his wisdom.

I was born in a town called Patara in a country that was then known as Lycia. It's a country that no longer exists, having been absorbed into the country of Türkiye long ago. According to the modern calendar, my birth date was March 15, 270 C.E. The calendar has changed a lot over the years before finally arriving at the one we all know now, though. I mention that only because it's possible that's not the day or the year I was born. People didn't keep great records that long ago like they do now. But it's a date that works as well as any. The point is, at the time of this writing, I was born almost eighteen centuries ago in Patara, Lycia.

My parents were Greek and named me Nicholas, a name from their native language that means "victory of the people." Why they picked that name, I've never known. I imagine it is just a name they liked very much. No one back then had middle or last names. I was simply "Nicholas" to all who knew me or "Nicholas of Patara" to anyone who perhaps knew more than one Nicholas and the other was from a different town. I was given all of my many other names much, much later in life. But we'll get to that part in good time.

I grew up reasonably wealthy for the time. My parents were merchants selling goods out of a shop in our town. Our town was a sort of hub for travelers, and many people found success there selling things. Because my parents had a shop and we dealt with people from all around, I was also relatively educated for the time. I learned to add and subtract to deal with money in my parents' shop. I had to learn several languages so that if someone came into our shop who spoke a language other than my native one, they would not leave to find a different merchant who could communicate with them, therefore taking their money elsewhere.

Being wealthy back then meant I had enough food to eat every day, a home with two rooms, and clothes that were washed once a week. I became very aware at an early age that not everyone had as much in life as my family did. So many people had no sandals for their feet, not enough food to eat, and slept in tents. Some weren't even fortunate enough to have a tent. Even as a child, this bothered me.

I remember one time when I was ten, I saw a boy around my age who had been walking around barefoot so long that he had terrible cuts on his feet and was limping. I took my sandals off, walked over to him, and gave them to him. It was the first gift I ever gave to someone who wasn't my parents. In those days (boy, I sure say that a lot, don't I? But I have to. I have to make sure you understand just how different the world was), charity to people experiencing poverty was almost unheard of. Oh, sure, some people helped out, but on the whole, most people were focused on their own survival and held on tightly to any small comfort that might have come their way. Because charity was so scarce, the boy couldn't believe I was *giving* him my sandals. He asked me what he had to do to get them.

"Nothing," I replied, grinning and thrusting the sandals into his hands. "Please, take them. You need them more than I do."

Tears welled up in the boy's eyes, and he threw his arms around me. He thanked me repeatedly before putting the sandals on his feet and taking off.

I whistled a happy little tune the whole way home that day. Nothing I had ever done before in my short life felt so good as giving my sandals to that poor little boy.

When I got home without sandals, my father took one look at my feet, and I saw his face grow grave.

"Nicholas," he said sternly, "where are your sandals?"

"I gave them to another boy," I replied.

"You *gave* your sandals away?" he asked.

"Yes," I said, confused by his demeanor.

"Nicholas!" My father wasn't a shouting man, but his tone was harsh. "You can't just go about giving things away! Those sandals cost money!"

"But father, I..." I began.

"No, Nicholas, do not speak back to me," my father said, cutting me off.

"Father, listen," I cried. "The boy, he was my age! Young! His feet...you should have seen them! He was limping. They were cut up so badly! He needed them!"

My father's features softened, and he kneeled in front of me to look me in the eye.

"You say the boy's feet were cut?" he asked.

"So cut," I said, wiping tears away that had filled my eyes. "Cut and dirty, and he was limping. And his clothes were dirty, too. He just looked like he needed sandals so badly. I knew I could get more, but maybe he couldn't get any, so I just took mine off and gave them to him! Please don't be mad, Father. I just wanted to help."

He embraced me, kissed me on the cheek, held me out at arm's length, and smiled at me.

"Nicholas, I am so proud," he said. "I'm sorry I spoke harshly to you. It's good that you should think of others and want to take care of them because they are less fortunate than you. But I wish you had asked first. Your sandals cost money, and I want you to understand that even though we have more than others, there is a reason for that. We put a lot of work into this shop. I thought you understood. Maybe I haven't had you do enough around here. So, even though I'm proud of you, I'm going to make you put in some more work around the business. If you want to give to others, you must work for it."

I happily made the extra effort, and my heart warmed, knowing that somewhere, that little boy was no longer limping on hurt feet. What was my "suffering" doing some honest work compared to that of that boy?

That's how my long journey began. That one simple act of seeing a little boy in the streets who desperately needed my sandals more than I did and giving them to him without a second thought. Even at ten, I knew I wanted to keep making people as happy as I had made that boy. Of course, I wasn't sure then how I would do that, and I couldn't have dreamed in my wildest dreams that I would still be doing it almost eighteen centuries later.

After that, I continued to find ways to help my village's poor people as often as possible. Most of the time, it wasn't something as major as the sandals I had given the first time, though I occasionally earned my way into an extra pair. What I more often gave in those early days was food and blankets. It might not sound like much, but if I gave a poor person a loaf of bread and a handful of olives, it often made their entire week better because I had given them more food than they had eaten in days. Or if I convinced a merchant to sell me a blanket for less than they had asked (bartering for a better price was big in those days), that blanket would be the highlight of someone's month because it meant they wouldn't have to sleep in animal pens for warmth. I always gave these gifts to fellow kids. Adults have always had difficulty accepting help, which I don't understand. Everyone needs help sometimes. But, because of that stubbornness, adults didn't want to accept charity, especially from a child. So, I gave to kids who were simply happy to have food to eat and share with their parents or a warm blanket to sleep under.

Soon, if my parents didn't have enough work for me to earn all I desired to help others, I went out to find more work around the village. By then, I already knew the value of good, hard, honest work. It never bothered me to be tired at the end of the day since I knew I got exhausted by helping others.

I spent five years that way, doing all the work I could during the day and aiding those in need in the evenings. Then, when I was fifteen, my father became ill and died. I mourned him deeply, but I also knew he had lived to what, at that time, was an old age, and for that I was grateful. Without knowledge of good nutrition or medicine, people died at what we now think of as very young ages. Fortunately, people have learned a lot since then and live much longer.

With my father gone, I took control of the shop. Women, sadly, were not allowed to be in charge of businesses and had to depend on men to take care of them. Even then, I thought that was ridiculous. Even though my father cared for my mother in the eyes of the public, she was always just as capable as he was at taking care of things. She could even read a little and do math, which women were not supposed to learn. But my father had been quite forward-thinking, and she and he had more or less been equal partners behind closed doors, and the community could not punish them. So, for the next year, my mother taught me much about the family business, and I helped grow our wealth.

Then, when I was sixteen, my mother also got sick and passed away. Today, no one would consider a sixteen-year-old an adult capable of living independently, but when I was sixteen, it was common. So I was alone in the world then, running the shop by myself all day, quickly finding myself with less time to go out and give gifts to those in need. I still managed from time to time, but my reputation as a helper of those less fortunate lagged, which caused a lot of disappointment. It disappointed me, too.

A couple of years went by in this manner, and then, when I was eighteen, one of my most famous exploits took place.

My First Gift Giving Adventure

If you research me and my history, one of the earliest accounts of my exploits you will find is the story of the coins I gave three girls so they could pay their dowries to be married. Over the many years since that happened, the actual facts of that story have been lost to all but me, which is why you will read it several ways and often read that it took place once I was already a grown man.

I had been running my family shop independently for two years and doing well at it. I had inherited all my parents' money and made a good amount of my own. However, another merchant had not done so well.

His name was Deniz, and he was a successful importer of rare spices for a good chunk of my life. But when I was seventeen, he made a significant investment in a shipment that was lost at sea. As such, his business went under, and he was forced to work in a stable for much less money than he had made before. The money he had saved was soon gone.

According to the rest of the village, the real tragedy was that Deniz's daughters could not get married as they had no money for dowries. Remember, at this time, women could not run businesses or be educated. They were, in essence, the property of the men in their lives: first their fathers and then their husbands. Because of this, a silly custom existed: fathers had to pay the men marrying their daughters a sum of money called a dowry. This way, the husband would have some extra money he could use to take on the responsibility of caring for a woman from her father.

Deniz's three daughters were indeed seeing some young men and wished to get married, but without the money for dowries, the young men would not even consider taking them as wives.

"It's too bad," I heard a man say to another in the inn one night while I was having dinner. There was no radio, television, or theater back then, so idle gossip was the main entertainment. "They're all going to age out of marriage before Deniz can raise enough money."

"Marriage age" in my youth now is rightfully considered appallingly young. Girls as young as thirteen were fine to get married, and if a woman wasn't married by nineteen or twenty, they were considered an old maid and not worth the time. As I said, people died pretty young in those days, and folks wanted to have families before they reached "old age."

As I sat there, popping olives into my mouth one at a time and slowly chewing them, savoring the texture and the salty flavor, I thought about this problem. I hadn't ever given a gift as big as a dowry, and I wasn't sure how I would go about it. I certainly couldn't just hand Deniz the money. And I wasn't entirely sure he would let his daughters take it if I gave it to them, either. I already told you that charity was rare, but so was accepting it. People, especially men, were too proud to accept charity. They thought it was insulting that someone would think they could not care for their family. Plus, there was the added complication of people knowing I had given it to them. If everyone knew I was handing out money, perhaps people would come begging at my door, even if they didn't need it.

And so was born the idea that I should give gifts in secret. It was perfect. If I could somehow slip the money to the girls without them knowing where it came from, they would know exactly what to use it for!

Looking back, I have to laugh because what I did next was basically case Deniz's house like a potential burglar. Now that I think about it, I suppose I was—of a sort, anyway—a reverse burglar, there to leave money rather than take it.

The first problem, I found, was that Deniz's house was very close to its neighbors. That would make getting the money into the house without being seen pretty much impossible. I had almost hoped I could walk by and toss it into an open window. In fact, if you look up this story now, the legend is that I did just that. Unfortunately, it turned out to be much more complicated than that.

Once I decided I couldn't just walk by and throw it in the window, I quickly realized that probably hadn't been a good plan in the first place. The house had four windows. I imagined two were for the family room, as they were on either side of the house, not too far behind the front door. But, as Deniz had once been a wealthy man and had not lost his home along with all his money, I assumed he had a three-room house with a bedroom for him and a bedroom for his daughters. If this was true, I couldn't be sure which room was the daughters' room and may throw the money into Deniz's room instead.

So I went home, and I thought. I was almost immediately convinced that I would have to give my gift in the dark of night when everyone was asleep. That would remove the risk of being seen by neighbors or passersby in the street. My main issue still was knowing which room was which. I couldn't just walk by during the day and see which room belonged to the girls. In my youth, windows were set high with the idea that smoke from fires in the house used for cooking and warmth would waft out of those high windows as it rose. It didn't really work that way most of the time, and when chimneys were invented a long time later, I thought back on the smokey houses from when I was young and wished I had a chimney as a boy.

It soon became apparent that I would have to climb a ladder, peek in a window, and hope I got the right one first—or at least not disturb Deniz if I looked into his window first.

I gathered three gold coins from the money my parents had left me. I figured these three gold coins, one for each daughter, would be plenty for a dowry—or, at least, I hoped. I wasn't sure how much was customary since I had no sisters. But since most things were paid for in lesser-value copper coins, I took a gamble that one gold coin each was sufficient.

Then, under cover of night, I crept to the inn where I often took my meals, slipped into their shed, and borrowed a ladder. I wasn't particularly big as a young man, so taking a ladder with me as I tried to sneak my way through the streets to Deniz's house wasn't the easiest task, but I managed.

Once I arrived, I went to the back of the house, propped the ladder against the side, and climbed to the window. When I peeked in, I could immediately tell by the dying light of the small fire I had, indeed, picked the wrong room on the first try. A single large form slept soundly on a sleeping mat in the middle of the room. I thanked my lucky stars that I had not disturbed Deniz's slumber, climbed back down the ladder, and went with it around to the other side of the house.

When I had made it up the ladder again and was looking into the right window, I was faced with another challenge: what to do when I dropped into the room to leave my gifts? After all, I needed a ladder to get to the outside of the window, so I could not climb back out when I was inside. From my perch, I spied the wooden door that separated the girls' room from the family room. I figured that if I was quiet, I could drop the coins by the girls' sleeping mats, rush to the door, crack it open enough to slip through and be out of their room and out of the house in a matter of seconds. Certainly, I wouldn't have to be in the house even a full minute. So, with that thought, I swung myself off the ladder, over the windowsill, and dropped into the room.

As soon as I hit the floor, I realized my mistake in assuming my plan would go smoothly. It wasn't the longest drop in the world from the window to the floor, but I had miscalculated and landed wrong. I felt a sharp pain as my ankle twisted. I let out a small yelp, lost my balance, and fell to the floor, almost landing right on one daughter as I did. I froze next to her sleeping mat, holding my breath, my heart pounding, sure I was caught. But none of the daughters stirred. I slowly let out the air in my lungs and made my way to my feet. My ankle throbbed, and when I tried to put my weight on it, a pain shot through it like lighting.

I hissed at the pain and froze again because the youngest daughter stirred, moaned, rolled over, and settled back into sleep.

I limped my way away from the girls into a corner. My heart thudded in my ears. I was terrified of them waking up and alerting their father, who would surely give me a severe beating for being in his daughters' room while they slept. I had to leave my coins and get out of there. But I was too scared to go back near the sleeping forms on the floor, sure that *boom boom boom* of my heart and my ragged breath would rouse them from their slumbers.

That's when the clothes caught my eye. Our town was a dry, sandy place. No matter the time of year, everyone wore long robes and tall socks to keep the sand off their skin. Then, perhaps one or two nights a week, when the robes and socks were quite dirty, we would haul buckets of water from the river, wash the sand from our clothes, and hang them by our nighttime fires to dry. To my great fortune, it had been wash day for the girls. Without wasting another second, I hobbled quickly to the clothesline, dropped a coin in one of each of the daughters' socks, limped to the door, and lifted the latch.

The creak the hinges made filled the room and stopped my breathing. To my horror, I heard a sound behind me and turned to see that the oldest daughter had sat bolt upright at the sound and was staring in my direction.

I stood in the doorway, frozen, waiting for a scream that didn't come. As I stared intently at her in the dim light, I noticed her eyes weren't fully open, and her expression was blank. She was still asleep! She had reacted to the sound but had not fully woken up! I had seen a local man sleepwalking through the street once, and he had worn the same expression. Even as I had this realization, she sank back to her pillow, and I unfroze. I slipped through the door, closed it quickly, ignoring the shrieking hinges, and made my way across the family room and out the front door as fast as possible. Then, my ankle screaming at me, I snuck around the house, collected the ladder, made it back to the inn, deposited it, and went home.

Finally, back in my own space, I examined my ankle by the light of my own fire. Though it felt like fire, it was only slightly swollen, so I figured I would be okay. I wrapped a strip of cloth tightly around it for support. I laid down on my sleeping mat but was too excited to sleep. I had done it! It hadn't gone exactly as I had planned. It certainly hadn't been smooth. But I had given the girls those coins! It exhilarated me, knowing in the morning they would wake up and find those coins in their socks and could plan their weddings! It would be a joyous occasion not just for them but for Deniz and the whole town! I might have gotten a few moments of sleep that night, but certainly not more than that. As soon as the sun showed itself over the horizon, I popped off my mat, went to the inn for food, and waited to hear news of Deniz's daughters.

It didn't take very long. People woke when the sun came up and went to sleep when it set. The first townsfolk were making their way through the door when the commotion began. The girls and Deniz came running down the street, holding the gold coins high.

"It's a miracle!" Deniz cried.

"We have been blessed!" the oldest daughter proclaimed.

Three weddings were performed in what seemed like no time, and the girls were happily married. And, with three fewer mouths to feed, Deniz eventually saved enough money to get back into a more lucrative business and improve his station in life. From my one gift-giving adventure, four lives (seven, if you include the men the daughters married) were happier. It made my heart light, and I knew that I wanted to make glad the hearts of my fellow humans for the rest of my life.

The Legend Begins

After the adventure of giving gifts to Deniz's daughters, I was hooked on the feeling of giving gifts anonymously. Many people still don't understand that the joy of giving a gift is not in the credit you receive but in the happiness it brings to the person who gets it. Sure, these days, everyone now knows I bring children gifts at Christmas and a few other select holidays like St. Nicholas Day, New Year, and Epiphany, so I get credit, but for most of my very long life of doing this, I did so in secret. Even now, I leave my gifts at night while people sleep and don't stick around to get showered with thanks. All the thanks I require is the happiness I bring.

So, after that first adventure, I kept my eyes out for other people in town who would benefit from gifts left in the night. At first, I did the same as I had done on that first night and left coins. I felt that people in need would know best what they were in the most need of and spend the money accordingly. But, after the first three or four times I ventured out in the night and left money, word got around, and many folks in town realized that rather than miracles occurring, some generous person was roaming around and giving away free money. Greedy people, many of whom didn't need money, spied out their windows or waited in doorways. More than once, I got caught sneaking around town by people looking for handouts, and I had to work hard to convince them it wasn't me leaving the money. My story was that I could not sleep and was out for some fresh air and perhaps also find the person leaving the money.

One time, I was shoved to the ground and nearly beaten up because a man did not believe me. By that time, I had been caught enough times at night that I had sewn a hidden pocket inside my robe and could show the man that the visible pockets on my robe were very much empty, and he left me there on the ground without so much as a token apology.

After all my near misses, I decided on two very important things: first, I would have to leave things other than money. If a family were ragged, I would leave robes. If a family were hungry, I would leave food. If money wasn't mysteriously appearing in homes, I reasoned, greedy people would be less likely to wait up to catch me or, worse, beat me and rob me. The second thing I decided was to venture outside my hometown and make it less evident that the person leaving the gifts was a resident. As a merchant, I would have reason to venture to other places to purchase goods for my store or perhaps sell some items in a new market.

This worked out well for me. After sneaking around town, leaving bread, cheese, vegetables, and clothes for a few weeks, people slept in their homes again as usual. Plus, the legend spread of gifts left for those in need at night. Often, I could slip in and out of doors (there weren't many locks in those days, just the occasional heavy bar laid across the inside of a door). Even more often, I would go into the tents that housed the poorest of the poor who lived on the very outskirts of town.

While it was easier to enter quietly into a tent as there were no squeaky hinges or heavy doors to slam, it was harder to remain undetected once inside. Tents don't have a lot of space for the people living in them to spread out, so I had to be extra careful not to step on or trip over anyone.

On one very memorable occasion, I went in, left some food and sandals, and tripped over an old man as I went to leave. I fell forward, stumbling through the tent, scrambling to grab hold of something to keep myself upright. Unfortunately, I grabbed the fabric of the tent itself, which, instead of keeping me up, came with me as I fell, and the whole tent came down with the poor, confused, frightened family inside. I am embarrassed to admit that, instead of staying to help them untangle themselves and get their tent back up, I ran as fast as I could, afraid of being mistaken for a robber and being beaten with clubs.

On another of these early nighttime adventures, I had a pretty nasty encounter with a dog. The poor nomad families in the tents at the edge of town often had dogs with them, as dogs were a good source of protection for what little they had in their camps. Before going to these camps at night, I made sure I spied during the day to see if the family I planned to visit had a dog. If they did, I often slowly approached the camp as though I were just passing by and wanted to say hello, to see if the dog was friendly. If it was, I pet it and played with it a bit as I made small talk with the family. This way, I knew I would be safe to return at night because the dog would know I was a friend. But if the dog seemed vicious or unsure of me, I would not return.

On this particular visit, though, I had not noticed a dog during my daytime visit to the camp. I don't know where it was then, but it certainly had not been where I could see it. So, thinking I was safe, I crept to the tent with my bundle of gifts. As I lifted the flap, I heard a growl to my left. I turned that way, and a large dog was there. Its teeth were bared and looked to me as big as daggers. A large dollop of drool hung from its jaws, glistening like a silver thread in the moonlight.

I dropped the flap and backed away slowly, whispering calming things like "nice dog, good dog, pretty dog" and hoping it wouldn't rush me. But my luck did not hold. It leaped at me, and I turned to run. Running from a dog is never a good idea because it is their instinct to chase, and no matter how fast you run, you will not run faster than the dog. Before I knew it, I felt teeth on my backside. They barely grazed my skin and mostly got fabric, but I still yelped and pushed myself to go faster. I heard a rip and felt most of the back of my cloak tear away. I'm still thankful it was chilly that night, and I wore that cloak. It not only provided me with extra protection from the dog's teeth as it was an additional layer of fabric between the teeth and my skin, but it also protected me from running all the way home in the dark, half undressed! I supposed the dog was happy to have caught anything at all because I made it away from the camp without it continuing to follow me, but I still stayed in for the next couple of nights, frightened to go back out and maybe have another call that close.

Traveling to other towns helped cut down on the number of people waiting up for me at night in my hometown. It also spread the legend of a mysterious gift-bringer who helped those in need. As I said earlier, generosity was not abundant back then, and gossip was the primary source of entertainment, so leaving gifts at night was strange and worth talking about.

When I got to different villages, I would spend the first day or so in the local market, purchasing goods under the pretense of bringing them back to my shop, mostly cloaks and sandals. I would usually bring food with me since buying the amount I needed would attract attention and give me away as the gift-giver. No one would buy food in one market to bring and sell in another. It wouldn't be good when I got it back to sell!

So, after a few years, my entire region knew the tale of the nighttime gift-giver who so loved the poor that they left food and clothes and, once in a while, a bit of money for them in their homes. And, because I lived in a town frequented by travelers from very far away, I often heard that I had been visiting people as far away as a hundred miles. Of course, I never actually made it that far. Frequently, I was lucky if I could make it thirty or forty miles, and those journeys took up the better part of a month by cart and by foot. I thought then and still believe that most of those stories were just stories. Legends that spread from town to town eventually had me traveling distances I couldn't make in those days. But, I also think now that, probably, other kind folks like myself had taken up the mission of helping the poor secretly at night. This is something that continues today, especially at Christmas. Where I might bring a child only a few toys, parents might give them even more but still put my name on it, choosing to credit me instead of themselves. As I said before, the joy of giving a gift is not in the credit you receive.

"Bishop" Nicholas

Now we come to the part of my story where deviation from the official record begins. When you look up my "official" history online, you read that, at a young age, I became involved with the church, eventually becoming a bishop. As bishop, I supposedly performed all kinds of amazing feats, such as guiding ships into port in a storm by appearing glowing in the air before them and leading the way. One very gruesome story had me bringing some children back from the dead. One story even claims I spent several years in prison when the Romans were persecuting Christians and I chose to be jailed rather than stop practicing my faith. These tales would later have me go down in history as Saint Nicholas, patron saint of sailors and children.

The thing about these legends is that none of them ever took place. I can't speak to exactly where they came from, but when I was in my early thirties, I did become involved with the Christians, just not the way history says I did. It's part of why I am most associated with Christmas, but not the whole reason. I'll talk more about that later.

I have mentioned more than once that charity was scarce in my youth. However, one organization that helped the poor was the Christian church. It's important to understand that, at that point, Rome ruled most of what we called "The Known World." Of course, we knew nothing of many parts of the world, such as the lands of Southeast Asia and the two American continents. However, most of Europe and the Middle East were part of the Roman Empire.

The Roman Empire had many official religions over its time as a major power in the world. I won't go into all those details. They are fascinating, but you can look them up yourself. They don't all have an essential part in my story. I will say that, because the Romans changed their official religion so much, my family had never really paid much attention to matters of faith. When, one year, Rome told you to worship Jupiter, Saturn, and other gods they had taken and renamed from the Greeks; then a few years later, told you to worship Mythra, a Persian sun god, it became tough to figure out which religion was true or best. Because of this, when a religion called Christianity began to spread, my family paid little attention to that one, too. And, I am sad to say that several Roman emperors paid it too much of the wrong kind of attention by making it against the law and mistreating Christians. I have always thought it's terrible to tell other people how best to live their lives as long as they aren't hurting anyone and even more horrible to mistreat them because they aren't living exactly how you think they should.

I'll return to the topic of ever-changing religion a little later when I tell you how I came to give gifts at Christmas rather than any other time of the year. My point at the moment is that, for all my life, I was more concerned with tending the family business and helping the poor than I was with religion.

However, as I became an adult and continued my nighttime gift-giving missions, I thought a lot about how I could help even more people. Being one person and visiting only one or two families at a time wasn't cutting it as far as I was concerned. So, I thought about enlisting other people.

I quickly decided that the problem was that the more people involved, the harder it would be to keep a secret. I definitely wanted it to remain a secret who was leaving the presents, so I got another idea.

As I said before, the Christians were gaining a reputation that few people or groups had back then: one of helping those in need. Priests were supposed to be poor, but *churches* had a lot of money. They had a lot of land and received donations. Many bishops were using church land to grow food and church money to buy blankets and clothes.

Knowing this, I got up one day, went to the church in Myra, which was not far from where I lived in Patara, and asked if I could speak with the bishop. I waited while one priest asked if he was free and was soon led into his chamber.

The bishop and I knew each other casually as he had seen me in the market and often did business with me. He smiled warmly when I entered and greeted me.

"Nicholas!" he cried. The bishop was a rather loud man. He was hard of hearing and leaned in close to you when you spoke so he could hear, but he also spoke loudly so he could hear himself. "I'm glad to see you! Come, sit!"

"Thank you, Bishop," I said as I pulled the other stool in the room over to me and took a seat.

"What brings you to the church today, Nicholas? We don't see you here ever. Come to join us?"

"Oh, no, Bishop, not to join, sorry. But I would like to speak with you about helping the church and, by extension, people in need."

"I see. What is it you have in mind?"

"Well, Bishop, as you know, I have a very successful shop in Patara, and I would like to use my good fortune to give back to the community. So many around us are much less well off than I am."

The bishop laid his hand on my shoulder and said, "I'm glad you see it, Nicholas. Many a fortunate man doesn't witness the situation of his fellow citizens. It's right and just that you should want to help."

"Thank you," I said, knowing I had come to the right place. "What I am thinking is that I can donate all the supplies the church uses to help the needy. I know that you and other bishops in other towns use church lands to grow food. Let me purchase and donate the seeds. Please let me also purchase and donate the clothes and blankets you give away. And if you need extra hands at harvest time, I will gladly help in the fields. And if you visit the needy with supplies, I will happily go with you."

"Nicholas!" the bishop cried again, spreading his arms wide. "So generous, my son! This is indeed a wonderful plan! I am sure other bishops in other churches in neighboring areas will be just as happy to hear this news as I am!"

"I am glad," I said. "It is already almost harvest time, so I obviously can't supply you with seed now, but I will venture out to markets in other towns on buying trips over the next few months and bring back as many blankets and clothes as possible. It's a start."

"Indeed, it is!" the bishop said with a smile and opened his arms again, this time for an embrace. I hugged him, and the deal was done. I left with my heart full, knowing now I could give to people day and night.

That is how it went for many years after that. Several men became Bishop of Myra after that first, but all were glad to have my donations of supplies, time, and labor. While I never became a member of the church, much less the clergy, the priests, bishops, and the people we served became so fond of me that they gave me the nickname "Bishop Nicholas" as a term of endearment and honor for all my good work.

So it was that, even into the modern day, I became known as Bishop Nicholas of Myra. But, as I said before, I am the only person who remembers how it began. Records weren't well kept all those years ago. Even as word of "Bishop" Nicholas spread across the land, the fact that I was never a clergy member was never put to parchment anywhere, and that fact was lost. As more and more years went by, it became accepted as fact that I had been Bishop of Myra and performed miracles. I suppose, in my little way, I did. But nothing was ever as grand as the stories told about me. But, long before TV and video games, as I said, gossip and stories were all people had. And, because people's lives were so hard, stories of heroes, good people, and magic gave them hope things would get better and that the world wasn't all bad. So, if they believed Bishop Nicholas of Myra was commanding crops to grow with a word and a wave of his hand rather than plain old Nicholas the ShopKeep of Patara donating seeds and harvesting the crops, well, that's alright with me.

Leaving Home

I know that, up to this point, my life has probably struck you as pretty ordinary. But, mostly, it was. Perhaps you were expecting magic from the beginning of my story, but that isn't how it went. I suppose I could have started at the part I am about to relate to you, but I think you must understand that, besides my fondness for helping people and giving gifts in secret, I didn't start life as someone extra special. Who I am now is a mixture of my good-natured attitude to all my fellow humans and an accident of magic. If you understand the beginning of my story as a pretty average person with an above-average desire to do good in the world, I hope you will realize you can make an impact, too. You may never have the magic enter your life that I have had in mine, but you will still have the extraordinary magic that comes from being kind and generous and being known for those qualities.

Still, I can just hear you now: "Yes, Santa, that's all well and good, but, well, you're *Santa Claus*! There's so much *actual* magic in your life I want to read about! It's why I picked up this book!" And, to be fair, you are right. I have written quite enough about my earliest days. The most fun and wondrous parts of my life are yet to come! So I will get on with it.

Most of my pre-magic adulthood was spent as I have laid out: giving gifts in secret at night and doing good deeds for the community at large with the help of the local church by day, all while still running my business. I lived happily for many, many years in that manner. But, as happens to everyone, I grew old. My hair and beard changed from being as black as night to white as the clouds in the sky. I developed deep wrinkles around my eyes and mouth from smiling and laughing merrily for years on end. My waistline expanded considerably, which was not common in those days. But I was invited to many celebrations and feasts by those in the community who wished to thank me for all my good work. And, since I have always loved to eat, I would never say no if they urged me to eat seconds or even thirds if the crops had been excellent that season.

As I entered my sixty-third year in 333, I thought about all I had done with life. I knew that, at sixty-three, my time was growing short. I was already lucky to have made it as far as I had. In a time before modern medicine, if people caught something nasty when they were young, even something people now would consider not a big deal, like the flu, they often would not recover and would pass away. At sixty-three, I was quite old indeed. I am happy these days that at sixty-three, people typically have quite a lot of life left in front of them to enjoy.

But, at that time, I had no idea just how unusually long my life would be, and I decided I wanted to spend what I thought were my last remaining days in places further from home than I had ever been. For example, I had never been to Constantinople (now called Istanbul), the city which had been named the new capital of the Roman Empire and was in my own country. I had never been to Rome itself, for that matter. I knew there would be many people in those places to whom I could bring gifts if only I could make it to them in time.

So, quietly, I sold off and donated items from my business and closed up shop. I settled all my accounts around the village. This was not uncommon for an older man to do, and my friends in town all wished me well and let me know they would say prayers for me. They all presumed, rightfully so, that I felt I was nearing my end.

I didn't tell anyone I planned to leave except for the newest bishop at the church. When I brought him the final load of goods, I asked to speak with him in his chamber. I let him know I wished to spend my remaining time doing good in some other parts of the world, that I wanted not to make a big deal of leaving, that I planned to slip quietly out of town, and asked if he could make excuses for me once I was gone. He said he could, wished me well, and told me he would pray for me. This was a decision I had made with great determination, a decision to follow my heart and make a difference in the world.

I had not chosen a time to leave. I was still trying to decide when to go when I went to bed the night before I ended up leaving. At the time, the date meant little to me, but the date I left home, December 6, would go down in history along with the rest of my story. In modern times, December sixth is known as The Feast of St. Nicholas or St. Nicholas Day and is one of the days children awake to find gifts left by me in the night. More on that later.

On December 5th, I went to bed not long after sundown, as I always did, but I had a terrible time sleeping. I tossed and turned, my dreams chaotic and strange. Like pretty much everyone, I forget my dreams soon after waking, so now I don't remember what exactly I dreamed of, but I remember lots of walking and vague shapes running by and swirling colored light.

I woke with a start just before dawn and knew I wanted to leave at that moment. I could see a tiny sliver of grey light on the horizon. Everyone in the village would still be asleep. I could make it quite far away, perhaps to the next village, by the time the sun was up. The unknown was calling to me, and I couldn't resist its allure.

I packed up some supplies in a canvas sack, lined the hidden pockets of my cloak with all my money, and walked out my door for the last time, the sack slung over my shoulder. I strolled out of the village, taking it all in. I had spent sixty-three years calling this place home and was sad to leave it but also very excited to be embarking on such a daring and new adventure at such a late stage of my life. To use an ancient cliche, my stomach was filled with butterflies.

When I finally left the edges of the village behind and struck out on the road for real, I was going at a very average pace. I figured I would probably need to stop to rest every few miles, and I had possibly over-estimated myself a bit when I thought I could be there by full sun up. I had no idea how wrong I was or what a long and incredible adventure awaited me.

The First Magic

I wasn't aware something strange was happening at first. I was so wrapped up in heading off on my journey and planning out how I might get to the places I wanted to go that the fact it was staying dark didn't sink in.

But, after I had walked much further than I had expected and still hadn't felt the need to stop for a rest, it hit me. I walked a few more steps, then stopped in the middle of the road, whirled around, and took in my surroundings. I had been this way before frequently and soon realized I had walked halfway to the next village. Despite that, there was only a slim streak of grey light on the horizon, the sky overhead still black and filled with stars.

This was impossible! Walking halfway to the nearest village should not only have made me quite tired and in need of a rest, but it was a walk of almost two hours, and the sun had not come up! I am not ashamed to tell you I was terrified. One thing we learn very early in life when we are just babes is that the sun rises every day. If all I could see was a bit of light on the horizon, had something happened to the sun? To the planet? I almost fled back toward home. Even now, I can't tell you why I didn't. I was scared and wanted to see people, and it would stand to reason I would want to see people I knew and loved in such a frightening moment. But I did not head that way. Instead, I turned and ran as fast as I could (which, I won't lie, at my age and my weight was not so fast. It may have even been the last time I ever ran. I can't recall a time since) in the direction I had been heading when I realized this terrible thing was happening.

To my surprise, for it seemed even in my shock at the sun not rising, I was still capable of surprise; I reached the village without stopping once to rest and made it in what seemed to me to be an incredibly short amount of time. Without the sun to keep track, I had no way of knowing how many hours had passed on my journey or how long it had been since I started running, but I had a vague idea that it took me no time at all to get to my destination compared to what it should have.

In town, I found no one up yet. It was still dark there, after all. Dawn still seemed a long way off, although I thought I saw a slight bit of color on the horizon now, where I had seen only a streak of gray light before. But I was no longer sure of what was real and what wasn't. I was so confused and afraid I thought I might be imagining the color.

I began pounding on doors, my voice trembling with fear. "Help!" I shrieked. Tears streamed down my face, a testament to my sheer terror. "Oh, someone, please! Help! Something is dreadfully wrong! Someone! Anyone! Please, come see!" But no one stirred. No one responded to my desperate pleas and frantic banging.

I had set out from home in search of an adventure, but instead, I found myself in a living nightmare, a world where the sun refused to rise. It was inconceivable! How could no one hear the commotion I was making? Was the village deserted? Was I the sole survivor on Earth?

It was then that I spotted a dog. It was sitting by the corner of a home, not looking in my direction. It struck me as strange that I could make so much noise and not attract the animal's attention. But there it was, sitting, staring into the distance in a different direction, not giving a care in the world about all the noise I was making. I thought maybe it was deaf. I approached it slowly, not wanting to frighten it and get bitten by a scared dog defending itself. I crept around the side to stand in front of it and was shocked, yet again, when it *still* did not register my presence. It didn't yelp or bark or wag its tail or growl. It didn't even twitch a single muscle. It just continued to sit there and stare as though it were made of stone. This could not be happening.

Without a thought, I reached up with one hand and slapped my cheek very hard, wondering now if perhaps I *was* having a nightmare and was still home asleep in my bed. That idea went out of my head as soon as my palm made contact with my face and a red-hot pain exploded there that made my eye water. I was very much awake.

I whirled away from the dog, away from the direction from which I had come, and took to running again, off toward yet another town. I did not know what I expected to find there after this place yielded no answers and no comfort, but I knew I had to do something, go somewhere. So I ran at my plodding pace, never once stopping to rest despite my, until then, increasingly tired and achy body needing to take frequent breaks if I so much as went for a long, gentle walk.

#

Again, I am not sure how long it took me to reach the next village, but I still felt that it hadn't taken me nearly as long as it should have, even at my slow running speed. As soon as I saw the first building, I yelled for help, for anyone to answer me. I noticed as I ran into town that, indeed, the color I had seen in the sky in the last village was real and that it had, in fact, grown brighter. The vibrant hues of the sky contrasted sharply with the eerie silence of the village. I sobbed with relief when I saw the colorful light on the horizon. The sun was finally rising. But, by my internal reckoning of time, it should have been up *hours* ago, creeping toward mid-morning by this point. I was two villages away from home and had gotten there on foot, not by some horse or donkey-pulled cart, which would have increased my travel speed but not enough to account for how quickly I had arrived here.

Once again, I pounded on doors, my voice echoing through the empty streets. "Is anyone there? Please, I need help!" I pleaded for someone, anyone, to acknowledge my existence, to share in the bizarre reality I was trapped in. But, as before, my cries fell on deaf ears. The village remained shrouded in silence and darkness.

I slumped to the ground by the side of what appeared to be a shop much like the one I had run all my life, drew my knees to my chest as best I could with my ample waistline, and wrapped my arms around them, shaking and crying. Never before (or since, for that matter) had I been so scared. I was desperate to see someone, anyone.

Just as I had that thought, I saw something out of the corner of my eye. A flicker of movement! Proof that someone else was out there with me! Another person!

"Hey!" I shouted, my voice echoing through the empty streets. "Wait! Please!" I sprinted toward the shadowy figure, my heart pounding in my chest. The figure seemed to melt into the darkness, elusive and uncatchable. "Please don't go!" I pleaded, my voice desperate. I turned the corner of the building, my eyes scanning the area, but there was no one. No shape, no shadow, no sign of life.

Villages then were not like towns and cities now. There weren't many buildings close together for someone to get lost in or find a space to slip away and hide. I walked down the path and looked around the edges of the scant few buildings, but I still didn't see a sign of life.

Once more, my knees grew weak, and I sank to the ground. The weight of my fear and confusion was unbearable. I had imagined the movement, I thought. Later, I found out that this wasn't true. But, at the time, I thought that, in my confusion and fear, I had seen what I wanted to see. I laid down on my side, my body trembling, and cried some more.

There is a well-known saying, "fight or flight", describing what are said to be the two natural reactions to fear: stand your ground and protect yourself or run away to protect yourself. But there is another reaction to fear that is often forgotten: freeze. Sometimes, you are so overwhelmed by a situation that your body doesn't know what to do, and you lock up, stay in place, and do nothing. This is what my body did at that moment. I lay there on the ground, my mind racing with fear and confusion, quietly crying until I became so exhausted that I fell asleep.

\#

I awoke to the feeling of being gently prodded in the side. I jolted upright and saw a young boy stumble back from me, apparently caught using his foot to poke at me. It took me a moment to register this. A boy. A *moving* boy! Who had been using his foot to kick me softly! In the same instant, I became aware that it was *bright*! The sun was up! Full up! As I tilted my head to the sky, I noticed it must have been just past breakfast time! And I heard sounds! I hadn't realized how quiet it had been since I had first woken up that day, but with the hustle of folks beginning their day around me, it sunk in that I hadn't heard so much as the sound of a bird until that point.

I scrambled to my feet, the boy already turning to flee. "Wait!" I blurted out, desperation lacing my voice. "Please, just a moment!" He hesitated, curiosity and caution in his eyes, and I seized the opportunity. Reaching into my pack, I retrieved a small copper coin, a token of my gratitude for his unexpected wake-up call. He stared at it, his gaze shifting between the coin and me.

"Please," I said, my hand still outstretched. The joy of seeing a moving person, of being part of a living world again, was overwhelming. I wanted to give him a gift, a token of my gratitude for waking me up. He came a little closer, grabbed the coin from my hand, and looked at it closely.

A grin spread across his face, and he looked from the coin to me, back to the coin, and then back to me. "Thank you, sir!" he cried, then turned heel and ran off.

I looked around me and saw people walking up and down the streets, shop owners propping open the shutters and doors of their businesses, people—real, live, moving people—and sunlight.

What had happened to the world while I was on my trip here? What had happened to *me*? I was here, so I knew it wasn't a nightmare. I had gotten up from my bed some time ago and began walking. In that time, however long it was, the world had stood still. The sun had not risen. A dog had sat still as a statue. I hadn't heard a single sound. But I had moved about, bearing witness to the strange event. And, apparently, I was the only one. As I moved about the people in town, I didn't hear anything that indicated anyone knew anything had happened or been even slightly different from any other day.

I was grateful to have the world back to normal, my fear slipping away. But in its place, a new emotion stirred: curiosity. What had happened? Why had I been the only one to witness it? The fear that had gripped me during the event now transformed into a sense of wonder and fascination. As I sat on a blanket, eating some food, I pondered the events of the early morning hours and wondered: was it a unique occurrence, or would it happen again?

Little did I know I would get my answer soon.

The First Benefit of Magic

Days went by after the incident with time standing still. I roamed about, leaving gifts at night in the villages I came to. In the mornings, I would hear of the miracles that had taken place and the happy cries of families who now had food to eat and clothes to wear. I tried to attract as little attention as possible, because I worried that a stranger coming into town with gifts following soon after arrival would give away the mystery and awe.

But, of course, people inevitably noticed me wherever I went. Not many, but one or two people. Soon, the gift giver was known to be an older, plump, white-bearded man. I can't recall precisely where I was when I realized my reputation had preceded me, but I remember pulling the hood of my cloak up to hide my face when I heard about a miracle man matching my description who had been leaving gifts for the poor all over the region. But, being noticed and being *known*, I realized, were two different things. I certainly didn't introduce myself to too many people in my travels, so no one knew who I was beyond a kind stranger. And I never stayed once I left my gifts. I moved on before anyone could remember seeing me and put the pieces together.

And so it went, village after village, until I reached Constantinople, which, you will remember, was the capital of the Roman Empire and the biggest city I had ever visited.

I was taken aback at what a dirty place it was in so many sections. Nothing in those days was particularly clean, but Constantinople had slums; large sections of the city meant to be home to the poorest of the poor, and they were pretty run down and filthy indeed. I'm sorry to say such places still exist today and are hardly much better kept. I had never seen so many people in so much need, and I was almost immediately discouraged by the task before me. I had, I felt, a task of many nights in front of me to make sure I brought even a little happiness into the lives of all who needed it in this place.

I found a room at an inn and planned how to manage my task. I would have to visit multiple shops over several days to get all the food and clothing I needed without attracting attention. Fortunately, there was a wide variety to choose from, and I figured I could hit two or three a day for maybe a week, gathering first the clothing and then the food so I wouldn't have it kept in my room so long it would spoil.

I spent a week in this manner, and the day before the night I planned to give gifts, I took inventory of everything I had. I thought I could give gifts to as many as a dozen families in such a densely populated area. Each one wouldn't get much, but it would be something. I loaded everything into a giant canvas sack and laid down to nap before my night's work.

During my nap, I again had vivid and strange dreams, much like the night I first left home. I remember that and not much else. I remember that, in those dreams, I had a sensation of very intense speed, and I saw a lot of shapes rushing by and swirling colors. When I finally sat bolt upright awake in bed, the sun had sunk below the horizon, and it was dark outside. I did not know how long I had been asleep but knew it was time to get up and complete my mission.

I gathered my canvas sack and quietly went from my room to the street. I immediately knew it had happened again. The night was too quiet. In a place with so many people, there were still sounds of life and activity even after dark. But not now. I was again trapped in that eerie state of the world being frozen around me.

Like the first time this happened, I felt instant panic. But almost as quickly as I felt fear come over me and make me want to yell and cry for help like the first time, I felt myself calm down. I remembered that panic and fear had not helped me last time.

I sat down by the side of the building, took a few deep breaths, and gathered my thoughts. I even talked to myself, trying to both think my situation through and hear any noise at all, even if it was my own voice.

"Okay. I've experienced this before. It's going to be okay. Everything eventually made it back to normal last time. It will this time, too. Just...just need to decide what to do now."

It wasn't much of a decision. I looked at the sack of gifts sitting next to me and knew what I would do. I had come here to give gifts to those in need, and, time standing still or not, that's what I was going to do.

I stood back up, brushed myself off, heaved the sack over my shoulder, and began my walk to the slums.

On my way there, I learned something new about my situation. As I didn't know the city well and wasn't used to so much clutter, I tripped a lot in the dark over things people had left in the street. The first time I tripped, I saw an amazing sight as I went sprawling and looked back to see what I had tripped on. It seemed I had tripped on a bucket of water. But, rather than the bucket tumbling over and spilling everywhere all at once when my foot hit it as would have been expected, I watched, astounded, as the bucket ever so slowly tipped. I saw single water droplets rising over the lip and floating gently through the air. I kept watching. Eventually, the bucket reached a point where the water began to slosh over the side and spill, but it flowed like honey, slow and oozing, unlike water. Even as I, at a regular pace, picked myself up off the ground, the bucket was still not fully tipped and spilled.

This slow movement of the bucket was my first, best clue to what was happening to me. It wasn't that everything had stopped around me, just that everything was moving incredibly slowly. Einstein was a very long way from being born, let alone from discovering that if something were moving very fast, everything around it would look slow, or I may have realized what was really happening. But since I seemed to be moving at normal speed, I assumed the world was moving very slowly around me. But more on that later.

Arriving at the slums of Constantinople, I embarked on my mission of distributing gifts. Each parcel, whether it was food for one family or clothes for another, was a small beacon of hope. As I emptied my big canvas sack, I couldn't help but feel a sense of fulfillment.

However, when I had delivered my last gift, I stood in the street gazing around me, thinking unhappily of all the families I still had not graced with a little something to ease their suffering. I was happy I had reached any at all, but I still thought of all the people who would wake up tomorrow and wonder why their neighbors had been blessed with food and clothes, and they had not. I turned to walk back to my room when a thought struck me: I had no idea how long it would be until morning! Quickly, on the heels of that thought came a second thought: *I can still give more gifts tonight! I have time!*

But, I remembered, my supply of gifts was gone. It was the middle of the night. I couldn't buy more. Unless...

"No," I said to myself as the thought hit me. "No, that wouldn't work. Would it?"

I had coins. Though it was night and no one was around to buy from, no one was around to stop me from helping myself, either. I remembered my first gift-giving adventure when I climbed the ladder and went through the window to leave coins for the girls. I could go to the market, climb through a window or two, gather what I needed, and leave enough gold and silver behind to cover the cost.

Looking back, I'm somewhat ashamed of the idea. It wasn't right of me to do, even though I paid for the goods I took. You wouldn't go to Walmart now after they were closed, let yourself in, go shopping, and leave money. You would wait for them to open. That's what I should have done then. But I was excited, caught up in the moment, and excited at the prospect of serving so many other people in such great need. I'm much, *much* older now and at least a bit wiser, and I have learned

I was wrong. This is another thing I will talk about later, learning from mistakes, as they relate to a part of my legend that I am not fond of. (I really must stop bringing up subjects I don't mean to get to right now. I apologize.)

With not one, not two, but *three* full canvas sacks of goods, I returned to the slums to spread more love and joy. It didn't strike me that night that I flung three heavy packs over my shoulder like they were filled with nothing but straw, but I remembered it later and marveled at yet another bizarre thing that had happened to me that magical night.

I left a gift for every family and individual I could find. If anyone did not receive something from me that night, I never heard of it. I exhausted my supplies, visited every person I found, and returned to my room at the inn full of happiness. I grinned all night long as I gave my gifts, grinned all the way back to my room, and, I think, kept grinning as I finally came down from the rush of my adventure and drifted off to sleep.

When I woke the next day, I knew immediately that whatever had happened to me the night before was still happening. Unlike the last time when I had woken up and found myself back in the world as usual, this time, it seemed I was still under the spell, or whatever it was. I knew because, despite the sun streaming through my window, I heard none of the sounds that would let me know a typical, busy day was taking place. No voices, no animal sounds, no sounds of work being done.

The calm I had felt the night before dissipated, replaced by a growing sense of fear. It was one thing to be the only moving being at night when I was leaving gifts, but it was another thing entirely to be the only one moving during the day when the everyday hustle and bustle of life was supposed to take place. The eerie stillness and the absence of familiar sounds intensified my unease.

I jumped from my bed, threw on my day clothes, charged out of my room, and almost ran directly into a man standing in the hall.

"Excuse me," I said to him, "I didn't mean to almost run you over!" I was so relieved to see another person that I didn't notice until the words were already out of my mouth that he wasn't exactly *standing* there. He was *frozen* there, mid-stride, like a mannequin. But then I realized that wasn't right, either. He wasn't frozen; he was moving so slowly that I almost couldn't see it. His right foot was creeping toward the floor like he was taking a step. Eventually, I saw it connect with the ground and looked to his left foot to see his heel, equally slow, begin to rise.

"Hello!" I said to him, waving my hands. Can you hear me? Can you see me?" I circled him, waving my arms and trying to elicit a response. I thought I saw his eyes begin to turn, but I couldn't be sure, so I left, feeling a mix of confusion, frustration, and a lingering sense of loneliness.

Everywhere I went was the same. I judged it was pretty early morning as I saw shopkeepers getting their day going, young boys sat in a circle around a man who looked to be teaching them math (girls, sadly, weren't allowed to go to school), and to my delight, the poor people I had visited the night before frozen amid big celebrations of their good fortune.

But I didn't see a single person I could interact with, no one who was moving as I was, no one I could speak to. Faced with this strange and lonely situation, I decided to leave Constantinople, heading toward the next place where I could bring happiness to people, hoping to find some answers along the way.

Timeless Wanderer

I lost track of how long I wandered alone, the world around me moving only fractions of inches at a time as I kept up my usual pace. It's hard to keep track of any sense of standard time when nights and days seem to last forever. Eventually, I even lost track of where I was. It wasn't like I could ask anyone.

My interactions with the world around me were limited to being able to touch and taste. I could leave coins and take supplies I needed for gifts and to feed myself, but I was even running out of coins because I couldn't do any work to earn more. Even though I left home quite wealthy, no amount of money would last forever.

Because I was running out of coins, I taught myself to become an artisan. If I took raw materials, I could leave fewer coins. The finished product was, and still is, rightfully more expensive because the time and skill it takes someone to make those things is worth something. So, I taught myself to sew and carve. I also left less food and more clothing items since I needed to save money, and I reasoned the clothing would last longer and, therefore, be more valuable to the people getting my gifts.

My first products were very rough. To learn to sew a cloak, I had to take apart my own cloak to use as a pattern because I did not know what shape the pieces were supposed to be. I kept the first shoddy, poorly stitched cloaks to wear myself rather than throw them out or give away products I didn't consider perfect. The people receiving my gifts were poor, but they were still worthy of getting the best, the same as those who could afford to buy their things.

I also learned a few exciting things about the extraordinary situation I had found myself in. I was much stronger than I should have been for my age and than I had even been in my youth. Remember before when I told you I had lifted those three sacks like they were nothing? Well, I never became Superman, but I could lift a lot. It was like that if you have ever turned on the TV and watched a strongman competition with men lifting heavy logs or rocks and moving them around. I couldn't explain it.

I also didn't get tired the same way I used to. I could sew or carve for hours and hours without a break, without my hands or wrists becoming too sore or weak. I could walk vast distances with no need to sit and rest. During this period, I first visited more than one town in one night. I built myself a wagon, piled it as high as possible with gifts one night, and just started walking. I delivered to all the poor people of the village I was staying in, realized I had more to give, and walked to the next town. Even then, I had more time left but not enough presents to deliver, so though I didn't feel I needed to rest, I stopped for the night and went to sleep.

By this point, since I couldn't interact with innkeepers to rent myself a place to stay, I had made myself a tent. I camped on the outskirts of towns for days, making my gifts. When I had enough, I would go out at night and deliver them. I repeated this process over and over. But, as happy as I was to bring others joy, I got very lonely. I missed the voices and company of others, the bustle of life being lived. I never found another person experiencing life as I was in those days. I occasionally thought I saw movement out of the corner of my eye, and once I swore I saw a child running off down the street, but I never actually caught sight of or met up with anyone else.

As I said before, I only have a vague idea of how long my life was like this. I just kept going, on and on, from town to town. I saw places I never dreamed I would. At certain points, I would realize I had crossed into other countries simply because I noticed little differences in dress, in the way things were built, and in the few written words I saw along the way that showed to me that these people spoke or wrote differently than the people in other places I had been. This kept my spirits up. I longed to talk to the people I saw, to learn about them through direct contact, but it still fascinated me to know about them in the ways I could.

By this point in my wandering, I had reached Greece. Remember, my parents were Greek, and I knew the language, so I knew where I was when I saw it on signs. I got to see the beautiful city of Athens for the first time and, from my studies, knew that if I got on a ship, I could sail the Mediterranean Sea and reach Rome. But I did not know how I would even exist on a boat in my current state. I would be stuck just walking back and forth endlessly while everyone around me, and perhaps even the ship, seemed almost not to move at all. I wasn't even sure how to figure out which ship was going to Rome since I couldn't walk up to someone and ask. I wanted to see Rome and knew I could walk there if I had to, but I was also very curious about sea travel since, having been born in the desert, I knew nothing about sailing.

So, at the port, I sat down on a crate and thought. As I sat there, I closed my eyes and thought hard about the most logical steps to take. Then, without warning, I got a feeling of stopping suddenly. You know when you jolt awake feeling like you have just fallen out of bed but haven't? It was just like that. It seemed like I had come to a crash landing on the crate. Just as abruptly and jarringly, sound rushed back into my world. I was startled, and my eyes snapped open, and I jumped to my feet. The world was moving again! I almost covered my ears because I hadn't heard a sound other than myself in so long that I found the world very loud!

What had just happened? I couldn't figure it out. I had lived in a world of near stillness for a long time, and now everything was back to how it had been most of my life!

I impolitely snagged a passerby and asked him the date. He looked at me like I was someone who had lost their mind, but he told me, and I was amazed to learn that I had come all the way to Athens, with innumerable stops along the way to craft and give gifts, in only four months! I wasn't sure how much time I had expected to learn I had been on my mission, but it certainly felt like it had been much longer than that! I thanked him, let him go, and turned back to the ships.

Something had let me find myself back in the position of being able to board a ship for Rome. I did not know precisely what it was, but it had happened just as I put my mind to solving the problem of *sailing* to Rome rather than walking. I wasn't even afraid of not returning to my state of...whatever it was...to keep bringing gifts to more people than I had ever thought possible. It just *felt* like I would return to being in that magical (for that is what I now believed it was) living space.

So, I asked people which ship was going to Rome and which ship might book me passage in exchange for work since I no longer had coins to offer. Several ships were going that way, but most people in charge looked at me and assumed I was too old to be useful since sailing required a lot of physical labor. But one kind man named Gaius, a merchant from Rome, told me he was about to shove off for home and could use a hand on board. I thanked him profusely, and before I knew it, I was heading to sea for the first time.

Sea travel was a challenge for me, a struggle that began with the onset of seasickness. The first couple of days were a blur of discomfort, and I found myself repeatedly apologizing to Gaius for my lack of usefulness. As I confessed my inexperience with sailing, he reassured me, promising that I would acclimate to the sea's rhythm in due time.

"The rocking of the ship bothers many people who have spent all their lives on dry land," he said, clapping me on the back as I leaned over the side and tried not to throw up on his boat. "But I promise pretty soon you'll walk a straight line like the boat is standing still."

He was right, of course. And once I finally felt like myself and could lend a hand, I found I enjoyed it. I have never in my life been averse to putting in a good day's work to earn my keep, and all the other men on board marveled at how I could heave-ho on an oar when the wind died down a bit and how I could lug big heavy ropes with the rest of them. I marveled a bit, too, because even though I knew I could do miraculous physical things while I was on my travels, I hadn't been sure I could now that I was back in the ordinary world.

While on the ship, I heard the legends that had begun about me when I could not talk with people. It was big news that someone (or someones, because many didn't believe it was just one person) had been slipping into the dwellings of people in the night and leaving things for them.

I heard that many believed it was an angel or other supernatural be-ing doing the good work, perhaps even a human being blessed by a god (whichever god they worshipped, I suppose. Remember, many gods were still in existence at the time) to be supernatural and generous. Few people believed it was a group of people, I was told, because the idea of generosity was so sadly scarce and communication so slow to spread across nations that it seemed unlikely to many that an entire group of such selfless givers could come together and work as one.

"I heard the gift giver can turn into the wind and blow under doors or through cracks in walls," one sailor said one night as we were gathered to eat dinner.

"Nah," replied another. "Walls don't matter to a being like that. They can walk right through them!"

"I heard they could fly," said yet another crew member. "They're making it to so many towns in one night! They must soar like a bird does to get so far!"

When I heard that, it made me chuckle because, of course, I couldn't fly! No one could! Flying requires wings! It was such a silly notion. Now, as you know, I fly over the entire world, as does everyone else. It's funny the things we think are impossible when we haven't yet learned how to do them.

When we finally docked in Rome, I was sad to leave all my friends I had made on the journey. I thanked Gaius profusely and told him I wished I could do more for him. We hugged, and I struck out into the city, my heart brimming with excitement and anticipation for the adventures that awaited me.

In Rome, I discovered my ability to manipulate magic. As I leisurely explored the city, immersing myself in the vibrant tapestry of human life, my thoughts were never far from my mission and how I would accomplish it.

I knew I would be able to. I just didn't know how. I thought back to being on the dock in Athens and about how, when I really wanted to solve the problem of booking passage on a ship, I had just closed my eyes, and the world had snapped back into motion. I once again found myself in a situation like that. So, hoping it would work, I sat and closed my eyes.

I focused very hard on wanting time to crawl almost to a stop around me, on wanting to walk around people unnoticed so I could keep bringing presents to those in need. All at once, I felt like I lurched, and I got a feeling of incredible speed. I heard sounds rush past my ears, sounding like they were getting further and further away until the world was still and quiet again. When I opened my eyes, a world again surrounded me that, at a glance, was as still as a statue.

"Fascinating," I said to myself as I stood up, gathered what little I had with me, and walked off searching for supplies.

A Very Brief History of Christmas, Pt. 1: Ancient Winter Holidays

Let's leave me discovering I can control the magic and walking off into the streets of Rome for now. My story is getting to a part where it gets very "wash, rinse, repeat," where I do the same things repeatedly for quite a long time, and that isn't very interesting to talk about. But I don't want to skip too far ahead without telling you a bit about Christmas.

Now, I don't want this to become a boring history lesson with me just telling you names and dates and such. You can look up Christmas's long (and, in my opinion, fascinating) history on your own if what I tell you catches your interest, but there are a bunch of articles and books on the subject already, so I don't want to take up too much space in this book retelling it. But I can't explain my story and connection to Christmas without telling you at least a little about history.

Winter holidays, with their ancient origins, hold a fascinating history. They were a beacon of joy during the long, dark, and cold days of winter, reminding people that the sun's warmth would return in the spring. These celebrations often coincided with the winter solstice, the shortest day of the year. Picture this: a grand feast, a symbol of the forthcoming abundance of food. Sounds familiar, doesn't it?

Another thing these winter holidays sometimes included was the giving of gifts. One such holiday was called Saturnalia. It was a holiday that celebrated the Roman god Saturn and lasted from December 17th to the 23rd. Romans loved to celebrate and during Saturnalia, everything was closed but those shops that sold food, drink, and small gifts. On top of eating and drinking, gift-giving was part of Saturnalia. Friends and family would give each other small tokens of their love and appreciation for each other: patches for clothes and sandals, small toys for children, new straw for brooms, that sort of thing. Often, during Saturnalia, wealthy slave owners would welcome their slaves to their tables, and they could eat, drink, and be merry as if they were free. Of course, it would have shown even greater kindness not to own one's fellow human beings at all, but it's useless to talk about how it could have been rather than how it was. These enslavers felt they were being extra kind and generous, allowing their slaves to take part in the season's joy, and to a certain extent they were, so it's the best example of the spirit of the season actual history has for me to offer.

In the year 270, a new emperor took charge of the Roman Empire. His name was Aurelian, and he did not worship the traditional Roman gods (which they had borrowed from the Greeks and renamed, but that's a different story). Remember, earlier in my story, I told you that my family wasn't religious because the religion of Rome changed quite a bit. This was one of those times. Aurelian worshiped a god that had been borrowed from a Syrian religion. That god was named Sol Invictus, which means "Unconquered Sun." On December 25th, 274 C.E., Aurelian made The Cult of Sol Invictus the Roman Empire's official religion. However, since he let people keep having a celebration, most people didn't care if they were celebrating Saturn or Sol Invictus. They renamed Saturnalia the Festival of Dies Natalis Solis Invicti. It carried on very much as it had when it was Saturnalia but focused more on December 25th, which was said to be Sol Invictus's birthday. During this period, people actually celebrated both holidays, though, as it took some time for the religion of Sol Invictus to catch on and replace the old Roman Gods.

Though the Roman Empire covered most of Europe, not everyone worshiped the Roman Gods or Sol Invictus. The Germanic people, who occupied a good chunk of central Europe and Scandinavia, worshiped other gods. Some of their names you probably recognize from modern pop culture: Odin, Thor, Loki, and Heimdal.

During the period surrounding the winter solstice, these people celebrated a season called Jol (also spelled Jul in some places), which, later on, would come to be spelled Yule, which you may recognize as a word now associated with Christmas, like in the song lyric "sing the ancient Yuletide carol," where the word "Yuletide" means "Christmas time." We still observe a few of the Yule traditions today: the Yule log, the Yule goat, the Yule boar (which you probably know as the Christmas ham), and Yule singing, or wassailing, also known as caroling. In modern-day Finland, I am still known as Joulupukki.

Also, in that time, Celtic people hung holly, ivy, and mistletoe, which are green winter herbs, and would kiss under the mistletoe as a symbol of prosperity and fertility in times to come.

I am telling you about these holidays so you can understand a bit about how Christmas came to be so important and how my part in it was a natural extension of the spirit of love, joy, and generosity that already existed in December. Winter festivals were the most popular because a lot less farm work had to be done during this period of the year, and people were eager to look forward to spring and longer days.

You'll notice I have said nothing about the celebration of Christmas here as I tell you about the ancient winter holidays. That's because it wasn't a thing yet. During the times I am talking about, Christianity was a tiny religion. In fact, during several periods in the existence of the Roman Empire, it was illegal to be Christian, and people who were Christian were mistreated. So, until Christianity became the Roman Empire's official religion and spread through Europe, they didn't celebrate or worship openly. And they hadn't decided to mark the birth of their Lord yearly yet, though there is a record that a celebration of Jesus' birth took place "eight days before the first of January" in the year 354. We'll talk a little more about how Christmas became the dominant holiday later in my story. But it's essential for you to remember that winter holidays were already very much alive during my earliest adventures and were some of the most joyous occasions of the whole year. December has always, it seems, been a time when people want to gather with friends and family and be kind to their fellow humans, if only for a little while.

The Hidden People

Before the little break to talk about the history of Christmas, we left me entering the city of Rome for the first time. As I said at the beginning of the last chapter, this part of my story plays like a song on repeat for a good period. I wandered alone for a long time, crafting and leaving gifts as I went. I don't need to tell you about all those times, so I will skip to the next important event in my story.

Eventually, I made my way north to lands I hadn't even heard about before. I didn't recognize the languages I encountered when I interacted with others and began to learn them. At some point, I realized I knew more languages than anyone I had ever heard of, and I was amazed that I could hold so much knowledge. I added that to the list of my abilities, I couldn't explain.

In what is now Austria, I saw snow for the first time. I had heard of snow before but never encountered it. The cold, soft blanket over the ground that made everything look glistening enchanted me. I fell in love with it immediately. I had spent much of my life surrounded by sand and found the snow magical. I never wanted to live in a place without it again. The cold that came with the snow didn't bother me a bit. I felt like I was in a place where I was supposed to be.

Over the years I wandered alone, I often continued to catch glimpses of movement and what I thought to be other people when I was moving and the world stood still around me. Every time I did, though, I was never sure of what I had seen because it would dash away out of sight, and I could not find what I had thought I had seen.

By the time I wandered into the land of what is now Germany, I had been on my own for ten years. I was much older than I ever expected to be and showed no signs of aging or slowing down. Indeed, I felt better than the day I had left home. I barely slept because I hardly ever felt tired. A couple of hours a night seemed to do the trick in refreshing me. And though I did not look like a young man, as far as I could tell, I hadn't gotten a single new wrinkle in the previous decade. Plus, despite walking more miles than any human being ever had before me and eating generous portions of food at every meal (okay, and often between meals), I never gained or lost weight. I seemed to be as stuck in time in my own way as the people I passed frozen in the streets every day.

My life took another spectacular turn in Germany. For, you see, it was in Germany that I first befriended elves.

It was in the Black Forest that I first met an elf. I had made myself a little camp among the trees, crafting gifts for nearby towns. As I carved a crutch for a man I had noticed earlier that day who only had one leg, I saw more of that movement I kept seeing occasionally. A shadow popped out from behind a tree, was visible for a couple of seconds, then went back behind the tree. I pretended not to notice and kept carving, thinking if I didn't acknowledge what I had seen, perhaps it would happen again.

Sure enough, a few moments later, I heard a rustle and saw a shape dart from behind the tree, run a little way, then hide behind another tree. This time, I was sure I had seen it. It wasn't a big shape, more like the shape of a child. My heart beat a little faster. I was excited that someone else may be like me. But I was also concerned. How scared must the poor little one be if it was a child?

I whistled a happy little tune as I carved, a song I remembered from when I was young. I wanted whoever was out there to know I wasn't dangerous. The next time I looked up from my carving, I gave a little start because there, right out in the open, was a small person.

He wasn't a child; that much was clear. But he wasn't a full-grown man, either. I had encountered a few little people in my time, but not many because, sadly, they were thought to be evil and often shunned by their communities. But this person was not a little person, either. At least, I didn't think so. Because I noticed, his ears came to a very pronounced point.

He was dressed in shades of green and brown. His green tunic was long and fell to just above his knees. His pants, I thought, were comically puffy. On his feet were brown boots, and a long stocking cap was perched on his head. He had sparkling blue eyes, and the hair poking from beneath his cap was thick and black. He was of an indeterminate age. As far as I could tell, he could have been anywhere from thirty to forty.

"Hello," I said to him in the region's language, keeping my voice soft and non-threatening. He gave me a little nod in response but said nothing, so I spoke again. "My name is Nicholas."

This time, he spoke. "Adelgard," he said, indicating himself with a poke of his finger to his chest.

"I'm pleased to meet you, Adelgard," I told him. There was a pause, and neither of us said anything before I broke the silence. "Would you like to have a seat with me?" I asked. I have a little food I could share."

He eyed me briefly, then stepped closer and sat across from me. I set down the crutch, reached into my pack, and pulled out a loaf of bread, a small pouch of berries, and a bit of dried meat. I offered him some of these things, and he took a hunk of bread and some berries but declined the dried meat.

"Elves don't eat meat," he said to me. "The animals are our fellow living beings. It's cruel to kill them to eat."

"Oh," I said, flustered, and shoved the meat back into my pack. "I'm sorry. I...I didn't know."

"No," he said, "you wouldn't. Humans seem to think of animals as lesser creatures than themselves."

"It's not that," I said back, "It's just...just...well...huh..." I trailed off, not sure of a defense I could mount. I had never thought of it before, but he was right. I loved animals, but I always ate them out of habit. I was brought up that way. It never occurred to me before that moment that maybe it wasn't okay to eat them.

Having no response to what he had said, I changed course. "Elves?" I said, the question evident in my voice. "I haven't heard of them before. Is that the name of your tribe? Your people?"

"No," he said, popping a berry into his mouth and chewing it slowly. "Elves are my *kind*. I guess *my people* is correct in a way. We differ from humans. Different from you. We live in this realm." He gestured broadly at our surroundings.

"The forest?"

"No, no, this *realm*. The *Hylgan Rikalt*," he replied.

I stared at him, completely lost. It must have been apparent on my face because he chuckled. "That's elvish for the Hidden Realm," he said.

I stared at him blankly and shook my head. "I don't understand."

"You know," he said, "the space you've been living in, too. You can't tell me you haven't wondered how you've been carrying on as you have with the world mostly standing still around you."

"I thought..." I started, then paused. I wasn't sure *what* I thought was going on. "Well, I guess I didn't really think anything. I thought magic was happening to me."

"Well, you're not wrong," he replied. "Magic is the closest word for it. See, the *Hylgan Rikalt* is Earth, but also its own world. You know how you can still see everything as you have always seen it and even touch it, but everything is just slow to the point of seeming to stand still? That's because the *Hylgan Rikalt* is also its own place, just to the side of the human world, so to speak. It's why humans rarely ever see us. We're not invisible, exactly. We're just...sped up."

"I don't understand," I said again.

"Okay," he sighed, "let me see if I can explain this right. I've never had to explain it before. I've never met a human. So, you know how you have been walking around, feeling like you are moving at your normal speed and the world is moving slowly?" I nodded. "Well, actually, the world is moving at its regular speed. To the humans, I mean. The *Hylgan Rikalt is*, I don't know, faster, somehow. We, you, can travel very far in the same time humans only travel a few miles. We can accomplish more in one day than a human could in months. They aren't moving slowly; we're moving fast. At least, to them we are. That's why they don't see us. We whoosh right past them. Maybe they see a hint of color, like if a fly went by, but that's it."

I gaped at him. Then I stammered for a bit, having trouble understanding what I was hearing. Finally, I exclaimed, "But how did I get here? Why can I still interact with others if I focus really hard?"

"The answer to how you got here is: I don't know. No one does. You're quite a legend, you know."

Now, I was baffled. "Well, I know people are talking about my gifts, but I didn't know anyone knew…" he cut me off.

"No, no, Nicholas. I mean, yes. I mean…oh…yes, humans are talking about your gifts, but that's not the legend I'm talking about. To *elves*, I mean! No human has *ever* crossed over to our realm before. Sometimes we cross into yours, but no human has ever come to ours! You can still interact with humans because it's possible to cross in and out of the realm by accident or on purpose, which is how humans know about elves, but it's never happened to a human as far as anyone knows!"

"Hold on a moment," I said to him, holding up a hand. "Others know about me besides you?"

Here, he blushed and hung his head. "Yes. Like I said, you're something of a legend."

"Well, where have you been?" I almost shouted at him. "I've been wandering the world for ten whole years! And for a long part of that, I never spoke to another soul before I realized I could control the magic!

If I'm such a legend, why did no one tell me this sooner? It sure would have been nice to know!"

Adelgard lifted his head, his cheeks still bright red, but with his eyes confidently looking into mine. "We were afraid of you," he said softly.

I deflated. I never expected to hear that someone might have feared me, not when I worked so hard to be so kind.

"Like I told you," he continued, "no human had ever crossed into our realm before. We don't interact with humans very often. I hear some communities further north interact with humans more, but we keep mostly to ourselves in this part of the world. I'm sure you know this, but there has been a lot of fighting over the years as Rome has tried and succeeded in taking over more and more land. We may not be seen much by humans, but the things they do affect our lives just the same. Elves haven't had a war in *thousands* of years. We're peaceful. We're happy. We live quietly and help each other, sometimes even helping humans. But sadly, humans are often mean and violent. When word spread that a human had entered the *Hylgan Rikalt*, well," he shrugged his shoulders and gave another sigh, "everyone just decided to stay away from you. But everywhere you went, you were watched. I heard you almost caught some of us from time to time." I realized he meant all the times over the years I thought I had seen movement that I really had, that it had been elves watching me.

"Okay," I said to him, "I understand that. But it's been *ten years*! How did you not realize until now that I mean no one any harm?"

"Fear runs deep in us," he admitted. "But, friend Nicholas, you have a right to be upset. That's why I'm speaking to you now. Someone should have done it sooner. No elf alive that has heard of you can remember ever encountering a human so kind and generous, and elves are very long-lived. I'm sure you've noticed by now that you are, too." Again, I must have looked confused because he went on. "Have you not noticed that you aren't changing?"

"I...well...yes," I said, mystified.

"You are truly one with the realm," he said, equally awed as I was. "Amazing."

"One with the realm?"

"Like you belong here. Like it is your natural habitat. Tell me, do you sleep much? Do you tire? Do you feel strong?"

"I feel very strong," I said, "and I sleep very little, but I hardly ever get tired."

"Astounding," he said, his voice still full of wonder. "Simply amazing." He paused, resting his chin on his hand. "Oh!" he nearly shouted, "I remember what I was saying! Yes, Nicholas, because you have been observed to be so kind, loving, and generous, someone should have come to you sooner and explained things to you sooner. On behalf of elfin kind, I cry your pardon!" He swept off his cap, held it to his chest, and bent into a low bow. I became very embarrassed.

"It's okay, Adelgard, it's okay," I blurted, "please, stand back up, you're forgiven." He stood and placed the cap back on his head.

"It's my hope you'll come with me to my village," he said. "I'm...sort of in charge. We don't really have rulers among the elves, but we take turns being...organizers, for lack of a better term. If we have decisions to make as a group, someone needs to ensure everything goes smoothly and every voice gets heard. At the moment, that someone is me. We had a meeting, and we'd like to be the ones to welcome you officially."

We walked a little through the forest before approaching a large clearing. I gaped in awe at the village that spread out before me because it was unlike anything I had ever seen. All the buildings were crafted in the Germanic style of the area, but all were a fraction of the size of the buildings I was used to. Also, everything was painted brightly. Things were rather plain in those days. Pigments to make colors for paint and fabric dye were costly, so people often left things in natural shades, with bright colors like purple, blue, and red being reserved for the rich. Apparently, elves had no such limit in their realm because they painted buildings all colors of the rainbow, and the clothes were dyed to match.

Adelgard, in a plain tunic and somewhat absurdly puffy pants, both in earthy shades, was one of the plainest dressed people in sight. I saw elves with elegant embroidered patterns on their clothes. There were hats of all shapes and sizes: long stocking caps, pointed cone hats, hats that looked like crowns, and so many more.

As we stepped out of the forest and into the village, the bustling activity around us stopped. All eyes turned towards me, and a hush fell over the crowd. The weight of their collective gaze bore down on me, and I felt a wave of unease wash over me. I leaned towards Adelgard, my voice barely a whisper, 'Why is everyone staring at me?'

"Like I told you," he said to me, "you're a legend."

We walked on. They greeted me with many smiles and timid waves. I smiled and nodded back, doing my best not to let on how uncomfortable and confused I was. As we passed by, elves fell into line behind us and followed.

Eventually, we reached what seemed to be a town common. There was a small stage, and Adelgard climbed up on it and motioned for me to follow. I did so, hoping I wouldn't break it. It wasn't big, but it was very sturdy. I turned and looked at a sea of about two hundred elfin faces staring expectantly up at us. As I looked at them all, I couldn't help but notice that none looked particularly old or young. Every face I saw looked like a person in perhaps their thirties or forties. Though, as I learned later, they were all so much older than that.

"Hi, everyone!" Adelgard said to the crowd, a sly smile creeping onto his face. "As you can see, I didn't have any luck convincing the human to come back to the village with me." A laugh rose in the crowd, and I, too, couldn't help but laugh. My new friend looked at me and winked. I felt some of my discomfort melt away. When the laugh died down, Adelgard went on.

"Everyone, this is Nicholas," he said, gesturing my way, "the human we have heard so much about. I spoke to him, and he didn't know about elves or our special realm. He has been wandering alone all these years, confused and sometimes frightened by what has been happening to him. We all know that humans can become violent and lash out when they are scared and confused. But not Nicholas. Nicholas has looked at his situation, overcome his fear, and carried on with a hopeful, happy spirit! When faced with the reality of being able to move among his fellow humans undetected, and at a great rate of speed, Nicholas used this to help others! He does indeed craft and bring gifts to the most in need. If someone is in rags, he clothes them! If someone is hungry, he feeds them! If they are lame and cannot walk without help, he brings them canes and crutches!"

A cheer rose, and I felt my face flush. I never once gave a gift to receive credit or attention, and having a light turned on my deeds was intensely embarrassing, although I can't say why exactly. I have gotten over it in the past several centuries, but at that moment, my face was hot and, I'm sure, the color of a ripe tomato. But I smiled and nodded and gave a little wave to the crowd.

Adelgard motioned for them to settle, then carried on. "Nicholas may not be unique among humans in his willingness to help those in need, for we know that most humans *are* good and do their best to be kind. However, he is unique in his boundless love for his fellow people and unwavering gentleness. While no human has ever before passed into our realm, I think we can safely say that, now that one has, we are truly fortunate that he is so good, humble, and like us in spirit! Let's welcome Nicholas to the *Hylgan Rikalt* and tell the world that Nicholas is our brother!"

More cheers erupted, and Adelgard's arms enveloped me in a warm embrace. Unexpectedly, tears welled in my eyes, and my heart swelled with joy and love. I returned his hug, feeling the love and acceptance radiating from the crowd. The cheers, applause, and whistles grew louder, and in that moment, I felt a sense of belonging I hadn't experienced since my childhood.

Adelgard led me from the stage, where I was immediately swarmed by elves who wanted to shake my hand or hug me, and all wanted to greet me at once. Tears rolled down my face, and happiness exploded out of me as booming laughter.

After years of solitary wandering, I had finally found my place among these elves. I had found my people.

The Legend Grows

In the Black Forest, in that first elfin village, my mission began taking the shape of what you now know it to be. Until then, I had not settled in one place in ten years. I had merely wandered about giving gifts wherever my feet took me next. But once I was invited into the village, I didn't want to wander anymore. With the help of the elves, I built myself a simple two-room cabin that was my size on the edge of the village and took up residence there.

I still gave gifts, but only in areas around the village, where I could walk and be back in the forest by morning. I did this several nights a week, picking a direction and walking until I ran out of gifts, then heading back. During the days, I would carve and sew, and soon, I had many friends in the village who wanted to help me while I worked.

A seamstress named Erminlinda made beautiful, rugged cloaks for me to give. A shoemaker named Odalric made me the finest boots I had ever seen out of canvas and leather when he had some. Adelgard told me during our first meeting that elves don't eat meat because they don't believe in killing. Because they don't believe in killing, they use very little leather and fur in the things they make compared to clothes in the human realm. However, they felt okay using the hides of animals that had met death naturally. They used a lot of wool, though, because wool didn't involve hurting the sheep. They kept a small herd in the village that they loved and treated very well. I even could bring more food than

I had been able to in years because the elves were great bakers and had fine crops of berries and nuts they harvested in the surrounding woods.

But, even as I was delivering some of the highest quality gifts I had in many years, I soon grew sad thinking about all the places I was no longer reaching.

I brought this up one day to Odalric, who was teaching me the best stitch to use to keep the soles on the shoes. He bent his head for a moment, scratched his chin, snapped his fingers, and looked back up at me.

"I have an idea!" he said, setting down the shoe he was working on and getting to his feet. "Come with me!"

He guided me through the village, where we were met with warm greetings, smiles, and waves. I was struck by the elves' perpetual cheerfulness. They faced challenges with determination but never lost their composure. It was a sight I had never seen before, and I felt incredibly blessed to be a part of their community.

We came to the workshop of Waldhar, the leading builder of the village. Odalric knocked and called for him to come outside because I could not fit in the elf-sized building. The sounds of hammering from inside stopped, and the door opened, and Waldhar came out.

Even by elf standards, he was short but wide, with solid arms and legs. His auburn beard was in three braids and hung to his belt. Curlycues of wood shavings were clinging to it. He smiled broadly at me and Odalric.

"Well, what can I do for you today, my friends?" he asked.

"Nicholas needs a wagon," Odalric said to him.

"A wagon?" I asked, peering down at Odalric, quite confused. "What on earth do I need a wagon for?"

"Didn't you just tell me you wished you could get further and bring presents to more people?" he asked me.

"Yes."

"Well, if you have a wagon, you can load it up with more gifts!" he exclaimed with a twinkle in his eye. "Since you're not running out of nighttime, just gifts, if you fill the wagon, you can distribute more presents before dawn! And if you have a horse or a donkey to pull it, you can travel faster, too!"

"Odalric! That's brilliant!" I said, dropping to one knee and hugging my friend.

"How big of a wagon, do you think?" Waldhar asked.

"My goodness, I don't know," I replied. "What would you suggest?"

"Hang on," he said, then turned and went back into the workshop. A moment later, he returned and had a ladder tucked under one arm, a piece of parchment in his mouth, a tape measure around his neck, and a quill and inkpot in his hands. I still can't believe he managed to carry all that.

He set the ladder next to me, thrust the quill, ink, and parchment into Odalric's hands, and told him to take down the numbers he would say. He then took the tape measure and measured me all over, calling out numbers as he went. When he was done, he took the parchment, quill, and ink back, looked at the numbers, scribbled down a few other numbers, nodded to himself, and then looked up at me.

"Come back in a week," he said. Then he glanced back down at his numbers, nodded again, looked back at me, and said, "That should be enough time for me to have it all done.

Waldhar was good to his word. I spent a week crafting gifts with help from my elf friends, and on the last day of the week, he found me and said I should follow him back to the workshop because the job was ready.

When we arrived, a large canvas tarp covered what I assumed was the wagon. Waldhar stood next to it, and a crowd gathered around it.

"I'm really proud of this," he said. "I don't want to brag, but this is the best work I have done in a long time. Nicholas, I present to you your wagon!" He gripped the canvas and pulled it theatrically from the form underneath.

It was a very handsome wagon indeed. It was a deep chestnut color that he had made shiny with some stain. It had a massive bed that could hold bags and bags of gifts for me to give. He even carved decorative swirls along the side to make it more attractive, which amused me because no one would ever see it but us. But I appreciated his dedication to his craft.

"Magnificent, Waldhar!" I said, grasping his hand and pumping it up and down. "I will travel far with this once we find a good steed to pull it!"

"I think," said Adelgard from behind me, causing me to turn, "we won't have to look too hard." As he spoke, two other elves emerged, leading a majestic white horse. Blue ribbons adorned its mane and tail, and a stunning red bridle graced its face, capturing the attention and admiration of everyone present.

"This is Vulfgang," Adelgard said, patting the horse's nose. "We had a little talk with him, and he would be happy to help you spread happiness by pulling the wagon."

"Well, that's wonderful!" I cried. "I'll start packing! We can head out tonight on our first run!" I hurriedly gathered the gifts we had crafted, carefully arranging them in the wagon. The anticipation of the first run filled the air, and I could feel the excitement building.

As I was loading up my wagon with the last couple of sacks of gifts, my dear friend Erminlinda, a talented seamstress, came to me with a box wrapped with a big bow. She held it out to me and said, "For your journey."

"A gift for me?" I said, my voice filled with surprise and touched by Erminlinda's thoughtfulness. I couldn't remember the last time anyone had given me a gift. I took it from her and admired the craft she had used to tie the bow. Then, I set it on the back of the wagon, undid the bow, and lifted off the lid.

Inside was a pile of green and brown, and because I knew Erminlinda was a seamstress, I assumed it was some sort of garment. But I was not prepared for the beautiful robe which I pulled out. It was a deep forest green, trimmed with brown bear fur. It had an oversized, lined hood to keep the cold from my head.

"Oh, Erminlinda," I said softly, "this is gorgeous."

"It should fit you," she said, grinning from ear to ear, her eyes green as summer grass sparkling with merriment. I got your measurements from Waldhar. It's wool from our sheep, and the fur was from a bear that had taken sick and died close to here. I assume you're going to be traveling to some places at least as cold as here, if not colder, so you're going to need something to keep the chill out!"

I dropped to one knee and hugged her. "That is so thoughtful, my friend. Thank you so much!" I stood back up and engulfed myself in the robe. It was just the perfect size and was incredibly soft and warm. Also in the box was a green silk sash, which I tied around my waist to close the robe.

Erminlinda clapped, giggled, and bounced with delight, her long, thick, vibrant red hair bouncing around her face. I gave her a theatrical bow. I was pretty delighted myself. I felt almost like a king in such a luxurious garment. I've never worried much about having nice things for myself or felt I deserve anything in return for my good work. But, at that moment, I felt that my life of good deeds was being rewarded in a small way. I had friends who cared enough to help me in my mission and gift me nice things, and I figured I had earned those things.

Pretty soon, a crowd had gathered to see me off. I hitched Vulfgang to the wagon, climbed up, took a seat, grabbed the reins, and waved to my friends. I flicked the reins, hollered, "Giddup," and we were off.

I wish I could adequately describe my joy as Vulfgang took off at a canter. The wind passing blew my beard around.

'Ho ho!" I exclaimed, my joy bubbling over. As we set off towards the first town, my heart was brimming with excitement and love, eager to share the gifts and spread the joy.

We arrived swiftly, and I leaped from the wagon, swung a pack over my back, and with glee all but ran around the town, leaving my small gifts wherever I found a less fortunate family. Before I knew it, I had visited every family that needed visiting, so I hopped back into the cart and was off again.

I repeated this over and over that night, traveling to towns and villages further away than I had ever been before. Anywhere I could go by horse and wagon, I went. When I had finally exhausted my supply of gifts and had to head for home, I still had plenty of nighttime left. I couldn't believe it! I had been traveling in the elf realm for more than a decade and was still amazed by how far I could travel so fast. I returned to the village long before the sun rose and was greeted by yet another crowd of elves, all gathering around me, asking questions, wondering how it had gone and how far I had traveled. I laughed and invited everyone to the town square to hear about my adventure, and I told my story until dawn.

I did my mission like this for a good number of years. My journeys into the night now only happened twice a month, with the rest of the time spent making gifts. Occasionally, I would pop back into the human realm and hear more and more stories about mysterious presents appearing at night to families in need. No one could figure out who or what was providing these gifts. Many thought it was gods or angels. I heard a time or two the idea that my friends, the elves, were responsible, which, of course, was partly true. But no one yet knew about me. That still came later.

The next big development in my story came almost eighty years after that first nighttime ride with my horse and wagon because that was when I shifted my mission full-time to bringing toys to children.

The First Toys

You are probably wondering about some things at this point in my story. For example, in my last chapter, I mentioned that I had a horse and wagon, not a sleigh and reindeer. I also mentioned my first elf-made robe was green and brown, not red and white. But remember, my life has been very long, and not everything about it happened all at once. Even today, some countries still expect me to wear clothes other than the red and white coat and hat you probably always picture me in. In some countries, I am still depicted as riding my old friend Vulfgang, the white horse, though his name is never mentioned. I'll explain in a bit how those customs came to be in those countries, but first I need to tell you about toys for children.

Until I was about one-hundred-fifty-five years old, I helped families in need: parents, grandparents, aunts, uncles, and, of course, children. I always gave the children a little more than the adults because I know children often experience feelings of wanting more than adults.

In the summer of that year, I was sitting out under a shady tree, whistling a tune and carving a fun new item I had not yet tried my hand at: a top. I often saw children spinning tops for fun and thought it would be nice to add to my gift-giving rounds so children could have something to play with. Toys were not plentiful in those times. People were still focused almost entirely on survival, making money, and finding food. Even children had to work hard, especially those of low-income families, who needed everyone to chip in to bring food home.

So children did not have the time they do now to play and enjoy life. Plus, there just weren't many toys. There were tops and hoops that children rolled around by pushing them with sticks, and in Egypt, I had seen wooden carvings of crocodiles that children played with. And, of course, what toys there were cost money, which most families either didn't have or couldn't spare for something they couldn't eat or wear.

Thus, I resolved to bring joy to the hearts of underprivileged children by gifting them toys. The idea of tops appealed to me, as I could craft each one uniquely, ensuring they spun perfectly and painting them in vibrant hues. I reckoned a top, nestled amidst the clothes and food I distributed to each family, would be a delightful addition.

As I sat there under the tree, my friend Adelgard came and asked if he could sit down next to me. I told him he could and went back to my carving. He watched me for a bit before he said something.

"You know, if you're going to add tops to your load, you'll probably have to go out less. Even if Waldhar goes to making tops full time and sets aside his other projects, we couldn't get enough done, and I don't think anyone else in the village is skilled enough yet at carving to lend a hand. Plus, we still have shoes to make, clothes to sew, and fruit to pick. It's a lot to do in such a short time."

I put down my top and my knife and sighed. "You're probably right," I acknowledged sadly. "It's too bad. I have so many families to visit."

Adelgard gazed at the top for a long time. I could see he was deep in thought about something important, so I sat quietly. Finally, he looked up at me and spoke what was on his mind.

Sometimes in life, there are ideas that are so good that you wish you had thought of them and want to take credit for them. But, the right and gracious thing to do is give credit to the person who really thought of it. Here, that's my old friend Adelgard.

"Nicholas," he said cautiously, "what if you *just* gave the toys?"

His suggestion left me utterly speechless. My jaw dropped, and my eyes widened in astonishment. It was a brilliant idea, so brilliant that I was at a loss for words. I think he mistook my silence for displeasure, as he hurriedly tried to explain his reasoning.

"You've always given more to the children than the adults, anyway. You've said so many times that you think they more than anyone else need reminding that there is love, kindness, and joy in the world..."

"And what better way to remind them there is joy in the world than bringing them the gift of play!" I shouted. "Adelgard, that's absolutely genius!" He blushed so hard that his face looked like a beet. I swept him up in a brief but intense hug before scrambling to my feet.

"Come on!" I said, scooping up my knife and the top. "We're going to miss a delivery or two, but it can't be helped. We need to teach anyone who knows even a bit of carving the proper way to carve a top if we're ever going to have enough!"

It didn't take as long as I thought for those in town who were already at least somewhat skilled at carving to get great. I learned that elves have a knack for learning, and soon, dozens and dozens of tops were being carved daily. Many others in town pitched in and painted the little toys in many vibrant colors, and in just a few weeks, there were so many tops I was sure I would have extra when I was done!

But this time, I was the one who had the idea. As I loaded tops into bags, and my friends did the same, I looked at the beautiful, happy load I was packing onto my wagon and thought what a shame it would be to waste them. I still could only go so far with Vulfgang and the wagon. Natural barriers like rivers and mountains stopped us from reaching some villages and countries. I turned to Odalric, who was next to me, and asked his opinion on the thought forming in my mind.

"I have so many tops," I began, my voice tinged with uncertainty, "far more than there are needy children, I believe. Do you think, my friend, that it would be wrong to deliver a toy to *every* child, not just the poor ones?"

Odalric pondered this for a moment. He had a habit of tapping his left foot as he thought, and I watched the toe of that shoe bounce as he did it. Finally, he ran his hand through his short blonde hair and spoke.

"Well," he said, sounding unsure, "I don't know much about human children. Do the ones who aren't poor have toys?"

"Some do, yes. But there aren't many toys in the world. So I imagine many parents don't even have access to toys to buy their children, even if they can afford them," I replied.

He hummed a bit, and his left toe tapped some more. I tried to explain my reasoning to him.

"The main reason I want to give poor children gifts is so they can know that happiness, kindness, and generosity exist. I want them to know that even a stranger can love and care for them and make sure they experience joy. But just because a child is rich doesn't mean they shouldn't learn the same lesson. If I give a gift to a rich child to show them that someone they don't know cares enough about their happiness to give them a toy, perhaps they can take that lesson with them as they grow up and be more generous to those less fortunate than they are than the generation before them was."

"Then," Odalric replied, his voice filled with conviction, "I think giving a toy to all children, regardless of whether their family is rich or poor, is a magnificent plan!" He gripped my hand and pumped it up and down in a vigorous shake, his enthusiasm contagious.

So it came to be that I would bring toys to all children. After the first delivery of tops, we embarked on a journey of creativity. We learned to make other toys. We carved animals of all kinds, each one a unique creation. We formed hoops, perfect circles of joy. We molded marbles out of clay, each one a tiny world of wonder. And Erminlinda, with her nimble fingers, sewed the first dolls, outfitting them with beautiful clothes that she stitched with love. We lived there in the Black Forest, making toys for many happy years, and once a month, I would take toys to as many places as I could reach, spreading joy with every step.

But, as you know, my mission was far from done growing and changing.

Leaving the Forest

After leaving toys for children for the first time, I spent a long time in the Black Forest among my elf friends. Things didn't always go smoothly. I got lost quite a few times. Even though Rome had conquered most of Europe many years before, there weren't many reliable maps. And though I was learning to navigate by the stars, it took me a long time to get good at it. Plus, it's impossible to navigate by the stars on a cloudy night. By the time GPS was invented, I had long since mastered finding my way around the world in the dark, but it would have been the best thing I could have ever received back then.

Because I got lost a lot, I often dropped out of the *Hylgan Rikalt* and spoke to people to figure out where I was and find my way home again. On these returns to the human realm, I got news of what was happening in the world and heard people talking about my exploits leaving gifts for children. It amazed people that not only were gifts being given by a seemingly supernatural being, but those gifts were *toys* for *children*! Some people thought it was silly and a waste of time for children to play with toys, but far more people were happy that someone or something was caring enough to provide their children with many happy hours of play.

I also learned I wasn't always traveling within the *Hylgan Rikalt*. I already knew that I could slip back into the human realm both on purpose and by accident, but I had apparently been slipping out without realizing it because I also heard many people saying that they had glimpsed the mysterious gift giver. However, I must have quickly slipped back into the elfin realm because I also heard that the gift giver could disappear. No one ever seemed to see me very well. I heard I was tall and short, fat and skinny, old and young. The young thing puzzled me because, by that point, my beard and hair had been white for over a hundred years. Probably closer to two hundred, really. The only description that remained pretty consistent was that I was dressed in fur. My beautiful green wool robe with brown fur had held up nicely, and I wore it on all my journeys unless it was hot.

One of the times I was lost, I learned I, by name, was famous. That surprised me quite a bit when I first heard it because I had left my village so long ago at that point that I assumed I was long forgotten. However, it seemed my village and the world had not forgotten me and wouldn't anytime soon. I was already being referred to as "Saint" Nicholas, and legends about me separate from my gift-giving were spreading (I wouldn't be associated with gift-giving until the year 1500, but that's a story for later).

Apparently, after I had left my village, people assumed I had died. At least, that is the story that got spread and took hold. I also heard I had lived in my home much longer than I really had because, you will remember, I left home in the year 333, yet I heard I had died in 343, ten whole years later. And, after my supposed death, what was remembered most about me was the work I had done with the local church helping the poor. Somewhere along the way, the fact that I had been called "Bishop Nicholas" by the church members had gotten confused with me actually being a bishop. Now, Bishop Nicholas of Myra and his work helping the poor was legendary. I had apparently miraculously healed the sick, caused crops to grow, and guided ships in from the harbor. I supposedly was still performing these miracles from beyond the grave, which is why they called me a saint. Of course, the story about my first gifts, the coins for the girls, was already the most famous tale. That is how, later, when I was made an official saint by the Catholic Church, I became known as the patron saint of children. But, like becoming associated with gift-giving, that came later, so I'll save that story for now. The point is that as Christianity, long since legal and by that time the Roman Empire's official religion, spread across Europe, so did tales of St. Nicholas.

The years went by there in the forest. I traveled as far as I could with my horse and wagon and brought toys to children. But in the next hundred-plus years, more and more humans ventured into the forest. Populations grew. More trees were cut down. Even though we lived in our secret realm, we couldn't take up the same space as humans. The village moved deeper and deeper into the woods.

In 476, the Roman Empire finally collapsed under the strain of trying to control such a vast amount of territory. Countries became independent. Having spent so long bringing joy to the same area of the world, I longed to see other countries and introduce my gifts of toys to different lands and other children.

Despite the allure of new lands, I found it hard to part with the elf village in the Black Forest. The thought of leaving my friends behind and embarking on another solitary journey was daunting after all those years.

However, in the year 506, I called a meeting in the village, and we all met in the square. I stood on the little stage there, took a deep breath, and delivered my news.

"My friends," I said, spreading my arms warmly. "I have some news for you. But first, please know that I have never been more grateful for anything in my life than your welcoming friendship. When I first came to this village a hundred-fifty-some-odd years ago, I had been on my own for ten years and fully expected to spend the rest of my days fulfilling my beautiful mission alone. You all took me in, embraced my mission, and helped make it better." Everyone clapped, and I waited for them to settle back down.

"But," I continued, "after living in this village for so long and visiting the same lands for all that time, I have made a tough decision. I believe it is time to travel further, explore new lands, and bring toys to more children in other places." A commotion arose, and I motioned for them all to settle down. "I will miss you all and the help you have given me."

"You must stay, Nicholas!" someone yelled.

"Who will help you make the toys?" asked another.

Then something happened that surprised me. Erminlinda, usually quiet and reserved, stepped from the crowd, mounted the stage next to me, and gestured for quiet. The crowd, clearly as surprised as I was, fell silent almost immediately.

Erminlinda turned to me and, under her breath, asked me, "Are you sure of wanting to leave, my friend?"

"Yes," I whispered back to her.

She nodded, then turned to face her friends and neighbors. "Nicholas has decided to leave the forest," she said, "and it is not our place to keep him here." There was a bit of a stir, and she gestured again for them to be quiet.

"Of course, we will miss helping him with his mission of spreading love and generosity to human children," she said. "However! I wish to present you with an idea! We have lived here in the forest for so long. We have seen very little of the world. Our village has stood among these trees for a thousand years! If Nicholas is going to venture out into the world to spread the magic of play and happiness to more and more children, perhaps, my friends, we could go with him!"

The crowd was silent for a moment. Then whispers went around as everyone softly voiced their opinions to each other. Erminlinda stood and watched. I did the same. I had not expected her to propose what she had. I certainly didn't mind the idea of my friends coming with me, but I didn't want anyone to feel forced from their homes. Finally, a voice spoke up, and I realized it was Adelgard.

"As you said, Erminlinda, we *have* been here a very long time. I suspect many here have grown tired of our village. Elves in older days wandered more and sought more knowledge and excitement than we have in a thousand years. I think your proposal is wonderful. The years since

Nicholas arrived, the times I have spent helping his mission, have been the best I have had in centuries. I know many of you, if not all of you, agree with me." More murmurs went around the crowd at this.

"So," said Erminlinda, "Adelgard is with me. Anyone else?"

As the realization of Erminlinda's proposal sank in, a wave of excitement swept through the crowd. Cheers erupted, hats flew into the air, and elves whistled and clapped. Overwhelmed with emotion, my eyes welled up with tears. I had never felt such a profound sense of gratitude and love.

"My friends! My friends!" I yelled, trying to get their attention. They all fell silent, and I went on. "I am so grateful for your decision. I am so thankful for your love, help, and friendship. I am honored you have chosen to come on this adventure with me. I love and appreciate you all!" More cheers arose. I left the stage and was swarmed by everyone in the village, hugging me, patting me on the back and arms, and everyone telling me how much they loved me and were excited to expand our mission.

A big feast was prepared in record time. Bonfires were lit. A huge celebration began. Elves love to celebrate. There were piles of fresh fruit, a superb selection of breads and pastries, and delicious savory vegetable hand-pies. Everyone ate, danced by the bonfire's light, and sang all night. The next day, the deconstruction and packing up of the village began. Within a week, we started our trek out of the forest, heading out into the world to bring our mission of peace, love, hope, and kindness to more of the world.

A Very Brief History of Christmas, Pt. 2: Christianization

Let's take another break here with me and the elves leaving the forest for another history lesson. We're getting closer to me becoming a part of Christmas, but first, I need to tell you more about how Christmas came to be.

In 313, a monumental event occurred. Roman Emperor Constantine the First, also known as Constantine the Great, legalized Christianity. This was a turning point, a shift in the tides of history. After that, Christianity grew swiftly and eventually became the empire's official religion by decree of Emperor Theodosius in 380.

Christians, like the practitioners of religions that had come before them, were not fond of people worshipping other gods. As the religion spread throughout the Roman Empire, they tried repeatedly to convert people to Christianity, squash other faiths, and stop practices they found inappropriate and ungodly.

The problem with that, besides trying to force their beliefs on other people just like other religions had done to them (two wrongs don't make a right, after all!), was that people were still very fond of celebrating their winter festivals. As I mentioned in Chapter Nine, *Saturnalia*, *Jol*, and the Festival of *Dies Natalis Solis Invicti* were all very popular. People loved them and didn't want to give them up! But the Christians thought these festivals were against God and that they encouraged bad behavior like drinking alcohol and, of all things, singing and dancing. The early Christians were very against joyful celebration. They felt it wasn't proper. So, it turned out, did some Christians who came along much later, but I'll tell you about them when we get there. The point is that Christians didn't want people to have their winter festivals, and people didn't like that, so they were not converting to this new religion.

I could write a lot about how the various winter celebrations came to be about the birth of Jesus, but I will try to be brief so I can get back to my own story as soon as possible. The short version is that there was a lot of disagreement in Christianity about whether the birth of Jesus should be celebrated at all. Some thought it was insulting to Him since He was the Son of God and was not a mere human who should have a birthday celebration. Others felt that celebrating His birth was just one more form of worship and celebration of Him, just like the Festival of *Dies Natalis Solis Invicti,* which was a celebration of the birth of Sol Invictus. The first record of a Nativity celebration says it happened on December 25th, 354. But it was a long time after that before it became a regular celebration, and even longer before it became known as Christmas.

To get more people on board with converting to their religion, Christians eventually caved to the idea of a winter festival. They told folks they could continue to have the holidays they had been having. But now, instead of long festivals, they would be one day: December 25th. And, instead of being about Saturn or Sol or Odin, they now would be a celebration of the birth of Jesus. This, of course, is an abridged and simple version of what happened, but it is the information you need to understand for this story. And, much like when *Saturnalia* had become the Festival of *Dies Natalis Solis Invicti,* people didn't care *who* they were celebrating, so much as they were happy they got to celebrate at all. Some researchers now think that, without Christians compromising on winter festivities, the religion may never have become as big and popular as it is now. As someone who was there, I agree with them. People need joy in their lives. People need time in life to have fun. As I said in Chapter Nine, these winter festivals were the highlight of many people's year. I can't think of much more fun than that, can you?

And, not all the things they loved about their old holidays went away, which is where I eventually have a part in the holiday, as do many of the things you love about Christmas. They still gave each other small presents to show they cared. They still got to feast. People who celebrated in the Celtic regions still hung mistletoe and holly. Those who had celebrated *Jol* still burned their logs and ate their hams. The religion changed, but the customs mostly stayed the same, and people were happy.

Okay, I think that's enough history for now. I'll have to tell you some more later, but not much more. Let's return to my elf friends and me heading out on our new adventure and to one of the most important moments of my life.

Lisette

When we first left the Black Forest, we weren't sure where we were going or why; we just wanted to explore new places and give more gifts to more children. But after a couple of weeks on the road, Waldhar, always a very practical elf, came to me with an idea.

"I think, Nicholas," he said, "that if we are going to be out here exploring, we should make accurate maps of the land so that you don't get lost as much. Maybe we don't need to settle anywhere special just yet, so we can map out as much as possible."

"Oh, my friend, that is a wonderful plan!" I said to him. "I really would love to know where I am and how to get home on nights I can't see the stars!"

So we held a meeting and decided the group would split up for weeks at a time, mapping out where they went, finding villages, and making toys. Then we would all agree to meet at a specific location where I would gather up all the maps and all the toys, then whisk around with Vulfgang and my wagon full of gifts for a night, bringing joy and play to the children of the surrounding areas before we moved a little further on and did the same thing in a new location.

It wasn't a small task, either. Even though we could move quickly and cover lots of ground, my friends taught me a lot about doing it right, which meant figuring out distances and keeping track of important landmarks. Measuring distances especially took a long time because it had to be done just right, or the whole map would be wrong.

I know now that with the internet, movies, TV, and video games, this probably sounds incredibly dull, like chores. But to me and the elves, it was an adventure. It was a chance to see new places, learn new things, and most importantly, solve new problems, which brought us a deep sense of satisfaction and inspiration.

Before we knew it, we spent more time making maps than toys, and I wasn't making as many trips to deliver those toys. But we didn't worry; we knew what we were doing with the maps was important, so we pressed on.

In 508, I was in Bordeaux, France, on one of these mapping adventures when another significant change in my life happened.

When I was there, Bordeaux was already a pretty old city, having been settled almost a thousand years before. I found it a fascinating place and walked around to see it. I even slid into the human realm to interact with those who lived there. It was a pretty place, right next to the Garonne River, and the day was bright and warm. I stopped at a little market to buy some of the local grapes, which were first brought to the city and planted by the Romans nearly six hundred years before.

As I dropped the coins into the merchant's hand, gathered my grapes, and turned to leave, I bumped into the person next to me, sending their food and my grapes spilling to the ground.

"I'm so sorry!" I said, bending to gather the food for the poor person I had knocked into. But, as I bent, so did the person next to me, and our heads collided, causing both of us to fall backward.

"Oh!" I yelped, one hand rising to rub my head just above my eyes, blocking my vision. "Oh, goodness, I am just so sorry!"

I lowered my hand as I spoke and finally noticed the person I had bumped into twice. Suddenly, my breath caught, and I couldn't say anything more.

The person I had collided with had had a hood on, but now they lowered it from their head. As she rubbed her scalp, I could see not only was she a woman, but the most beautiful woman I had ever seen in all my extraordinarily long life.

She had long, golden hair that fell to her shoulders and had just the finest touches of gray beginning to appear in it. Her eyes were a lovely shade of hazel. She was not skinny but also not plump. Just a rather ordinary build. Though she was sitting down, I could tell she was a bit tall for a woman but probably still shorter than me, if not by much. Though I couldn't be sure of her age, she looked to me in her mid-forties. Certainly no older than her late forties. But, if she was, her skin was remarkably clear and relatively unlined for someone of that age at that time, when no one did things like wear sunscreen or use lotion. By the time they reached their late thirties, many people had lived lives of hard work, often outside in the weather, and their skin showed just how hard their lives had been. Either this woman came from privilege or was just very lucky.

When she looked at me, I expected her expression to be cross. After all, I had not only just knocked all her food from her hands, but I had given her a good whack on the head to boot. But seeing a small smile touch her lips when her eyes met mine surprised me. I'm not sure, even all these years later, if it was just because of her kind and forgiving nature or if I looked absolutely foolish at that moment, stammering and staring. I'm rather inclined to think it's the latter.

"My good woman," I finally said as I got on my hands and knees and gathered her things. "I do hope you'll forgive me. I'm not usually such a clumsy old fool!" I don't usually say such harsh things about myself, but right then, I felt so awkward and embarrassed that I couldn't think of anything to say *but* that.

She, too, got on her hands and knees to gather things up, and she laughed and said, "Oh, sir, no, you're not a fool. I think we have both been the victims of horrible timing, each of us bumping into the other at the wrong moments. Don't feel so bad."

Her voice was musical, high, and sweet. When she spoke to me, I felt my cheeks get hot and kept my gaze pointed toward what I was doing so she couldn't see me blush.

Just as I collected the last of her things and began to climb to my feet, I saw her hand reach out to me and noticed she was already up, offering her hand to help me. I felt even more embarrassed, as it should have been me offering to help her up. I still thought I was the one who had caused this despite her assuring me she was equally to blame for the mishap. I was sure she was just offering to help up an old man out of pity, thinking I probably couldn't do it myself. Still, her gesture was probably meant in kindness, so I reached out and clasped her hand with mine.

As I took her hand, I felt a spark. My heart danced in my chest, and my breath caught again. I had experienced plenty of magic in my time, but no magic ever felt as...well...magical as grasping her hand. I had never held a woman's hand before. In my youth, I had been interested in girls in my village, but as I grew older and became more interested in my work, my interest in those girls slipped away. I realized here in the street with this woman's hand in mine that I had never been married or even courted a woman.

"Thank you," I mumbled as I climbed to my feet, afraid to say much more.

"No, sir, thank *you*," she countered. "Such a gentleman to help a lady gather her groceries from the ground!"

I realized then that I still held her things, so I stuck my arms out for her to take them. She did, then thrust out her hand with my bundle of grapes in it.

"My goodness, my grapes!" I stammered, now wholly overcome with nervousness. I took them from her and thanked her again.

"Well," she said, "I hope your head is okay."

"Oh, yes, yes, it is, thank you. How about yours?"

She laughed a little. "I've had worse. Growing up, my family had a stable with donkeys, and I was kicked by one of them once. I had a bump as big as an egg for a week!"

"That sounds awful," I said, not knowing what else to say.

"Yes, it was pretty painful for a while. But you know how it is when you're a kid; you get over things like that much faster."

"Very true," I said, then an awkward silence fell between us.

"Well then," she said, giving me another little smile, "I guess I'll be on my way."

"Ah, yes," I replied, "I suppose I should be, too." She turned to go, but at the last second, I practically yelled, "Wait a moment!"

She turned to me, and those hazel eyes stared back into mine. "I'm Nicholas," I told her. I realized just now that I never properly introduced myself."

"Nice to meet you, Nicholas. I'm Lisette."

"Lisette," I echoed, "that's a lovely name. Nice to meet you. Have a pleasant day, Lisette. I hope we meet again sometime."

"As do I," she replied, now not just giving me a little grin but a full, beautiful smile. "Good day, Nicholas." And with that, she walked off into the crowd, leaving me standing there with my grapes.

In the days that followed my serendipitous encounter with Lisette in the bustling market, my thoughts were consumed by her. It was a bewitching experience, to say the least. After a lifetime of experiences, I was astounded to find myself utterly captivated by a woman I had only just met, a woman who was, in truth, a stranger to me.

As I went about my regular days making toys, I found myself constantly daydreaming about Lisette. My work, once a source of pride, was now riddled with mistakes. My tops wouldn't spin right because I carved them crooked, and my dolls had legs that were different lengths because I didn't double-check my measurements before I sewed them on. I was more distracted than I had ever been in my whole life.

Of course, my friends noticed. I was pretty embarrassed to tell them why the quality of my work had slipped, but eventually, I turned to Erminlinda. While elves are not mean, they do sometimes engage in friendly teasing, and I wasn't in the mood to have my friends snicker at my childish crush. But I knew Erminlinda would not behave that way when I told her what was going on with me.

Well, I thought I knew. When I went into her sewing room to talk to her and confessed why I had been doing such shabby work, a grin immediately split her face, and she giggled.

"Why, Nicholas," she cooed, flipping her flaming red hair back playfully, "isn't two-hundred-thirty-seven a little old to be thinking about courting a woman?"

"Erminlinda," I said, more sternly than I meant to, "this is serious! Yes, okay, I am well over two hundred years old, but for the first time since I was very young, I'm taken with a woman. And I know she is a stranger. I saw her once in a market. But, isn't it possible I could go back to Bordeaux, see her again, and maybe, I don't know, woo her?"

Erminlinda, still smiling but becoming more serious, stared at me momentarily, her emerald eyes appraising me, then said, "Okay, let's consider the situation. Suppose for a minute you go back and find this Lisette. How do you intend to explain to her who you are? What your life is like? More importantly, do you think she'll even believe you? How long could you expect to have a relationship with her while hiding these things about yourself?"

"I don't know," I admitted, heaving a weighty sigh.

"I'm not discouraging you, my friend," she said, laying a hand on my arm comfortingly, "but you need to think about this carefully. Suppose you return to Bordeaux and engage this woman again to possibly start a relationship. In that case, you need to be ready for the very real possibility that she will laugh in your face if you reach a place where you tell her about your life. Belief in elves isn't rare, but it isn't universal. Some people think we are just legends. And who ever heard of a human *living* with us? You're the only one of your kind, Nicholas! She may find that hard to swallow."

"I understand that. I do. But," here I paused and stroked my mustache in thought for a moment, trying to find the right words. Finally, I continued, "But I feel almost like I did when I first came to terms with being in the *Hylgan Rikalt*. I'm scared, but I'm also pretty sure I'm where I'm supposed to be. I don't know if it's destiny or if there really are soul mates in the world; I just know that I have lived what any reasonable person would assume is an impossibly long life, and in all that time, I have never felt as drawn to another person as I am to Lisette."

"Then I believe you should heed that feeling, Nicholas, and follow it to wherever it may lead you," Erminlinda said, her voice filled with understanding and support. She then hugged me, picked up her sewing, and playfully added, "Now shoo! Your silly little love life has caused you to mess these dolls up, and I have extra work to do!"

Now I was in a better mood and more open to being teased. I laughed heartily, thanked her for listening and the advice, and left for Bordeaux.

Every day in the city of Bordeaux was tinged with anticipation, a fervent hope to see Lisette again. It was a rare break from my usual work routine, and I filled my time with leisurely strolls through the markets and along the waterfront, indulging in the town's delectable grapes. Yet, my heart yearned for another encounter with the woman who had captivated my thoughts.

I was beginning to feel foolish and a bit creepy, wandering the streets to hopefully meet a woman I had only met once when I finally saw her at a fish vendor's cart one day.

As I approached her, I couldn't help but wish I had sought more advice from Erminlinda on engaging a woman without sounding dull. My palms grew clammy, my heart raced, and my nerves were in a frenzy. The fear of uttering something wrong was almost paralyzing.

Just as I was about to try to get her attention, she turned from the fish vendor, saw me, and smiled. My breath caught. She was beautiful. I hadn't just built that up in my mind.

"Hello again, Nicholas!" she said, approaching me.

"Oh, hello," I said, trying hard not to stare down at my feet. I suddenly felt very bashful.

"I expected I wouldn't see you again," she said. "I tend to see the same people all the time, them being my neighbors and all. I thought you were a traveler passing through when we first met."

"Well, I am a bit of a traveler. But my travels have brought me back here. I'm glad to see you again."

"And I am glad to see you. I hope you have a good visit to Bordeaux."

"Thank you," I mumbled, unsure what else to say. There was a heavy, awkward silence where we just smiled at each other.

"Well, I must be getting this fish home," she said. "Have a wonderful day." Then she turned to leave.

"Wait!" I blurted, and she turned back to me with a slightly puzzled look. "I...well...this might be very forward of me. I know I'm quite a bit older than you, and we don't know each other, but...well...I was wondering...that is, I was hoping...would you...would you dine with me this evening?"

Her lips curved into a smile, and for a moment, I feared she was about to mock me. But then, she uttered the words that filled me with immense relief and joy, "Well, I got an awfully large fish for just me. Of course, it wouldn't be appropriate to invite you, a man I barely know, into my home. But it's such a lovely day; I imagine it would be alright if we dined outside. Care to walk home with me so you know where to come later?"

I said I would like that very much, and we walked off together toward her home. I was so delighted that she had agreed to dinner with me; I couldn't even bring myself to tell her I didn't eat meat and that maybe she shouldn't prepare that fish. It wasn't a long walk, and I paid attention to everything around it so I could find my way back later. She told me to come back in a few hours, and I gave her, to my embarrassment, a slight bow before I left to wander about, passing the time until dinner.

"Why did I bow?" I mumbled to myself as I headed off down the street. "I've never bowed to anyone in my life!"

I returned to Lisette's house at the appointed hour. She had already placed her table and two chairs in the street in front of her house. Just as I was about to knock, the front door opened.

"Nicholas, your timing is perfect!" she said, thrusting a large bowl into my hands. "Kindly put this on the table."

As I turned to do so, a tantalizing aroma wafted from the bowl, making my stomach rumble. It was filled with herb-covered potatoes, glistening with what I could only imagine was butter. My hunger, which I had neglected in my nervousness, suddenly overcame me.

I set the bowl down and turned to see her coming out of the house with a plate loaded with carrots and string beans. These, too, looked to be coated in oil and herbs.

"This all looks and smells so wonderful!" I said, my stomach rumbling with hunger and anticipation. I was nervous but also excited to spend this time with Lisette.

"I'm glad you think so," she replied, giving me another of her beautiful smiles. "Hold on one moment, and I'll get the fish."

"Oh..." I said sheepishly. "About that. I...I really should have told you this sooner, but...oh, I'm sorry about this...I don't eat meats, only fruits and vegetables."

She flapped a hand at me and gave a little laugh. "Well then, it's a good thing I cooked so many potatoes and carrots! I wish there could have been more string beans, but my crop wasn't good this year, and I had trouble finding any in the market. Don't worry about the fish; I'll give what I don't eat to Marjorie, the poor homeless woman who usually sleeps nearby. I try to give her food as much as I can. It's so sad that few people have helped care for her." With this, she turned and went inside, leaving me even more love-struck than I already had been. This woman was a gift-giver! She cared for the poor and people without homes!

As our dinner went on, I learned about her family and how she came to be an unwed woman in her forties living alone (remember, women at this time were still expected to get married and be supported by their husbands. That Lisette lived on her own was very unusual!) Her independence and determination were qualities that I found incredibly attractive.

"I never found a man I wanted to marry," she said. "It was a big fight with my father and mother for a long time. Their marriage was basically a business deal. My mother's family owned one of the most profitable vineyards in the area. Since she had no brothers to take over the business, my grandparents wanted to get her married so the business would still be well cared for. Anyway, when I was also an only child and a girl at that, my father expected that since he had married my mother to take over the business, I would need to marry as well. But I had been around long enough to know how to run the vineyard! Oh, sure, girls aren't allowed to learn much beyond housekeeping, but when your father is always doing business in the house and talking about business while you're running around the farm playing, you learn anyway.

"'I can run this business just fine and marry a man *I* see fit to marry!' I said to them many times. I know they wanted me to be happy. Still, they also never wanted to appear different in the community, and letting their daughter take over the business without a man was too far out of their idea of being normal. They told me I would learn to love a husband they picked out for me like they had learned to love each other, but I fought them the whole way.

"Eventually, my father caved in and taught me more about running the business than I had learned just by living around him. I got very good at it. When my mother and then my father died, I was more than capable of running the business on my own."

"Let me guess what happened next," I said, jumping in. "The men who worked in the vineyard didn't want a woman for a boss."

She pointed at me, gave a little wink, and then said, "Exactly."

"How sadly typical," I responded.

"So, rather than have the business fail because all my help quit, I sold it off for a hefty profit. I bought this house, and I've lived here ever since. I make a little extra money doing some sewing and sometimes selling baked goods, but I mostly do those things because I enjoy them, not because I need the money," she told me.

"Well, I certainly have a lot of respect for you for following your own path," I said, feeling yet another kinship with her since I had followed my own unique path so many years before.

"How about you?" she asked. "What is your line of work?"

I paused for a moment, completely unsure of what to say. I had no clue where to begin to tell her about my real life. "Well," I finally said, "mostly I create children's playthings. Toys."

"Really?" she said, leaning forward. "That's a fascinating job! You don't see many toys around! How did you come to do that?"

"That's a very long story," I told her truthfully.

"Well, I've got plenty of time. I'd love to hear it."

Just as I struggled to decide how or even if to tell her my tale, a woman came walking down the street, and Lisette said, "Hold on a moment, that's Marjorie! I want to give her the rest of this fish while it's still nice and fresh." She hopped up and carried her plate off to greet the homeless woman.

"Okay," I said to myself, "now what?" If I told her my real story, she would think I was crazy. But if I wanted to keep seeing her, I would have to tell her at some point. But how?

Just as I was getting myself all bent out of shape, she came back and lightly touched me on the shoulder, jerking me back to reality.

"Nicholas, I'm so sorry," she said, "but Marjorie is feeling poorly, and I would like to take her to an herbalist to get her something that will help her feel better."

"Oh, of course!" I cried, slightly relieved. "It's so kind of you to help her. Thank you so much for the meal and your wonderful company!"

"I'm happy to have had you here," she said. There was a pause. We both shuffled our feet, not sure what to do or say. Then she said, "I hope you don't think this too forward of me, but I would like to see you again."

"That would be wonderful!" I said, probably too loudly and more excitedly than intended. "Would you like to walk with me tomorrow by the river?"

"That sounds lovely," she said. "Now, if you'll excuse me, I hate to run, but…"

"Of course! Of course! I shall call on you in the morning." With that, we parted. I turned as I walked away and watched, a broad smile on my face, as she hooked Marjorie's arm in hers and led her off.

"I believe I'm in love," I said to myself, then turned and headed off for the night.

Later that evening, I sought advice from Erminlinda again. I wanted to keep seeing Lisette but had no idea how to tell her about my real life.

"I see your problem," Erminlinda said after I told her what was on my mind. She was making yet another beautiful doll, this one with a delicate blue silk gown, and set it down to turn to face me and give me her full attention.

"I don't have any hope of making this work, do I?" I said, already convinced this relationship was doomed to fail before it started properly.

"Well," Erminlinda responded, a note of hesitation in her voice, "I'm not sure. A woman living on her own is a very practical woman indeed and may not be given to believing in elves. If you tell her all the truth about yourself, I suppose there is a good chance she will think you're quite mad."

"I thought so," I said, slouching down in my chair.

"But that doesn't mean you shouldn't try!" She reached out and patted my arm. "If you really like this woman, you can't lie to her, my friend. If you did, how far would the relationship go? I know you've never had these feelings before, and it's scary to think it might not work out, but take it from me; the sting doesn't last forever." Her words, filled with understanding and support, gave me the courage to face my fears.

"You mean you've…" I began before she cut me off with a laugh.

"Oh, Nicholas! You think I've never been in love? But the one I loved was in love with someone else. It hurt for a while, and I was certainly sad. But that was several hundred years ago now! If you're going to live a life as long as an elf's, you have to start thinking in elfin years! Take a risk on love!"

"Thank you, my dear friend," I said, leaning over and patting her on the shoulder. "Your wisdom and support mean the world to me. I knew I could count on you."

The next morning, I arrived at Lisette's house, determined to tell her all about my life. I knocked on her door, and she came out dressed in a lovely white shirt and long green skirt, her blonde hair cascading around her face. I offered her my arm, and she hooked hers around it, and we strolled toward the water.

I made a lot of small talk at first, asking about Marjorie's health (doing better), commenting on the weather and the beauty of the scenery, and asking her about the business of growing grapes and making wine. My stomach was doing gymnastics as I thought about finally revealing my whole story to her.

Eventually, we came to a place where someone had put a roughly carved bench overlooking the river, and we took a seat. We sat there in silence for a bit, just watching the birds.

Finally, I turned to her and said, "Last night, before you took Marjorie to the herbalist, I was about to tell you all about myself."

"Yes, that's right, you were."

I took a deep breath and dove in. I recounted my life back in Lycia and how I had first given gifts of money and eventually left and began wandering around, bringing gifts to poor families and, eventually, just to children, skipping the parts of the story about magic and elves at first.

"What a magnificent life!" she cried. I realized, at some point, she had taken my hand. She squeezed it and said, "Nicholas, you are the kindest, most giving man I have ever met."

I blushed, now more terrified than ever about telling her the rest. My mouth went dry, but I carried on. I was afraid of losing her, of her rejecting me once she knew the truth. But I knew I had to be honest with her, no matter the cost.

"Well, there's more." Then I told her about the magic. About time moving slowly, crossing vast distances at incredible speed, befriending the colony of elves who now helped me on my mission, and, finally, about how I apparently did not age.

"By normal measure," I said, "I am two-hundred-thirty-eight years old. Yet I don't look or feel any older than when I left home at age sixty-three."

Silence fell between us. Lisette stared at me, mouth slightly open, looking stunned, not saying a word. I licked my lips, not sure what to do or say. Then, without warning, her face darkened, and she jumped up and yelled at me.

"I can't believe you! Do you think I'm a fool? Do you think I would fall for such an outlandish tale because I'm a woman living alone?" Lisette's voice was filled with hurt and anger. I felt a pang of vulnerability, unsure of how to respond.

"No! No! I..."

"I was starting to think you were special, that I was falling in love with you! Then you tell me a story like that! I don't know why you would feel the need to lie to me like that! Good day!" She turned and stormed off.

"No!" I shouted after her and then jumped up myself. "No, I swear! It's the truth!"

Without a thought, I reached out to grab her by the arm and, at the same time, felt the familiar sensation of slipping back into the *Hylgan Rikalt.* Just as my hand took her upper arm, the world slammed to a standstill. I hadn't planned it, and even as it was happening, I wasn't sure it would work, but there we both were.

She didn't realize it at first and whirled around, shaking free of my grip. "I will not have you grab me like that!" she yelled. Then I saw her expression change, and her eyes went wide. I turned to see where she was looking and saw a bird paused in mid-takeoff from the ground.

I turned back to her and, a bit embarrassed, said, "I'm sorry. I didn't plan this, but..."

"Oh!" she yelped, her hands rising and covering her mouth. "This...this can't be!" She spun in a circle. All around us, the world was still and quiet.

"It's okay," I said, gently placing my hand on her arm. We're in the *Hylgan Rikalt* now. That's elvish for 'Hidden Realm.' I didn't mean to plop you right down in the middle of it like this, but..."

"It's *real*!" she exclaimed, her voice filled with wonder. "Oh, Nicholas! Oh, I'm so sorry!" Her tone softened, and before I could react, she had thrown her arms around me.

"You don't have to be sorry," I said after a moment, holding her away from me at arm's length and looking into her eyes. "I expected your reaction. You don't know how afraid I was to tell you."

"This is...well, it's *magical*! It's magnificent! I can't believe it!" She took off at a run and went right up to the little bird, walking all around it and examining it.

"Be careful!" I called to her. "We can still interact with things! If you knock into the poor thing, you're liable to knock it down and hurt it!" She took a step back and continued to stare at it. "If you stand there long enough and don't blink, you'll eventually see its wings move, but you'll be here a while."

"I'd like to see more," she said, returning to me.

"Anything you'd like," I said and offered to take her hand. She allowed it, and we walked off back toward town, hand in hand.

My friends were delighted when I brought Lisette to meet them that day. They immediately made a huge feast to celebrate, which I found embarrassing. This was only the second time Lisette and I had spent time together, and holding a celebration felt premature to me. I wondered if it would to her, too. But she fell into comfortable conversation with my elfin friends almost immediately and insisted on helping with the cooking.

At one point, Waldhar came to me and gave me a very light, jovial punch in the arm, a huge laugh, and a wink.

"What?" I asked him.

"You're going to be married!" he said.

"I...what?" I sputtered. "I am no such thing! I just met this woman! What makes you think we're going to be married?"

"You brought her here! Not just to the *Hylgan Rikalt*, but right here to meet us! To your family! And look at her!" He turned and pointed at Lisette, who was laughing and cooking with several elves.

"So she's polite. She's enjoying herself. How does that equal marriage?"

"She's like you, Nicholas. She belongs here with us, with *you*." He winked at me again, turned, and left.

I watched Lisette continue to enjoy the company of my friends, and eventually, we sat down to eat our feast. When we had all eaten to almost bursting, several elves brought out instruments and played.

All my friends hopped up and danced. Lisette laughed and jumped up to join them, whirling and twirling to the music. Then, to my absolute horror, she danced over, took my hands, and yanked me up out of my seat to dance with her.

I have never been a good dancer. I lacked (and still lack) any sense of natural rhythm. When the elves danced, I was content to sit, watch, laugh, and clap along but never to get up and dance. Now, here was this beautiful woman I was falling in love with, taking me in the middle of the dance floor with her!

As she whirled about, her dress making lovely swirling motions, I did my best to clap, shuffle my feet, and sway in place, which delighted her to no end.

"Come on, Nicholas!" she said through a laugh. "Do a proper dance with me!"

"But I..." I began to protest, but she grabbed one of my hands, put the other on her waist, and put her other hand on my shoulder.

"Just follow what I do," she said, doing a few simple steps in a circle. I couldn't help but smile.

Waldhar's right, I thought, *we are going to be married.*

After a few months of courting, we were. We've been married ever since.

"Saint" Nicholas, The Middle Ages & The Renaissance

Now comes the part in my story when I have to skip over whole chunks of time. I can't very well keep repeating over and over again that many years were uneventful and passed much like the years before.

After Lisette and I married, we all fell into a comfortable routine of exploring, mapping, and making toys. When we had enough toys for me to make a gift-giving run to a specific area, I did so. These runs were not without their challenges. I still hadn't figured out a regular delivery schedule in those days. I simply picked an area, figured out how many gifts I would need, and went out and gave them. I was making several nighttime runs of toy deliveries a year, navigating through the darkness and the unknown.

This went on for a very long time. Eventually, we had extensive maps of Europe and changed them accordingly as towns changed names and new towns and cities were built.

Sadly, it was also a time of much suffering in Europe. Fighting happened constantly. Different tribes, clans, and nations fought and went to war. People often decided they wanted land others already lived on, which started more wars. I never understood why anyone wanted to kill for land. I had been to enough places to know there was plenty of room for everyone to live. But, sadly, there have always been people who never feel like they have enough: enough stuff, enough land, enough power. Those wars always made my job challenging, and I always treated the children of war-torn lands with extra love and generosity so they could remember how much good still existed in the world despite the scary things happening all around them. Historians refer to the period between the fall of Rome and the beginning of the fourteenth century as "The Middle Ages" and "The Medieval Period," but you may have also heard it called "The Dark Ages." On top of war, there was also quite a lot of sickness. People didn't have any knowledge of medicine yet. It was a sorrowful time for most people in Europe, so we did our best to raise people's spirits.

You'll notice I keep talking about how we were exploring Europe. At that point in time, Europe and parts of the Middle East, where I had been born and grown up, were what we called "The Known World." We had heard of far-off places like China, but we knew very little of the land and the people who lived there (and they knew very little of us). Travel was challenging. The Romans had built a lot of great roads (some of which you can still travel on today), but there still weren't enough of them to make traveling all over the continent easy and fast. Even at my super speed, I still had to deal with obstacles like mountains, valleys, forests, bodies of water, and poor roads. I can't tell you the number of times one of the axles or wheels on my wagon broke from the rough conditions I raced over! I lost entire nights of gift delivery, leaving my wagon by the road and going in search of the materials to fix it. I would have carried repair supplies on the wagon, but I needed every bit of space to pack all the presents I was bringing. I should have learned to give just a little space to repair supplies after the first few times I needed them and didn't have them, but I never could bring myself to not load the wagon as full as possible with things to give away rather than things I might need on my journey.

During this time, Christianity was also spread. It rapidly became the leading religion across Europe. I didn't know it then, but this religion would soon become a significant part of my legend and mission.

And make no mistake, I was already a legend at that point. No one had yet connected "Saint" Nicholas to the giving of gifts, but all over the continent, people knew that a mysterious nighttime visitor would periodically come and leave toys for the kids in the night. The more years that passed, the more children went to bed at night dreaming that they may wake up to a beautiful new plaything in the morning. Most of them did at one point or another, too. I say most because I realized over the years that some people did not wish to have me in their homes, leaving gifts for their children. It made me sad they would deny their child the joy of a new toy and the lesson of love and generosity that the toy represented. Still, I didn't want to upset anyone, so we kept lists of where I was not welcome to visit, and I always respected those wishes. And still do, of course. But more on that later.

Cities got bigger and bigger. They would still seem quite small to modern-day folks, but they were amazing then. They were crowded, dirty, and smelly, and too many people were impoverished. Everywhere we went, that seemed to be the state of things.

As populations spread and villages and cities popped up in more and more places, we moved further and further into remote regions where no people were. Even though we were in our hidden realm, we still needed the space to grow our homes and work areas to make more toys. We did this slowly, over hundreds of years, picking up and moving every few decades. This kept us out of the way of civilization's growth and kept civilization from intruding on our work.

Despite the hardships during this period, people still joyously celebrated Christmas. People still were thrilled to feast and give gifts, and it was during the Middle Ages that I, specifically, began to be associated with holiday gift-giving.

My legend spread like wildfire during that time. I think people were happy to have a story about a "saint" they could tell their children about. A lot of other saints, I'm afraid, have violence involved in their stories. However, parents could share stories about "Saint" Nicholas giving gifts to children and, for some reason, guiding ships safely into the harbor during vicious storms. I never learned where that story came from. But when life is hard, people need stories to keep themselves happy.

Until the 1100s, part of the Christmas season involved children going door-to-door to demand gifts rather than receiving them at home. But in the 1100s (I'm not sure of the exact date as I wasn't there), nuns in France began leaving gifts for children on the night of December 5th for them to find when they woke up on the 6th, which had officially been declared "St. Nicholas Day." If you'll remember, December 6 was when I left home and began my new life in 333. Though I am not sure how it came to be, apparently, in the years since then, the story had changed to be that I had died on that day in the year 343, ten years after anyone I had known in my homeland had last seen me. When Christian missionaries discovered tribes in Germany celebrating Yule in the Middle Ages around the same time as my supposed death day, they Christianized Yule and the tribes by creating St. Nicholas Day.

So, for the first time, I had a day on which my gifts were *expected*, which helped my mission a lot since I now knew there were whole segments of the continent I could visit on the night of December 5th. Since snow was often on the ground on that date, Waldhar built my first sleigh. On the night of the fifth, Vulfgang would gallop furiously across the land, towing me and my sleigh full of toys to the homes of children I knew were dreaming of shoes filled with toys and treats.

Inevitably, I suppose, people caught glimpses of me. I've never been as good at staying hidden as the elves. I sometimes accidentally slip into the human realm, which is how people learned what I look like. It's how, even today, you can see depictions of me riding a white horse in many European countries during celebrations of St. Nicholas Day. I'm not sure why my sleigh never made it into the culture of those places, but my old friend, Vulfgang, did.

Eventually, much to my happiness, the world lost most of its interest in war (though, as you know, that interest still hasn't totally gone away) and became more interested in things like art and education. This period began in the early 1300s and is known as the Renaissance. Unfortunately, starting in the year 1347, a sickness known as The Black Plague swept Europe, killing an incredible number of people. All told, about half of the population perished from this terrible disease.

Seeking yet further privacy and wishing to escape the horrors of The Black Plague, we pulled up stakes yet again and headed further north than we had ever been, into the country of Finland, to a region known as Lapland. My elf friends had heard of a huge settlement of elves in that region, and we hoped to join them.

This journey would have some of the most significant, most lasting impacts on my mission and legend ever.

The Search for Alfheim Begins

"My friends," I said to the gathered elves in the year 1348, "although there is so much land in Europe we could live on, the number of people that live here grows all the time." I did not yet know that early in the Black Plague how many people would, unfortunately, die of that terrible disease, actually decreasing the population of Europe.

"Plus, the people here are facing a horrible plague," I continued. "And even though we seem to be untouched by disease, the horror all around us, as you well know, is making it harder and harder to do our work. I know the world is bigger than the lands we have traveled and explored, so I propose that we again pick up and move." At the time, we were living in the land that would someday become Poland.

Odalric raised his hand. When I nodded to him, he stood. "Nicholas, I think I speak for everyone when I say that our work is needed now, perhaps more than ever, to comfort scared and suffering children. If you think we can do this good work better in a place other than here, you can be sure we'll go wherever we must."

Applause thundered through the hall, and many cheers went up. Lisette reached over and squeezed my hand. I looked at her, and she graced me with a beautiful smile. I knew she supported me fully in this. We had discussed it several times over recent months, and she had pushed me to call this meeting.

"Thank you, my friends," I said to them when the cheering and applauding died down. "I hope, after all the time we have lived and worked together, you know how much that means to me. I love you all so much. But I have no idea where we should go! We could, perhaps, go back toward my homeland, or down into the continent of Africa, or travel east toward China. We have so much more of the world we should learn about! Part of the reason I called you here is that I hoped that, if we all agreed on moving again, we could figure out some plan on where to move."

To my surprise, an elf named Starchilt, who didn't speak up much during meetings, raised her hand and bounced a bit to get me to notice her. I acknowledged her, and she jumped up.

"*Alfheim*," she said, then sat right back down. A murmur went through the crowd.

"Excuse me?" I replied.

When she didn't immediately answer, Waldhar piped up for her, "There is an old elfin legend, Nicholas, of a promised land where elves could forever live happily and away from too much interaction with the human world. This place is called *Alfheim*. It lies to the north. No one is quite sure where. All that is said about its exact location is that it can be found when you have traveled so far north that the North Star is directly overhead."

"Ah," I said, trying to think of a better reply. I looked back at Lisette, and she cocked an eyebrow at me. I could tell no words would come from her, but she knew I had to choose mine carefully. "I appreciate the suggestion, Starchilt, but I'm curious if anyone perhaps knows if any elf has ever reached *Alfheim*?"

The gathered elves sat quietly and exchanged looks. I saw shoulders shrug and heard some whispers. Eventually, Waldhar spoke back up.

"No one in our community," he said, "but there are more communities of elves than us. Many of them live further north, much further north than anyone here has ever been. I believe there are some in a land across the Baltic Sea called Lapland. When you found us, our community was one of the more adventurous communities that had moved into that region and lived there for many years. But, it's been said that elf kind began much further north, and most stayed, so the population up there should be much greater. Perhaps they know more about *Alfheim*."

All around Waldhar, elves were nodding their heads. I could see eyes beginning to glow excitedly and smiles lit up many faces. I hated to be in a position of crushing those dreams, but I also wasn't sure that moving north to chase a legend was a good idea, either. I was about to speak when Lisette caught my hand and pulled me to the side.

"One moment," she said to the crowd, tugging me further away from them. "Before you go ahead and refuse them outright," she said in a hushed tone, "I want you to stop and think about it."

"I wasn't going to..." I began, but she put a finger on my lips.

"Nicholas, I have known you far too long for you to get away with saying something so obviously as untrue as 'I wasn't going to say no.' Just hear me out on this. Let's go along with this idea." I opened my mouth to respond or defend myself. I couldn't begin to tell you how I thought I would do that, but she pressed on before I could. "The fact is that we need to move somewhere where we can have privacy, so why not go north and look for this *Alfheim*?"

"But we don't know if there even is such a place," I protested.

"You didn't believe elves existed until you met one," she responded reasonably. "I didn't believe your story until you crossed me into the *Hylgan Rikalt* and showed me the magic."

She was right. I have always been able to count on her to think more clearly and rationally than me. It's one of the many things I love about her.

"Okay," I said, getting on board with her, "I'll grant you it may exist. But suppose it doesn't? What then?"

"What's the worst that could happen? We find a quiet, remote area up north and build a new home. Even if *Alfheim* isn't a literal place, who says we can't make our own *Alfheim* wherever we end up?"

I smiled and hugged her. "If *Alfheim* is a promised land, my dear, then, as far as I'm concerned, wherever you and I call home is *Alfheim*, anyway. Come on, let's not keep them waiting anymore."

We walked back and stood once again before the community, who were waiting intently to hear what we had discussed and had to say.

"Well, gang," I said, placing my hands on my hips, "it seems we have a lot of work to do and a long way to go! Let's get packing! We're going in search of *Alfheim*!"

None of us had ever sailed before. I had been on a ship once and lent a hand, but I didn't know how to sail. But when we reached the coast of the Baltic Sea, Waldhar looked at the ships the area's residents had, took notes, and made drawings. He and several others even spent some time going onto boats with humans, doing their best to learn how to work a ship (which, as you can imagine, wasn't easy since the crews of those ships mostly seemed to stand still to them). Eventually, though, they felt confident they could sail, and Waldhar gathered up some of the best builders our community had to offer and set to work building us a ship of our own that would take us across the sea into the land now known as Finland. There was a way to reach this country by land, but it was a longer, more difficult journey, so we took the shortcut across the water.

The elves were sure we would find other communities of elves there, especially in the northernmost part of that land, which they called Lapland, and the elves we met there would know more about *Alfheim* and how to reach it.

It wasn't exactly an easy voyage. The journey was fraught with hard work and rowing. We had thought about actually sailing, but in the *Hylgan Rikalt* even the wind stands still, so we had to row. Also, even though we had left Poland in the fall and had all our winter clothing and supplies with us, we were unprepared for just how cold it got the further north we sailed. We built small fires but obviously could not set a blaze large enough to really warm us because we would set the boat on fire.

"I think we may have made a big mistake," I said to Lisette, my teeth chattering as we huddled under a few blankets below deck. She was shivering, and I expected her to agree, but she didn't.

"When we land on shore, we'll be able to get more supplies and build fires. We can make it through this. It's not forever. Now hug me tighter and keep me warm, and let's get some sleep!" she said, gripping me closer.

She was right again, of course. We made it through. It took a while, at least by our standards of speedy travel, but eventually, we landed on the shore of Finland in the city of Turku. We immediately set to getting more supplies to make blankets and winter clothing and learning about this new land.

I was excited to be in a new place, ready to bring gifts to children I had never visited. The long trip across the sea concerned me a bit because I knew it would make it more difficult to keep making my deliveries back in the lands we already knew and loved. Still, I was sure there was a way to make it back there by land swiftly enough with Vulfgang and my wagon so we could still get the job done. I didn't know then just how much my job would change on this journey to *Alfheim* and that not only would Vulfgang, my faithful old steed, retire, but that soon I wouldn't ever travel by land or sea to complete my mission again.

Lapland

When we landed in Finland, we did so on the southernmost coast. From maps, we knew that we could have sailed up the Baltic Sea to the region known as Lapland, which was our ultimate destination, but we wanted to travel by land through this new country and explore more. Our journey took us through picturesque towns, where we sampled local cuisine and Lisette and I interacted with friendly locals. We marveled at the stunning landscapes, from the rugged coastline to the rolling hills and dense forests. Each day brought a new adventure, and we were captivated by the charm and beauty of Finland.

So we took our time and wandered about, updating our maps as we moved north. We kept our eyes peeled for signs of other elf villages, but we never saw any in the southern parts of the country.

Finland is a beautiful country; it just got more beautiful the further north we moved. When we crossed into the southern portion of Lapland, we found it full of lush forests of pine and spruce trees. It was snowing by that time of year, and the scenery took my breath away. We saw the Northern Lights for the first time, bands of green, blue, and purple light streaking across the night sky. The sight was so mesmerizing that we all lay down in the snow and stared up at them, forgetting the cold and wet. The Lights even make a sort of crackling sound, a soft whisper that added to the magic of the moment.

"You were right," I whispered to Lisette the night we first saw the Northern Lights. "This was a good move. This place feels special. I don't know if it's the place the elves are looking for, but I feel a connection here. I could see myself living here for quite some time."

Not long after that night, a new chapter of our journey unfolded as we finally encountered another colony of elves. These days, the city where we met them is called Rovaniemi.

We had just woken up and were preparing to embark on another day's exploration when Adelgard tapped me and whispered, "Someone's watching us. To your left."

I casually turned that way and saw a head pulling back behind a tree some fifty feet away.

"So they are," I said. "Do you think we should say something?"

"I don't see why not," Adelgard said.

I cupped a hand to my mouth. "You there! Behind the tree! There's no need to hide! Why don't you come on out so we can all get to know each other?"

There was a moment when I thought the elf would stay hidden, but he slowly emerged from behind the tree and walked over to us. He had very light blonde hair, almost white, that stuck out from below his blue wool stocking cap. He was dressed in a blue tunic and a black coat that he wore open and hung to his knees. His pants were reddish-brown pants. He looked all around at the other elves, then looked Lisette and me up and down, clearly surprised to see humans among his kind.

"I'm Nicholas," I said, then gestured to Lisette, "and this is my wife, Lisette. Oh, and this is Adelgard. I'm sure you have some questions."

"One or two," he said with a wry smile. "I've never seen humans living with elves before."

"I'm told we're the only ones," Lisette said.

"Fascinating," he replied.

"And you are...?" Adelgard prompted.

"Oh! Sorry! I'm Tuka."

"A pleasure to meet you," I said.

"Your Elvish sounds funny. Strange accent," he said.

Adelgard laughed, "so does yours! We're from pretty far south. Germany."

Tuka's eyes grew wide. "You're one of the Wandering Tribes!" he exclaimed.

"I've never heard that," Adelgard said, scratching his chin thoughtfully, "but it's fitting. I suppose we are."

"You're some of the ones who left the homeland long ago and went further than any elf had ever gone! You're famous!"

"If you think our ancestors traveling south was amazing, just wait until you hear all about what we've been up to with Nicholas!" Adelgard replied with a grin.

Over the next few hours, we shared the past few centuries with Tuka, from when I met Adelgard in the Black Forest. He sat wide-eyed in amazement as he listened to all our tales, and when we were done, he clapped his hands together once and declared, "You must come to tell the others! They will be so eager to hear your stories!"

"Where are the others?" Lisette asked him.

"Oh, they're not far. Just outside the human city. To the north."

Lisette and I followed him away from our encampment. So many of the elves wanted to come, eager to meet more of their kind and share stories. But we ultimately figured that, for now, they should all stay behind so we could scout out whether this village of elves had room to accommodate us all.

"We don't want to impose on them, do we?" I asked the gathered elves. They reluctantly said that, no, of course, they didn't want to impose.

"Oh, plenty of room for a couple hundred more!" Tuka insisted, but we didn't want to trudge our whole group into the village on the word of one very excited elf.

We were amazed at its size upon approaching and entering the elf village. Our group consisted of two hundred thirty-three elves and two humans, so we took up a decent amount of space wherever we settled and called home. But this place was practically immense by the elf standards we had grown accustomed to. It had small buildings, of course, but it was spread out over a great deal of land with streets and shops.

"How many of you are there?" Lisette asked.

"Population six hundred forty-one," Tuka replied, leading us through a gate onto what appeared to be the main street.

It was full of elves bustling back and forth, but not long after we passed through the gate onto the street, they noticed humans were walking among them. We drew stares, and a crowd followed us.

"Um, Tuka," I said in a low voice, "shouldn't we stop and explain ourselves to everyone?"

"Nah," he said, waving a hand back toward me as he kept walking. We'll be at the main stage soon—the town meeting place. Once we're there, I'll ring the bell to bring everyone out and introduce you."

True to his word, he led us around a corner to the right, then another to the left, and we stood at the top of a large amphitheater. The semi-circle of seats ran down a hillside to a stage, all under a large roof. Tuka approached a rope leading up to a large bell mounted on a post and rang it. He let it clang five or six times, then waved us on and walked us down to the stage.

Even before he rang the bell, the elves who had been following us had taken seats. Soon, others came in, took seats, and whispered to each other when they saw two humans standing on the stage. It wasn't long before every seat in the house was filled, and all eyes were on us.

Tuka stepped up to the front of the stage and cleared his throat.

"Well," he began, "as you can see, we have guests! Everyone, this is Nicholas and Lisette. Now, I do have to tell you something about them you may not have noticed: they're human."

This got a laugh, and I smiled at the joke our new friend had made.

"I suppose you're wondering what humans are doing here. It turns out they have a fascinating story, and I think you'd all like to hear it. Oh, and one more thing: they're traveling with one of the Wandering Tribes."

This caused a murmur of excitement in the crowd. Tuka let it die down, then gestured Lisette and me to the front of the stage. He nodded at us and stepped back.

I began telling them my story, and Lisette joined me when she entered it. They all sat as rapt as Tuka had, taking in every word.

When I finished, Tuka stepped back up and stood beside us.

"Well, my friends," he said, "you heard their tale. Now, a question remains. I told them we have plenty of room for them to join us here, but they didn't want to impose on us. They were worried about barging in and taking up space. Does anyone here feel like they will take up space?"

A resounding "no" rang out from the crowd. Clearly, these elves wanted to spend more time with the humans and meet the famous Wandering Tribe.

Tuka turned to me with a big smile and said, "Well, that settles it. Get your friends. You're moving in!"

Once we joined the Lapland elves, we helped them erect more houses and added workshops to their village to continue making toys. For the first time in a long time, it felt like we had a place where we could set down roots and not move from for a long time.

"I think we found *Alfheim*," I remarked to Adelgard one day. We were working together on a beautiful small wagon that a child could pull things in or perhaps give a friend a ride in. I painted the pieces in a lovely, deep blue as Adelgard finished crafting them.

"No," he said as he gave a wheel a good test spin to ensure it worked properly, "I don't think this is *Alfheim*. The North Star isn't right overhead. It still lies north. But, I must say, I am quite happy here. So is everyone else. If the human population doesn't come this way, we could live here and do our work for quite some time!"

"I think the travel is going to be tricky, though," I replied, my voice tinged with concern. "I don't know if you've noticed, but there is a lot more snow on the ground here than anywhere we have ever visited. And while Vulfgang is a great horse, and I love him dearly, I'm afraid he's too big and heavy to make it through all this snow as fast as I need him to. We might need to find an alternative mode of transportation."

"I think I have a solution to that," a voice behind us said. We turned, and Waldhar was standing there. He flicked his head toward the door, turned, and walked out. We followed.

Outside, he pointed off into the yard. I saw two reindeer walking through the trees behind the workshop in the direction he indicated. I say walking, but of course, they were not in the Hidden Realm, so they looked to us to be frozen in the act of walking. Still, they seemed to be making their way through the deep drifts with almost no problem.

"I've noticed how they walk so easily when I slip into the human realm to observe and take in a bit of nature," Waldhar said. "I have even seen people with them hooked to sleds."

"That's true," Tuka said, joining us. "They're not too hard to train, and they make great transportation."

"Do you suppose we could bring a couple in and have them pull my sleigh like Vulfgang has for so many years?" I asked.

Tuka and Waldhar exchanged glances, and Tuka shrugged.

"Yeah, it shouldn't be a problem at all," Tuka said.

"They aren't as big or strong as Vulfgang," Waldhar added. "I should see about making you a sleigh out of a lighter wood." He pulled a piece of parchment from his pocket and a piece of charcoal from behind his ear and made a note of it. He nodded, folded the parchment, and stuck it back into his pocket. "Better go round up some help. I've got some trees to cut."

With the help of Tuka and three other elves named Kylakki, Nyllo, and Lars, I eventually found two reindeer that seemed suitable to be tamed and trained to pull the sleigh that Waldhar had made. They were the fastest in their heard but also were the most calm and approachable.

Let me tell you about reindeer. There are several subspecies, or varieties, of reindeer. The ones we found were of the type now called the Finnish forest reindeer, one of the largest types and probably the reindeer you picture when you think of my reindeer. There's also the mountain reindeer, also called common reindeer, which are native to Norway. You may also imagine them when you picture my reindeer. They are brown and sometimes have some white on them, which is how my reindeer are always portrayed in art, television, and movies. But they are actually not the type of reindeer that the famous eight are. We'll talk more about that later.

Kylakki, Nyllo, and Lars named the two reindeer Flossie and Glossie, elvish for kind and caring, respectively. They were spirited and full of energy but also very gentle, curious animals. We spent days training them, teaching them to respond to commands and work together. They were ready to pull the sleigh by Saint Nicholas Day Eve of 1348, a testament to their quick learning and our effective training methods.

Waldhar had meticulously crafted a stunning sleigh with a sleek pine-green paint job and polished brass runners that gleamed like gold. He had even padded the seat like a fine chair cushion.

I even got a brand new outfit as a gift from my new Finnish friends. I had long ago worn out the first outfit I got from Erminlinda that I mentioned earlier in this book, the green one with the brown fur. I had worn a lot of different special outfits since then in a rainbow of colors, but this one was the first one that resembled what you probably think of as a "Santa suit." Crafted in a traditional Finnish style like the elves' clothes, it had green pants, a white linen shirt with red embroidery patterns, a red wool vest with large wooden buttons, big brown boots, and an ankle-length red wool coat trimmed with white. It even had a matching hat. The coat and hat did not have fur, though. The white trim was made of braided fabric.

As Waldhar and Tuka said, the reindeer proved perfect for drawing the sleigh through the deep snow. Their large, broad hooves acted as snowshoes, stopping them from sinking too far into the snow, and their antlers helped them plow through drifts we encountered.

While we're discussing antlers, here's a fun fact: unlike other species of deer where only the males grow antlers, both male and female reindeer grow antlers, a new set every year. The antlers will grow through the spring and summer, then drop off, and a new pair will grow. However, the males drop their antlers much sooner than females, usually sometime in November. The females, on the other hand, lose their antlers between January and February. So, as you can probably guess, all my reindeer are female! That's why, if you spot me on Christmas Eve, you'll see my sleigh team with antlers!

But I can hear you now: "Santa, why are you talking about antlers? You were talking about two reindeer pulling your sleigh through the snow! On the ground! Don't your reindeer fly?" Well, not Flossie and Glossie. Only a specific type of reindeer can fly. I'll talk about them when we get there.

Still, Flossie and Glossie could run faster than my old friend Vulfgang, and when they jumped, it was close to flying. I was astounded the first time we leaped over a wide river, and I had to grab the reins extra tight to keep from being bumped up and out of the sleigh when we landed.

"Ho ho!" I laughed. "I guess I better have Waldhar put a harness in here to hold me in if we're going to pull stunts like that!"

The first St. Nicholas Day deliveries with my two new friends went so well that I used them every year after that. But, as you know, Flossie and Glossie eventually retired, their hard work and dedication rewarded with a life of luxurious relaxation, joining my friend Vulfgang in well-deserved rest.

After the first year of living in Lapland, a decision was made to move again, but this time, it was not far.

The Lapland elves had been living near Rovaniemi, and when we joined them, we made the village bigger. But in that first year, we realized that we perhaps were too large of a town to live so close to human civilization.

"But where should we go?" Adelgard asked from the crowd as I stood on stage at our village meeting. As I said earlier, there are no real leaders in elven society. We believe in consensus and the wisdom of the collective. I know everyone pictures me being the boss, but that's not really how it works. I was leading this meeting because someone had to, and I was the one who had been picked.

"Well," I responded, "I have been thinking about that, and I've asked around for suggestions from our friends who have lived here their whole lives. There is a mountain north of here called Korvatunturi that I am told is covered in a thick pine forest and surrounded by frozen lakes and land over which herds of reindeer roam. It seems like a place that will remain untouched by civilization for a long time to come, allowing us our privacy to do our work."

Kylakki stood up and said, "Not only that, Nicholas, but we Lapland elves have long believed Korvatunturi is a special place. It has a unique shape, almost like an ear, that allows voices from around the world to be heard there. It's said that's how the original elves learned people's wishes across the land and helped them come true."

"If that's true," Lisette said, "then that would be very helpful to our mission. It would let us know what sorts of things children wish to play with!"

"Well, then," I said to the united elves, "all in favor of embarking on this new chapter at Korvatunturi?"

A resounding cry of agreement arose from the gathering, and just like that, we were going to move to another new home.

Moving up the side of a mountain proved to be a daunting task, as you can probably imagine. The steep slopes and harsh weather tested our resilience. It took us the better part of two months to tear down the village, move it, and then set it back up. But eventually, we got settled, our new home standing proudly on the mountain peak.

It turned out the stories were true. Something about that mountain drew voices from near and far. Soon, we knew what children all over the place were interested in, and we began to keep lists. It was hard to tell which children specifically liked what, but we had a very good idea about what children wanted to play with. This unique feature of Korvatunturi, the ability to hear children's wishes, became a crucial part of our mission, guiding us in our efforts to bring joy to children's lives.

Korvatunturi made us a great home. We were pretty set to live there forever after just one year of being there, and we stayed for another fifty before something happened that made us move on yet again.

Iceland and the Huldufólk

I don't know how word eventually got out that we lived on Korvatunturi. Not precisely, anyway. I have a basic idea, though.

The *Hylgan Rikalt* is thin and somewhat porous, you see. While the elves and I can mainly remain in our hidden realm and only enter the human realm when we want to, it is possible to sometimes slip out of it accidentally in places. It's mostly how humans knew of elves at all, although I'm sure some sightings of elves were of ones who had chosen to spend time in the human realm. It's also how people eventually came to know what I look like. On the nights I make my deliveries, I never purposefully move from the elf realm to the human realm. I'm in too much of a hurry to slow down like that willfully. But, occasionally, I slip into the human realm, and someone sees me, and I also lose precious time.

So, what I believe happened is this, though I have no way of proving it: sometime in the year 1398, one of the elves or myself slipped from the *Hylgan Rikalt* into the human realm and, thinking we were not being watched, made our way back to our mountain home at a nice slow pace, perhaps to enjoy a beautiful day. It happened from time to time. But, on that particular day, we *were* being watched and someone saw whoever it was of our village make their way up the mountain.

Once the word got out that the gift-giver and his elf friends lived on Korvatunturi, all eyes turned to the mountain. We noticed more climbers and people spending time around the mountain's base. Everyone, it seemed, wanted to greet me or an elf.

"Nicholas," Lisette said to me late in the year 1399, "I know people can't find us here with their eyes, but the mountain only has so much space that people can climb before stumbling upon us here. Eventually, whether they are in the human realm or ours when they do it, someone will walk through this village. Do you think we should remain here?"

"We've been here fifty years now," I said, "and we all thought we had found our *Alfheim*. But perhaps we need to move on yet again. I should call a meeting."

So, that's what I did. We all gathered in our large meeting hall. Lisette and I laid out our conversation and asked if anyone had any thoughts. Lars stood and spoke.

"This has been a good home for us, Nicholas, but you and Lisette are right. We can't stay now that the local people know we are here. I'm sure all of them are well-intentioned people who just want to meet us and thank us for what we do, but they also don't understand just how important living and working in secret and private is to what we do. They don't know that it requires every bit of time we have and that they would take some of that time away. We need to continue the journey you and the Wandering Tribe began fifty years ago and keep searching for *Alfheim* because only there will we be alone for all time."

Murmurs of agreement spread through the hall, and I nodded to Lars, who sat back down. Tuka then jumped to his feet.

"If we're going to move on, I think I know just the place."

"Do tell," I said, motioning for him to continue.

"There is another place elves supposedly went when many left the homeland. Another Wandering Tribe. Although, if what I've heard is true, they aren't exactly wandering, as they have stayed in one small location. It's a small island nation to the west of here, known as Iceland. It's possible our brothers and sisters there could be a big help to us." He sat back down once he had said this.

"Alright," Lisette said. "Iceland is on the table. Does anyone else have an idea?"

Silence filled the room, and I saw several heads shake.

"Okay," I said, clapping my hands together, "it seems we're moving to Iceland! Let's get to work!"

The elves poured out of the meeting hall and set right to packing. Over the next several days, we had meetings after meetings, deciding what to take with us and what could be left behind. Then, over several weeks, we packed up all we could before we eventually left. I felt a pang of sadness that we were leaving this beautiful place where we could hear the world's wishes, but it had to be done. To this day, if you visit Finland, you can go to the city of Rovaniemi, which has been declared my hometown, and also see Korvatunturi, where the Finnish people still will tell you that Joulupukki, their name for me, lives. The memories of this place will always be with me, a part of my heart that I carry wherever I go.

We made our way across Finland, then Sweden, and into Norway. Then, we traveled down the coast until we reached a point where it seemed like the boat trip would be the shortest possible. Even though the elves who had come from the south with me had learned about sailing on the journey to Finland, no one in our group felt particularly confident about doing it, and we didn't want to get on the open ocean and get lost. A large ship with a dozen oars was built, and we all boarded it.

Rowing, even with a dozen oars and three elves to each, was a grueling task. Each of us could only row for about half an hour, and as the time neared its end, our pace would noticeably slow. Despite our efforts, our progress was slow. The journey was a test of our endurance and strength.

Finally, we set foot on the shores of Iceland. Once again, I was captivated by the beauty of a new land, a land brimming with the promise of adventure and the joy of sharing my gifts with the local children. The sheer excitement was overwhelming.

Moreover, almost as soon as we landed, I felt the place was special. We all could. We could practically see the magic in the air.

"There must be elves here," Adelgard said, his voice full of awe. "The place practically glows."

"I know," I replied. "Even Lapland wasn't like this."

"It's incredible," Lars said, joining me and Adelgard in wondering at the landscape before us. "Here I thought Korvatunturi was the most special and wondrous place in the world!"

We spent some time there on the shore, taking apart our boat for the scrap material to use later, and then began our journey inland in search of the local elves.

It didn't take us long to meet the local elves. Just like the elves in Lapland had found my group when we first explored that land, the native population of elves found us faster than we could have found them.

The first elf we met was at the top of a hill we were cresting a few days after we had landed in the country. She was sitting on a large stone, wearing a lovely sky-blue dress with a red stripe down each side and alternating red and blue stripes along the bottom. Over the top of her dress, she wore a vest of the same shade of blue, adorned with white lace. On her head was a tall, white, cone-shaped hat that curved slightly forward at the top, almost like the crescent moon.

"Welcome, travelers," she said, raising her hand in greeting. Then she noticed Lisette and me; her hand fell, and her eyes widened. "Oh, my! You're human!"

"That's right," Lisette said. "The only ones in the whole *Hylgan Rikalt,* as far as we know."

"We've been traveling with Nicholas and Lisette for a very long time," Erminlinda added, "we would love to meet with you and your people and talk about it."

"Yes, of course!" said the elf on the rock. "My name is Snælaug. Please, follow me." She got up off the rock and walked down the side of the hill.

We followed her into a little valley and were greeted by the most unique village I had ever seen. All the homes were built into hillsides.

We could see ornate wooden home fronts painted all the colors of the rainbow, but they all led into mounds or the side of the hill, meaning these elves lived underground.

Waldhard seemed especially interested in these homes. "Isn't it more work to build the houses into the hills than to just build them regularly?" he asked.

"Sure," Snælaug replied, "but it gets freezing here, and living in the hills provides our homes with more insulation, so they stay warmer."

Lars clapped a hand to his forehead. "I can't believe we never thought of that!" he cried.

"Why?" Snælaug asked. "Where are you from?"

"It's a long story," Lars replied. "But the short version is that many of us are from Lapland, where it also gets bitter cold for a big chunk of the year. I really can't believe we didn't think of this. It's genius."

Just like when I first met the Black Forest and Lapland elves, this village's citizens gathered around to witness the newcomers, especially the two humans, whispering excitedly.

Snælaug led us to a particularly large structure, then started and turned to look at me and Lisette as if she had forgotten we were there.

"Oh," she said, "I'm afraid we can't go inside. You two won't fit! I had planned to take you into the meeting hall and have everyone come, but I am not used to having humans around. I guess we will have to hold the meeting here, outside."

"That's alright," Lisette said soothingly. "We completely understand."

So, the meeting was called. Not that too many elves were left to come since most had already gathered to see the humans and the foreign elves. I judged there were about seven hundred of them, give or take.

Just as we had when we met the Lapland elves, we told our tale, beginning with me and how I had started my mission many, many years ago, with everyone else joining in and telling parts as they entered the story.

When it was done, the gathered crowd was silent. I saw wonder on many faces. Finally, an elf stepped forward and introduced himself.

"My name is Syndry," he said. He wore a brown coat and black pants. The coat had many large, shiny brass buttons down each side and on the sleeves, and his pants had the same buttons. He wore a fir-green shirt with smaller but equally shiny brass buttons. A red kerchief was tied around his neck and on his head he wore a knit cap that was a similar color to his shirt that had brown stripes. A small tassel dangled from the top of the cap.

"I believe I can speak for all gathered here when I say it is an honor to meet you all," he said. "We, of course, all know of the tribe of our forebearers from Lapland, and the legend of the Wandering Tribes led our ancestors here to this land. We are called the *Huldufólk* by the locals, which means 'Hidden People,' and so we call ourselves. There are many villages across this land. I believe, and I welcome anyone here to disagree, that I am correct in saying that you are welcome to live here with us." A chorus of agreement greeted his words, but not a single sound of disagreement.

"Furthermore," he said, raising his hand to silence the others, "your mission to bring joy to human children greatly interests me and, I assume, my friends and neighbors gathered here." His words were met with enthusiastic shouts of agreement from the crowd, their excitement palpable. "It is interesting to me, Nicholas, that your mission should align so closely with some things we *Huldufólk* have taken to doing in this land. You see, we have noticed that while our lives are often quite joyful and easy, the lives of humans are just as often sad and difficult. Because of this, we try to help them in many little ways. We have been known to clean houses, mend shoes, and bake bread. We do all this under cover of night so that when the humans wake in the morning, they find that one or more of their tedious tasks is taken care of, and they might find a little more time in their day for more happy undertakings like music and art."

"How noble of you all!" I cried, spreading my arms as if to hug them all. The acceptance and understanding we felt in that moment was overwhelming, a validation of our mission and a promise of a fruitful collaboration with the elves.

"But this business of toys," Syndry continued, "is especially wonderful. I, for one, would be overjoyed to make toys with you!" he turned and faced his village. "How about you all?" Cheers rang out, and hats were tossed in the air. Suddenly, a surge of bodies came forward, every one of our new friends trying to embrace us in hugs all at once. I couldn't stop laughing as I tried to hug them all. I was too filled with joy to keep it inside.

"Someone must go tell the other villages!" Snælaug cried over the din of all the merriment. "I think they're going to want to know!"

An elf who was small, even for an elf, volunteered and was off like a shot even though night was falling. In just a few short days, my group met several more villages of *Huldufólk* and were accepted by them all as friends. We were overjoyed that they all wished to share in our gift-giving mission.

"I think we're going to have to build one large centralized city," Lars told me once we had met with all the other villages. He was looking at a map of Iceland and a tally of the populations of each town. With the eight hundred-seventy-six of us who arrived here and the one-thousand-three-hundred-sixty-five here in Iceland, our total number is two-thousand-two-hundred-forty-one. I don't think we will want to spread out across the country. It will add an unnecessary complication to our mission."

"Yes, I think you are right," I replied. Though, as you know, elf culture has no official leadership, I noticed Lars was particularly good at organization and time management. Everyone else had noticed as well and turned to him for guidance. In particular, Lisette, who was also very efficient, had seen, and between the two of them, they had begun in the last few years to schedule out what needed to be done when and by whom. Since it proved very useful, no one objected to them falling into unofficial leadership roles. So here Lars sat, trying to put together our plan for moving forward.

"We'll have to call together a lot of the *Huldufólk* to help with that," he said. "They'll know the best places to build. I like their local buildings, the underground thing. Building that sort of city will take a lot of land, and they'll know the best place to get to work."

Before I knew it, a spot was chosen, and Lisette and Lars had created a timetable and divided the labor. The best builders set about building our new city, and the rest kept up toy making. We had a lot of work to do before St. Nicholas Day!

A Very Brief History of Christmas, Pt. 3

During the Medieval Period, Christmas emerged as a beacon of joy and hope, particularly for those enduring challenging times, such as the poor. This festive season, with its promise of merriment and respite, was eagerly anticipated and celebrated by all.

Christmas spanned twelve days from December 25th to January 6th during the Medieval Period. This extended holiday, which inspired the song "The Twelve Days of Christmas," was a time for everyone to come together, rest, feast, and enjoy the company of friends and family.

People still carried on with their older traditions, though. In homes across the Christian world, people hung holly, ivy, and mistletoe. The old tradition of a Yule log was kept as well, and good Christians kept it lit for the entire twelve-day celebration. Since the point of the holiday was to celebrate the birth of Jesus, church services were held. These eventually became elaborate and featured candles, gilded altars, and Nativity reenactments.

People played a variety of games during the Christmas celebrations, such as cards and dice (and even engaged in some gambling, which will be important later), chess, checkers, and backgammon. These games provided entertainment and fostered social interaction. Carols were written and performed. Medieval carols were not the same as what they are today. They were big, elaborate dances in the street and very joyous.

Music was everywhere, and there were performances by jugglers and acrobats. It's easy to see how this became such a popular holiday!

And, yes, there were gifts given. These gifts, initially simple tokens of love and appreciation, took on a deeper meaning when they became Christmas gifts. They were meant to reference the gifts given by the Magi to Jesus. However, they were still just gifts given from one to another, symbolizing the love and devotion of the giver, which is all that eventually mattered to me.

The First Christmas Eve

Once we had built a centralized city in Iceland and all the *Huldufólk* from all the villages had moved in, it was full steam ahead on getting the toys done in time for that year's St. Nicholas Day. Waldhar almost immediately noted a problem with our new location, however.

"Nicholas," he said, some concern in his voice. "I don't suppose you have considered how to get to the mainland?"

I was distracted, carving away at a piece of wood to make a top, and didn't grasp his question when I responded, "What do you mean?"

"Well, we are on an island nation. There is a whole ocean between here and the rest of the places you bring gifts. Flossie and Glossie can swim, but not that far! And your sleigh isn't built to float!" Waldhar pointed out, his concern evident.

I dropped the wood and the carving knife as that fact struck me for the first time. The weight of the situation settled heavily on my shoulders, and I could see the worry mirrored in Waldhar's eyes.

"The ocean!" I practically yelled. "Oh, my goodness, the ocean! How *am* I going to reach all the children?"

"That's what I'm asking!" Waldhar replied.

"Sailing takes so long I'll never make it," I said, resting my face in my hands.

There was a long, uncomfortable pause as Waldhar and I sat there with the fact that our new home may have set us up for failure in our mission.

Then, behind us, someone cleared their throat. I lifted my face from my hands, and we turned to see Kylakki standing in the doorway.

"I have a thought," she said.

"Go on," I urged, eager to not fail the children who expected their gifts.

"Flossie and Glossie, as you know, can jump very far. Suppose, Waldhar, that rafts be built, sailed to sea, and spaced between here and the continent? Then, once Nicholas is done with the deliveries here, Flossie and Glossie can get a running start, leap to the first raft, run across, leap to the next, and so on until they reach land on the other side." Kylakki's plan was simple yet ingenious, and it gave us hope.

Waldhar stroked his beard and stared at the ceiling for quite some time. This is how he looked when imagining rough building plans and doing calculations in his head for a project he had never done before.

"I'd need to know just how far they could jump," he said finally, "so I could figure out how many rafts we would need. And how fast they need to be going to achieve their farthest leap so I could build the rafts big enough to get them to that speed. And we'd have to test-land them on some rafts to make sure the rafts don't split or tip too much. But, yes, I suppose it could be done!"

"Kylakki," I said, whirling to face her, "go hitch the deer up to the sleigh. We're going to go out and start measuring some jumps."

The three of us devoted the next several days to tests, and then Waldhar and his select team spent several more days building rafts of different sizes to test. Then we took the rafts to the sea, and they were spaced out for more tests. The first test went badly. The rafts were the shortest ones, based on the distance Waldhar had measured it took Flossie and Glossie, who were hitched side-by-side, to get to full speed for a jump. But he had measured to where their back legs took off from the ground, not where the sleigh took off. So, when they leaped off the raft, the sleigh was still on it and was dragged right into the water, causing my poor reindeer to plummet into the water themselves. Fortunately, a team of elves was in a boat with ropes and ramps to get us out, but we were still wet and cold.

Waldhar could not stop apologizing. "I can't believe I did that!" he said repeatedly. "I had a feeling it was too short. I should never have had you test those rafts!" I assured him multiple times that everyone makes mistakes and that I didn't blame him, but it still bothered him.

"Enough," I said finally as we sat next to the fire that had been built to help me get dry. "Feeling bad is such a waste of time. Look, I'm mostly dry and warm now. Let's focus on moving on to the next set of rafts to see if those work better." My determination was unwavering, and I could see it reassured my friend.

The next test almost ended up as badly as the first. For some reason I don't quite understand, but Waldhar could probably explain, something to do with the shape is all I know, when we landed on the first of the next test rafts it titled badly backward when the sleigh came down on it, almost resulting into a backslide into the water.

"Nope!" Waldhar yelled from the boat. "Stop right there! This batch will not work either! We'll tow you back to shore!"

The next batch of rafts was rowed out, and as I climbed into the sleigh, Waldhar said, "I have a great feeling about these."

When I was given the go-ahead, I gave Flossie and Glossie the signal, and they started running. Right at the shore, they leaped into the air, and the sleigh left the ground behind them. We soared in a great arc, almost like we were flying for a long distance, and then, with a *whump!*, the sleigh landed on the first raft. It wobbled a bit but was basically sturdy in the water. The deer kept running, and I held my breath and closed my eyes as they took off in another big jump, bracing myself to crash again into the cold ocean water. But I felt the sleigh lurch up and a feeling of near weightlessness, and I knew we would make it. The relief and joy that washed over me was indescribable.

"Waaahoooo!" I cried out as the sleigh arced back down and landed on the next raft with another whump. "That was great! Keep going, girls!"

Again, the deer ran full-tilt and took off at the end of the raft. We made it to the third and final test raft with no problem, and I pulled tight on the reins, drawing them to a fast stop before we went off the end into the water. From the watchboat, I could hear cheers and claps.

"Yes!" Waldhar yelled. "That was perfect! Hold tight, Nicholas, we'll tow you in!"

Once we were back on land, I hugged Waldhar, Kylakki, and all the rest of the build team. We were all overjoyed that the test had worked and that the mission could continue.

After that, it was work, work, and more work getting toys ready and rafts built and towed out to sea. There wasn't much time before St. Nicholas Day, and I didn't want to disappoint a single child.

The gift-giving went smoothly that year, and when I returned to Iceland, we had a big feast to celebrate. It was at this feast that Christmas first really came to my attention.

"We don't normally eat this much until *Pipermynta Daur*!" Snælaug said with a laugh as she popped a large pastry into her mouth.

"*Pipermynta Daur*?" Lisette asked.

"Peppermint Day," she said, translating from Icelandic Elvish. It's an old *Huldufólk* holiday we celebrate on December 24th. Like many old human holidays, it welcomes the time of year when the sun will be out for longer each day."

While every part of the world has short days in the winter, places near and above the Arctic Circle, such as Lapland and Iceland, have the shortest days. In my new home in Iceland, the sun was only up this time of year from about eleven in the morning to three in the afternoon, a meager four hours. This had also been true in Lapland, but the elves there had had no such holiday.

"Tell us about it," I said, interested.

"Well, mostly, we feast, dance, sing, and give each other small gifts. Then we head out to help the humans; typically, they leave us food, too.

Peppermint Day coincides with their holiday as well. It used to be called other things, but these days, we have heard it called Christmas."

"But why Peppermint Day?" Lisette asked.

"Because we use peppermint a lot in what we eat!" Snælaug replied with a laugh. "It doesn't really have a meaning besides that. I guess it could also signify a return of growing season, and peppermint is the symbol we use. But, mostly, since we make peppermint candies and peppermint pies and put it in drinks to celebrate, it seemed like a fun thing to call it!"

"Christmas, huh?" I mused, stroking my beard.

"Yes, it seems quite popular. The humans celebrate it enthusiastically. It's a very joyful time."

I pondered over that for a while. While I certainly cherished the tradition of giving my St. Nicholas Day gifts, the day itself didn't strike me as particularly joyful overall. But this newer holiday of Christmas sounded a lot like the other old holidays I remembered from my youth: brimming with song, dance, food, and tokens of love and friendship from one person to another. I honestly had fallen out of touch with a lot of the happenings in the human world. The last significant things I remembered very well were discovering the existence of St. Nicholas Day almost three hundred years prior and The Black Plague about fifty years ago. I was unaware of much of the progress in society, which, of course, was my own fault and, in hindsight, a bit of a mistake. Just because I lived among the elves didn't mean I wasn't also a citizen of the world and should know what was happening. This Christmas holiday seemed very much like something I yearned to be a part of.

"Snælaug, this holiday, Christmas. Do many people celebrate it?" I asked.

"I don't know about anywhere else, but it seems pretty widespread here—at least among those who call themselves Christians. As far as I can tell, it's a religious holiday for them, at least nominally. I see them pray to their god at a service on that day, but that isn't really the holiday's focus. I think they are celebrating the birth of their god or something. They seem to celebrate with a lot of merriment, though!"

"Well," I said, my brain forming a plan, "I can't wait to celebrate Peppermint Day with you all. Then I want to watch the celebration of this Christmas. Maybe hop over to the continent to see if folks over there like it as much as you say the people here do."

December 24th arrived, and I was excited to celebrate Peppermint Day with the elves. What a celebration it was! If there is one thing elves know how to do, it's have a good time.

Upon waking, I could already hear songs being sung throughout the village. I sat up and rubbed my eyes as Lisette came into the room.

"It's good to see you plan on getting up today!" she chuckled.

I glanced at the hourglass on my bedside table, which didn't appear any more empty on the top than it usually was when I woke in the morning. I needed the hourglass more than ever this time of year because the sun did not rise this far north until around what we would now call 11 AM and then would set a mere four hours later, making the early morning hours all seem about the same.

"I don't seem to have slept any later than I normally do," I replied.

"Well, the rest of us have been up for a few hours now! Hurry up, get dressed, and come join us!" Lisette's voice was brimming with excitement, and I could hear the anticipation in her words. I quickly dressed in my festive attire and joined the bustling streets.

The streets were a sight to behold, adorned with wreaths and garlands crafted from evergreen branches, and illuminated by a multitude of candles. The air was filled with the sweet aroma of peppermint, intermingled with the tantalizing scents of cooked food.

Adelgard approached me and yelled, "Catch!" I barely had time to raise my hands and snatch what he tossed.

I looked into my hand and saw a hard yellow chunk, almost like a pebble.

"What's this?" I asked him.

"Pop it into your mouth," he said with a little smile.

I stared at it a little doubtfully. It looked a bit like a blob of hard earwax. But I trusted my old friend and did as he told me. As the sweet and sharp taste of peppermint filled my mouth, I couldn't help but smile. It was a delightful surprise, and I was glad I trusted Adelgard.

"This is delicious!" I said.

"It's something our *Huldufólk* cousins created," he replied. "It's hardened honey that they have flavored with peppermint!"

"What a terrific invention!"

"I had a feeling you'd like it! Come on, we're going to have a big sing in the town square!" Adelgard's eyes sparkled with excitement as he led me towards the town square, his hand on my shoulder. The sound of laughter and music filled the air, and I couldn't help but feel a part of something truly special.

Never in my life had I experienced such a wonderful day. I always knew my elfin friends were full of merriment and knew how to celebrate, but the *Huldufólk* took it to another level. Bonfires were built everywhere around the town, and dances were going around each one. Gallons upon gallons of delicious peppermint tea were being drunk, and tables were piled so high with food that I thought my small friends might need stools to reach the top of them!

As the day drew to a close, long after the sun had set, Syndry found me enjoying my third helping of the *Huldufólk*'s special celebration roast. It was a delicious mixture of mushrooms, carrots, nuts, beans, and seasonings wrapped in dough and baked, then smothered in gravy.

"How are you liking the roast?" he asked, having a seat across from me.

"It's wonderful! I would happily eat this every day!"

He laughed. "well, a lot of work goes into making those roasts, so we usually save them for special occasions. We'll have them again in the spring for Seeding Day when we celebrate the return of the growing season."

"Well, maybe I'll make one or two between now and then for myself," I said, then forked another bite into my mouth.

"We're going to be heading out soon to mingle with the humans," he said, "so you might want to finish up. I know you're eager to see what their holiday is all about."

Though it was getting pretty late in the day when we ventured out to the human towns, there were still many homes with lights burning bright, and people were up and about.

Much like in our own settlement, the humans had food out, and we could see they were playing games and having a good time.

"We can return to the homes where people are awake later," Lars told me. For now, we will go into the homes where people are already asleep and do some things for them.

Like whispers in the wind, the elves spread swiftly and silently to the dark homes, and I followed Syndry into one. He carried a broom, and I brought a load of rags and a bucket of hot water. We planned to scrub this family's floor until they could eat off it. And, while I'm on the subject of eating, just like I had been told, there was a small plate of food left out. So, as we worked, we snacked. One strange thing I had realized since living in the realm of the elves was I hardly ever seemed to get full. I had been eating most of the day and was still happily snacking on pastries left out by the family in this house. By ordinary reckoning, I should have been impossibly fat from eating all the food I did, yet I had not gained or lost any size since I stopped living as a normal human. My pants always remained the same size. Yes, it was larger than most wore at the time, but nowhere near as large as it should have been based on my diet.

As we worked, some clothes hanging by the fireplace caught my eye. I assumed this family had been out playing in the snow, and these clothes hanging by the now extinguished fire had been hung there to dry when they had come in from having fun.

Hanging among the clothes were some children's clothes, including socks. Seeing these socks, my mind went back to when I was only eighteen, sneaking into Deniz's house to leave gold coins for his daughters. I had left those coins in their socks, and now I had an idea.

"Syndry, wait right here," I said, getting off my hands and knees and heading for the door. "I want to run back to the village and get some things. I'll be right back."

I rushed back to the village and loaded our extra toys from St. Nicholas Day into a big sack. Then I had another thought, and I took as many peppermint honey candies as I could find and put them in the sack. I hitched Flossie and Glossie up to the sleigh and rode it into the human town. I threw the sack over my shoulder and returned to the house where Syndry was waiting for me.

"What are you doing?" he asked.

"When I was a much younger man, the first secret gifts I gave were to three girls who needed money. I wasn't living among elves then, so when I snuck into their home, I was almost caught more than once, and I was scared. I had to hurry and leave the money somewhere the girls were sure to find it, so I dropped it into their socks and left. See here that this family has a child," I gestured to the clothes at the fireplace, "I am going to do just like I did all those years ago and leave a gift in this child's stocking. Only this time, it will be a toy rather than money!"

I pulled a small bag of clay marbles from the sack of toys I had brought and dropped it neatly into the child's stocking. Then, I dropped in several of the sweets.

Syndry's eyes were wide as he watched, and he said, "This is a fantastic idea! Come on, we have to find the other homes with children!"

And so, we set off on our mission. We hurried around, asking our friends who had been in the other homes where there were children to give gifts to. Not every home had clothes by their fireplaces, but in the ones that did, I was sure to leave the gifts in the stockings. In other homes, I left them by the heads of the children as they slept in their beds, where they would also be sure to find them in the morning. I had to wait a good chunk of the night for those staying up late to go to bed before I could get into their homes and leave gifts for their children, but it was worth it. When I had given away all the toys and sweets, a sense of deep contentment washed over me. I practically floated as I hopped into the sleigh and headed back home for more peppermint tea and another slice of celebration roast.

When I woke on Christmas Day, I decided I wanted to slip into the human realm and wander into one of the human towns to see how they celebrated this Christmas holiday. I dressed in my finest clothes, and Lisette dressed in hers, and we headed out together for our first proper outing into the human world in many years.

Guided by our trusty companions, Flossie and Glossie, we journeyed to the nearest town. The air was filled with a sense of anticipation as we arrived, the townsfolk already gathered in the church for their worship. We slipped into the back, our presence unnoticed, and observed the unfamiliar yet captivating Christian worship service. The room resonated with songs of praise and gratitude. As the service concluded, we joined the crowd, stepping out into the streets.

Of course, we were noticed as strangers in this small town where everyone knew everyone else's name. We introduced ourselves as newcomers to the country who had been out for a Christmas Day sleigh ride from our home in another town not far away. We were warmly welcomed and invited to take part in the caroling that was about to begin.

"We'd be delighted to join you," Lisette said with a smile, her eyes sparkling with excitement.

Don't forget, Medieval carols were large dances, not just songs like you know today. And I hadn't gotten any better at dancing since Lisette had swept me into her arms to dance the first time she met the elves! She knew this and laughed as she dragged me along to the carol with her, knowing that watching me try to keep up with the steps would be amusing. As much as she loves me, she does like to tease me!

While I certainly had trouble doing the dancing properly, I must admit I had a lot of fun! Then, when the dancing was over, games were played, and we watched as children ran about, showing off their new toys to one another.

"It's quite strange," one woman said when she noticed us watching the children. "All the children in town woke up with new playthings today."

"Why is that strange?" Lisette asked, feigning curiosity even though she knew quite well where the toys had come from.

"Because no one knows where they came from!" the woman replied. "Obviously, *someone* left them, but no one will say who! At first, we were all quite frightened that someone had been in our homes, but nothing seems to be missing and no one was hurt. All that happened was the leaving of toys for children."

"Perhaps the *Huldufólk* have a new tradition," I said.

"Perhaps..." the woman said, but she didn't sound sure.

But I was sure. Standing there watching the children play with their new toys, combined with all the happiness and celebration around me, I knew I wanted to be a part of Christmas every year, in any place it was celebrated.

Eight Flying Reindeer

Starting in 1401, I joyfully continued the tradition of bringing presents for St. Nicholas Day, a celebration I cherished. But it was my first full Christmas Eve journey around Europe that truly ignited my excitement. Wherever I discovered Christmas being celebrated, I eagerly brought toys. The elves, in a moment of collective inspiration, decided to officially change our major elfin holiday from Peppermint Day to Christmas. However, they also decided to keep Peppermint Day and moved it from December 24th to December 23rd, creating an extended holiday filled with joy and merriment.

In the following few years, I traveled to many countries in the human realm to learn more about Christmas and its customs. I learned that all over the continent, there was a lot of mystery and excitement surrounding the mysterious person who brought gifts on Christmas Eve.

Within a few years, I learned people were celebrating Christmas not only in European countries but also in Russia and parts of the Middle East. However, in the Middle Eastern countries, the main religions were Islam and Judaism, so most people were not celebrating Christmas.

This presented me with a challenge. Up until that point, my gift-giving had been indiscriminate, a symbol of goodwill, love, and generosity for all children. However, as I began to limit my gift-giving to certain times of the year and, eventually, the Christmas holiday, I faced difficulties. Initially, I left gifts for all children on Christmas Eve, regardless of their faith. But Jewish and Muslim families, understandably, were perplexed about why gifts were arriving on a Christian holiday. The following year, I attempted to align my gift-giving with holidays celebrated in their cultures. However, unlike the Christmas holiday, these religious holidays did not maintain the same spirit of gift-giving that the Christians had preserved when they phased out older holidays.

Eventually, I came to a realization. While my gifts were not tied to any specific religion, I understood that I could only bring them to children who celebrated Christmas. This acceptance was bittersweet. I was thrilled about Christmas and the joy it brought, but I also felt a pang of sadness that I could only share my message of love and generosity with a specific group of children.

"Look at it this way, Nicholas," Lisette said to me as I sat pouting by the fireplace not long after I had made this realization, "a substantial population of children are Christian and celebrate Christmas. So many people will still grow up knowing about the joy of your gifts and learning that a stranger can care enough to be kind to them. Then, they will grow up and put that lesson into practice in the real world, even with people of different cultures than they are. On top of that, it's not like those other cultures *aren't* teaching their children to be kind and generous! They are just doing it differently. It will all be okay in the end."

"Oh, I know that," I said, sighing. "I am just disappointed. Giving children toys is my greatest pleasure, and I hate that some children will go without my gifts. My toys are some children's only exposure to happiness and play in the whole year."

"That may be true, but it's less true than when you started," she replied. The world is getting better all the time! I know the last few hundred years were difficult times and that all the years when you were first starting were, too. But since the end of The Plague, things have been building back better than before. People are putting more effort into art, science, and philosophy, which enrich the mind and spirit rather than create horror like war does."

She was right. We were in the period historians now call The Late Middle Ages, coming swiftly into a time now called the Renaissance, which is looked upon as an extraordinary flourishing of artistic and scientific endeavors. It was when people began to consider humanism, a school of thought that stresses human beings' potential value and goodness, emphasizes everyday human needs, and seeks rational ways of solving human problems. In other words, the world was becoming more civilized. Things *were* improving. They didn't get better all at once. There were still plenty of difficult times ahead. But, in that moment, I felt some of the weight of the world I had felt for so long lift off my shoulders. I had spent so long feeling it was my sole responsibility to spread kindness because no one else was. I had always known that other people had just as much capacity for goodness as I did but believed they were too busy just trying to survive to do that good. It was the first time I felt they might find the time for it.

"You're right, my love," I said, taking her hand in mine and patting it with my other hand. "I was just having a selfish moment, I guess. Even if I can't bring my gifts to all children because their beliefs do not include welcoming me into their home, that does not mean those children will not know joy and love and generosity of spirit. I'm old and stuck in my ways, you know. I'm pretty used to being one of the few dispensers of happiness. But, of course, I can't be upset at the idea that more people will treat others well. If more people are going to spread happiness in their own way, how can I say no to that?"

She leaned in and kissed my cheek. "Okay, enough sulking," she said, letting go of my hand and standing up. "Christmas is still coming!"

We continued to live in Iceland for the next several years. But it is a tiny country, and we eventually found, like in other places we had lived before, that the human world was closing in on us. And, like before, we also needed room to grow. More children were celebrating Christmas, and we needed to make gifts for them, which required more space to craft and store toys. On top of that, I had also started bringing sweets to children when I brought them toys and exotic nuts and fruits we gathered from other lands. We needed space to store these, too.

So, in January 1410, we had another of our big meetings to decide what to do next.

"You told us when you met us you had been searching for *Alfheim*," Snælaug said. "And as much as the *Huldufólk* have loved our home here for as long as we can remember, this place is not *Alfheim*. I vote we continue looking for it. It is, after all, the promised land of the elves, and no human cities shall ever find us there."

"I second that vote," my old friend Adelgard said, his eyes filled with hope and determination. "I still believe Alfheim is out there waiting for us, just as you do."

"Well, then," I said, "all in favor, raise your hand."

The entire village, united in their determination, shot their hands into the air, and a resounding chorus of "aye" rang out. Once again, it was clear that we would tear down and move on together.

"I guess we better get busy," Lisette said to everyone. "We've only got eleven months to find a home and prepare for Christmas!"

We embarked on a thrilling adventure, carrying only the essentials for our long journey. Our ships, crafted from the very wood that once sheltered us, were our vessels of exploration. Guided by the North Star, we sailed north, our destination, *Alfheim*, still a distant dream.

We were at sea for a good long while, and we initially sailed northeast to avoid the country known as Greenland to the west of Iceland. We knew Greenland was a large place extending very far north, and we had initially thought that we should travel across that land to reach our destination. But we decided there would be fewer obstacles to carry our supplies through if we simply went north by boat.

This decision ultimately led to our discovery of a small cluster of islands we had not known about before, and it changed my mission and my legend forever.

Today, this small cluster of islands, or archipelago, is named Svalbard and is part of Norway, even though it lies quite a good distance north of that country. When we arrived, it was still winter, a time of perpetual darkness known as the polar night, where the sun never rises. As far as our eyes could reach, the landscape was a pristine white canvas blanketed with ice and snow.

"And I thought home was cold," Lars said, pulling a hood up over his head, which already had a hat covering it.

"No kidding," I replied, my mitten-clad hands rubbing together in a futile attempt to generate warmth. "I wonder if perhaps we are making a big mistake."

"You said that when we moved to Lapland," Lisette said, huddling against me and shivering, "and back then, I said you were wrong. Even though I'm freezing, I think you're wrong now, too. So we better hurry, get back on the ship, and stoke the fires. Hop to it, Nicholas! Get me warm!" She laughed a little at her playfully bossy tone, and I laughed, too.

"You heard the boss, my friends!" I said as I headed back up the plank to the ship. "Let's get ourselves rested and warm; tomorrow we can check out this place we have landed."

The next day (though we could only tell it was the next day by our hourglasses because it was still dark), most of the elves stayed on the boats around the fires, and I struck out with Waldhar, Odalric, and Tuka to do some exploring. The island we were on seemed vast, and though the north star still shone in the north, we were filled with a deep curiosity about this place and its untold possibilities.

As we walked, our lanterns held out before us, Odalric spotted large footprints in the snow.

"Looks like a bear," he said, hunching down and peering at the prints. "A huge one! These prints have to be as big as your head, Nicholas!"

"Then let's try not to run into it, shall we?" I said, looking around like the bear might be right behind me.

"Oh, stop," Waldhar said, slapping me playfully on the arm, "a bear won't see us! It's over in the other realm!"

"Well, I'd rather be safe than sorry," I replied. "Just because one hasn't come into the elf realm yet doesn't mean one won't! There was never a human here before me, after all."

Not too long after we saw the prints, we did, indeed, come face to face with the bear. I rounded a large drift of snow, and there it was, a massive creature. I'm not ashamed to admit I let out a scream and stumbled backward, dropping my lantern, which immediately went out.

My friends scrambled forward to help me as I pushed myself backward on my backside, away from the bear.

Suddenly, Tuka was laughing. I looked at him and saw he was doubled over, his hands on his knees, shaking with mirth.

"Nicholas," he said through howls of laughter, "it's just like we told you! The bear is not in the *Hylgan Rikalt*! Look!"

I got up to my feet again and walked toward Tuka. He was right, of course. The massive and pure white bear was frozen mid-stride, solid in the other realm. Odalric and Waldhar joined Tuka in his laughter, the three holding each other up as they howled like banshees.

"Well, I would have liked to see you three round that drift and not be scared!" I said rather sharply. I may not be embarrassed now, but I sure was then.

"Okay, okay," Waldhar said, still chuckling and snorting as he picked my lantern off the ground and relit it off his lantern. "That's a fair point. I'm sorry I laughed, old friend." He wiped a few tears off his face and regained his composure.

"I'm not," Odalric said, wiping away tears and with a grin so goofy I couldn't help but smile back. I knew none of them meant anything by their laughter.

"I suppose I did look pretty ridiculous," I conceded with a snort of laughter. Come on, let's see what else we can see."

We found some human settlements on the island, but nothing significant. We also saw a gorgeous fox, as white as the snow, just like the bear we had seen before. But, mostly, there didn't seem to be too much in the way of life.

Just as I thought it was almost time to turn back and head to the ship, I heard Tuka yelp from the top of a hill.

"Nicholas! Odalric! Waldhar! Come quick! You guys *have* to see this!"

We hurried as fast as we could to his side and looked where he was pointing. Spread out in the valley below us were hundreds and hundreds of tiny reindeer, all as white as the bear and the fox except for their brown antlers. We could barely see them by the moon's light, just beyond the light of our lanterns.

But it wasn't the sheer number of the reindeer below us that had caught Tuka's eye. As I looked at them, I noticed something incredible. There were traces of movement among the hundreds of bodies in the herd. It was very slow, but we had never once seen things in the other realm move when we were in our realm.

"They must be moving incredibly fast," Waldhar breathed. I saw his face tilt upward into his thinking pose, and he stared off into the sky for a moment or two. "At least a hundred times faster than anything in that realm *should* move, I think."

Just as he said that something even more extraordinary happened. The movement broke from the rest of the herd, and we saw eight reindeer, apparently in full gallop even though, to our eyes, they were still moving slowly, moving out into the open. Almost as one, they took a colossal leap and soared into the sky! And when I say soared, I mean they ascended higher than I had ever seen Flossie and Glossie jump and stayed in the air for what I was sure had to be an impossible amount of time.

"No way," Odalric said.

"Incredible," Tuka whispered.

"They're flying," Waldhar said, his eyes the widest I had ever seen.

"That can't be," I said to him. "They haven't got wings!"

"But they are!" Waldhar said, his voice full of excitement. "Look at them, Nicholas! I'm not sure how to explain this, but I'll do my best. You know how you can feel the air going by when you're going very fast?

Well, I've spent a lot of time watching birds and, basically, I think they can fly because when they flap their wings, it lets enough air *under* their wings to lift them to fly, like how a good strong wind can lift things into the air. If those reindeer down there were running as fast as I think they were, they got enough air under them to do the same thing!"

"I admit, I don't quite get it," I said. Waldhar had always been incredibly smart, and I couldn't always follow him. "But I know enough to know you usually know what you're talking about."

"Nicholas," Odalric said, "if we could get those reindeer and cross them into the *Hylgan Rikalt*, they would make the mission so much easier. No more platforms over the sea! We're moving very far away from human civilization. If you could take off and fly over the ocean, over entire countries, think of it!"

I looked down and watched as the eight reindeer below me came in for a landing, then took off running again and once more took off into the air. Odalric's words made a lot of sense.

"Let's go get Kylakki and Nyllo," I said. "They're the best with Flossie and Glossie; they know reindeer."

When we finally returned with Kylakki and Nyllo, the eight flyers were seemingly taking a break. We built a fire and settled atop the hill, preparing for an extended stakeout. But our anticipation was short-lived. Barely had we made ourselves comfortable when we witnessed a sight that filled us with awe. The reindeer, in all their unique glory, were off again. Kylakki and Nyllo, just as enthralled as we were, rushed into the valley, eager to interact with these extraordinary creatures.

Once we were down the hill and into the herd, we found that these reindeer, on top of being all white, differed from Flossie and Glossie in another way. These reindeer were tiny. Years later, when scientists began to study animals and publish what they knew about them, we learned that this type of reindeer, named Svalbard reindeer after the only place on Earth they live, is the smallest type of reindeer in the world.

The eight flyers were all female; their antlers still attached this deep into winter. Odalric, Waldhar, Tuka, and I watched Kylakki and Nyllo cross from the elfin realm to interact with the deer. Our friends, it seemed, could not move as fast as the deer because they stood frozen in place, staring up at the deer we could see slowly circling overhead.

"I guess we might as well head back to the ship and see what comes next," Waldhar said. "We could be here all day just watching them walk over to the deer once they land."

So we trekked back and waited. We made toys on board and turned the hourglass over four or five times until finally, from up on deck, someone shouted my name. I dropped the figurine I was carving and headed up to see what the fuss was about.

As I reached the deck, I saw Kylakki, Nyllo, and the eight flying reindeer walking up to the shore.

"We brought some new friends!" Nyllo called up.

"I can see that!" I responded. "Well done!"

"You've got to see it in real-time," Kylakki said. "It's amazing! Get the others and come ashore!"

Seeing Kylakki and Nyllo standing together, I was struck by how similar they looked. They could easily be mistaken for twins. They both had smooth, alabaster skin, crystal blue eyes, and short, white-blonde hair.

When everyone was lined up on solid ground, Kylakki and Nyllo let go of the ropes holding the deer, and each clapped their hands together sharply. The deer, startled, I suppose, took off running so fast they were almost a blur. We all oohed and aahed, barely able to keep our eyes on the rapidly moving animals. Then, before we could even register they were doing it, they took off into the air and were soaring out of sight, back toward the rest of their herd. The sight was so breathtaking it left us speechless.

"Ooops," Nyllo said, turning her head to look at Kylakki.

"We probably should have thought of that," Kylakki responded, rubbing her temple.

"Yeah," Nyllo agreed.

"We'll be back," Kylakki said. Then, they both turned and walked back toward the herd.

Once Kylakki and Nyllo returned with the eight flyers, they devised their training program, which began in earnest the next day. Once in a while, I would look off the ship's deck and see the two of them on small sleds being lifted off the ground behind one or more deer. They were so good with the animals, and I was impressed with how quickly things progressed.

During that time, I devoted extra care to my old friends Flossie and Glossie. They were more than just animals to me; they were companions who had served me faithfully. I made sure to remind them of this, stroking their noses gently (reindeer are sensitive creatures, their hollow hair making their bodies off-limits for touch) and treating them to extra slices of apple.

"Girls, it looks like you're going to have some new sisters and enjoy yourselves a very long, happy retirement," I told them.

Once the eight flyers had been in training for about a week, Nyllo called me over one day to watch their progress. I could feel the excitement in the air as we approached the training ground, eager to see how far they had come.

"Things are going really well," she informed me as Kylakki fed each deer a little slice of apple. "And we've given them all names, too!"

"Oh?" I replied.

"Yup!" She pointed to the right at three on the end. "Those three are the fastest of the bunch, so we've named them, from right to left: Dasher, Comet is the one in the middle with the big brown spot on her back, and Blitzen."

"Blitzen?" I asked. "What does that have to do with speed?"

"It means lightning," she replied.

"I see."

"Then over there is Dancer. She is a bit fidgety and looks like she's dancing. Then, next to her is Prancer. She walks like she's prancing about. Just behind her, with the big brown spot that is almost the same as Comet's, that's Cupid. She's super loving. Same with Vixen, who is standing there next to Cupid. And then finally, that one there, on the left, bellowing, we call her Donder, which means thunder, because she's always making some noise. Seems to like to hear herself talk!"

"Good names," I said with a smile. "I like them!"

"I know they probably look rather similar to you right now, but you'll be able to notice small differences in their appearance soon enough and be able to tell which is which. Especially their antlers. Every reindeer grows a set of unique antlers, and when they fall off, they'll grow back the same shape every year."

"How interesting!" I replied.

"We think we have even figured out a good configuration for them to be hitched up as a team. They'll be two-by-two in a line of four. Dasher and Dancer in front, Prancer and Vixen behind them, then Comet and Cupid, and Donder and Blitzen closest to the sleigh. That way, three of the four rows have one of the fastest deer. Wouldn't want them pushing or pulling too hard on the others if we put them all in the front or all in the back."

"Great work!" I said. "How much longer do you think you will need? We should probably head back out to sea in search of *Alfheim* before too long."

"Oh, maybe another two or three weeks," Kylakki said, joining us. I noticed she had not tied up the reindeer, a sure sign she knew they would not take off on us.

"That should be okay," I replied.

"They won't be fully trained by then, of course," she said, "but enough that it will be okay to bring them on the ship and not have them fly off on us."

"Excellent," I said, putting one hand on each of their shoulders. "You two are doing fantastic work. I appreciate it so much! This is going to make things much better going forward!"

And, of course, it did. As I write this, my eight flying friends have been part of my mission for six hundred twenty-two years,and I'm not sure how I ever could have kept doing this job without them.

Alfheim

We entrusted Kylakki and Nyllo with training the deer for three exhilarating weeks. As the days passed, the reindeer's mastery of commands grew, and I marveled at their ability to take off, circle the skies, and gracefully land.

"We can keep working on it off the decks of the ships," Nyllo said as she herded the deer up the plank when it was time to leave. "Jump them from ship to ship, off to icebergs, that kind of thing. They're getting great at this! Pretty soon, we can hitch them up to the sleigh and start getting them used to that."

"I'm looking forward to it!" I said. And I was. Kind of. The idea of actually taking off into the sky like a bird was thrilling and sort of scary at the same time. Even though Waldhar had explained his hypothesis on flight to me several times, I still wasn't quite sure how flight worked. I didn't know how I or the sleigh would even stay in the air if we actually got up there.

Leaving the comfort of the land behind, we embarked on a journey into the mysterious, uncharted north. The prospect of venturing into the unknown was daunting, yet it held a certain allure. We were treading where no one had ever set foot, and the uncertainty of what lay ahead was thrilling and intriguing.

Despite that, I enjoyed being out in the dark of the far north, gazing up from the ship's deck at the ocean of stars that hung above the sea of water we sailed upon. The vast expanse of darkness and twinkling lights made me feel tiny but in a good way. It made me feel like my fear didn't matter, which was comforting. Most people on Earth today have never seen that many stars because now the lights of the big cities pollute the skies and wash out the wonder of the universe above us. But some places are still dark enough to see it. I recommend you try to find such a place and go there if you can.

The northern lights would often swirl overhead and bathe the world in their vibrant greens, pinks, and blues. Their incredible beauty struck me every time. They were proof enough to me that we were headed in the right direction, to a special place where we could do our special work.

After several days of sailing, Adelgard approached me with a piece of news.

"There's getting to be too much ice to keep sailing," he reported.

"So, how do you think we should continue?" I asked, my voice tinged with uncertainty.

"Odalric has left the deck and is riding Flossie ahead, jumping across the ice. He thinks at some point, it must become one solid mass. He has gone to figure out how far until it does. If we can make it that far, we can leave the ships and travel further on foot."

"And if it's too far ahead?"

"Waldhar thinks we have enough material on board to make ice breakers we can attach to the front of the ships to sort of push the ice out of the way to make it if it's too far," he told me.

"Interesting," I replied.

"I guess for now, we can sail a little further ahead and then wait for Odalric to get back."

So that's what we did. I could hear the chunks of ice in the water grinding against the sides of the hull as we made our way through. When I went up on deck, I saw the sheer volume of ice floating on the surrounding water, which made it look *almost*, but not quite, like the water was already frozen solid.

Then, as I looked forward, I saw Flossie, Odalric perched on her back, bounding back to the ship. She took a final enormous leap and landed on deck. Odalric slung himself off her back and stood in front of me.

"Good news! It's only a few more miles north before it solidifies into a sheet of ice we can walk across."

"How many miles are 'a few'?" Waldhar asked. "I need to know if I need to get a team together to build icebreakers on the fronts of these ships. If we go too much further, we'll end up with holes in the hull."

"About five," Odalric said, "give or take."

Waldhar peered over the edge at our hull, then back at the other ship, scratched his chin a bit, then looked back at Odalric.

"How much worse does the ice get toward the edge of the ice sheet?"

"It's pretty much like this the whole way. If I had to guess, I'd say this part here was as solid as the ice sheet ahead just a few weeks ago, but it's getting on spring time so it probably cracked and drifted out this far."

Waldhar, his face etched with concern, stared at his shoes for a few more moments, then lifted his gaze and declared, "I believe five miles is a manageable distance. We've come this far. Let's hurry up and get there."

We reached the ice sheet with our ships unscathed. Stepping onto the ice, we loaded my sleigh with provisions and harnessed the team. Waldhar, ever resourceful, crafted sleds and hitched Flossie, Glossie, and Wulfgang to them, ready to tow more supplies. The thrill of our expedition was palpable as we prepared to venture further into this icy wilderness.

Contrary to my expectations, the snow was not as deep as I had imagined. I later discovered that in these northern regions, the air is exceptionally dry, resulting in minimal snowfall. Nevertheless, the snow was still deep enough to warrant the elves crafting snowshoes and skis to facilitate our movement in this unique landscape.

"Okay," Lisette chuckled as she tied on some snowshoes, "this time, I'll say it: we may have made a mistake coming all the way up here."

I burst out laughing, and so did she. I gave her a big hug and a kiss.

"You don't really think that, my love," I said, kissing the end of her nose.

She smiled at the northern lights swirling overhead and around us at our large family.

"No, not at all," she reassured, then playfully kissed the end of my nose. "Since the day I met you, our lives have been filled with joy and adventure. I have every faith that this journey will be no different. After all, I'm the one who encouraged you to take this leap."

We laughed again, struggled to our feet in our new snowshoes (I fell over once trying to stand, which led to more laughter), and turned to head even further north.

We trudged through the snow for several days, always following the North Star, which still lay just ahead of us but creeping ever further overhead.

Looking back on that time, we all have slightly different memories of how it went. Some say we only walked four or five days; some think a week or more. Time meant little up there in the dark, surrounded by nothing but snow and ice. If I'm honest, it was terrifying at times, not knowing where we were, every single direction looking the same. The uncertainty and fear were as real as the biting cold.

But, one day, however long into our journey it was, someone shouted, "Look!"

I had a hood pulled tight over my head and a scarf around my face. I had been looking down at my feet, watching where I was going so I didn't stumble and fall. I jerked my head up and saw one elf, though I couldn't tell who because we were all bundled up so tightly, pointing straight ahead.

Our entire company stopped in its tracks at the cry, and we all turned where the finger pointed. A murmur ran through the crowd at the sight before us, followed by gasps and excited whispers.

Ahead of me, maybe three miles, lay a sight I first took for some kind of mirage. The air was crisp and cold, biting at my cheeks as I squinted to get a better look. I quickly dismissed the idea of a mirage because everyone could see it. It was real, and it was unlike anything I had ever seen or, truthfully, had thought it would be possible to see.

The Northern Lights, which by now I was used to and thought I understood, were whirling into a vast circle in the sky. As we watched, a brilliant beam of green light shot from the sky to the ground, illuminating a vast swath of land in a cone of light.

"Amazing," Lisette breathed beside me.

"That must be it," I heard Erminlinda say somewhere behind me.

"Yes," I heard Tuka agree, "it must."

Agreement rippled through the crowd, and everyone spoke in tones of awe and reverence. I was in awe myself.

"Well," I said, "what are we waiting for? Let's get moving!" I could hear the excitement in my own voice, and I knew that the others felt the same. We were all eager to continue our journey, to see what other wonders lay ahead.

We pressed on, and the closer we got to the ethereal cone of Northern Lights that had descended from the sky, the quicker our pace became.

We crossed into the lights, and everyone began to chatter excitedly around me. I heard a chorus of "look, look," and fingers pointed to the sky.

I craned my neck upward, and beside me, Lisette did, too. I heard her gasp, and she clutched my hand. I grasped it back just as tightly. Directly above us, shining brighter than it had ever shown in all the time I had ever seen it, was the North Star, a beacon of hope and triumph that brought tears to our eyes.

"We're finally here," she said to me softly, her voice filled with a sense of belonging.

"So we are," I breathed back, almost too awestruck to speak.

"We made it!" I heard Tuka cry out. "*Alfheim*!"

"*Alfheim*!" everyone bellowed out in unison.

Then, before I even realized what was happening, dancing broke out. Everyone was hugging everyone else and swinging each other around. Almost everyone was weeping, including Lisette and me. Cheers rang out all around. Even the animals appeared to notice something special going on, and I saw them hop and kick happily.

"My friends!" I hollered out above the noise. "My loving family! Our journey is over! At last, we are home!"

#

The cone of light from the Northern Lights lit a vast space, and we used it all as our new home. So much work was done, and I won't bore you with all the details. We built houses and workshops like we had in Iceland, wood structures buried under mounds of snow for more insulation. We had to make a lot of trips back to places with trees to get enough wood.

When all was said and done, we had a proper city. We built homes for everyone, a dozen work buildings, a barn, and a half-dozen things Waldhar crafted he called greenhouses. Each structure was meticulously designed and constructed, with every detail carefully considered to ensure our survival in this new, icy land.

"You see," he said, showing Lisette and me around one, "there isn't any dirt here, just ice and snow. But we will still need to grow food. So, we hauled in dirt and built these gardens here in these long huts with glass roofs. In the spring and summer, when the sun is out, it will shine in and let plants grow. Along with a few logs on the fire for a little extra warmth, of course."

"Waldhar, I *love* it!" Lisette cried, giving him a big hug. "I love plants! Oh, I can't wait to get to work in here! We can have all kinds of good things!"

"This will certainly save us a lot of long trips for supplies," I said, patting Waldhar on the shoulder. "What a fantastic creation, my friend. Thank you!"

When the city was completed, the lights retreated to the sky, almost like they knew they had done their job. I can't explain it. It is just a thing that happened. That's magic.

Since then, we've added many more greenhouses and a couple dozen more workshop buildings. Some more homes, too. Because, as I discovered later in my journeys around the world, elves lived in other places, too, and many wanted to help. But that came later. After I learned to fly.

First Flight

Even working at our incredible speed, building our new home took up a considerable chunk of the year 1410 and left us very little time to prepare for Christmas.

One day in September of that year, I was busy carving a doll's face, trying to get the mouth just right, when a knock came at my door. I had built a little private workshop for days I felt like some quiet work time. I found that sometimes I did my best when I was alone with my thoughts, focusing on the work, perhaps humming a little tune. The room was rather plain, with a simple workbench, every wall lined with shelves to hold tools or completed toys. The toys, all brightly colored and cheerful, were all the decorations I needed. When I looked up from my work, I saw Waldhar, our chief engineer and my old friend, standing in the doorway.

"Just need to take a couple of quick measurements," he said.

"Of what?" I asked.

"Of you! I'm building a new sleigh that will take off and stay up better. The team is having a bit of trouble with the old one. It's shaped a little wrong. No big deal. But before I build the new one, I need to measure you and make sure I get everything just right."

"I feel like we've done this before," I said, setting the doll's head down.

"We did. But that was so long ago. It doesn't hurt to double-check!"

"Oh, I suppose," I reluctantly agreed, my voice tinged with hesitation, and got up to follow him.

He took several measurements of me and finally said, "Alright, come on, I have to weigh you!"

"Weigh me?" I asked.

"Yes. I need to ensure the deer can pull the sleigh and you, get you into the air, and stay there. That means I need to know what you weigh so I can make sure the sleigh I build is light enough. I wouldn't want you up there only to come crashing down!"

"Oh!" I said, horrified at the thought. "Oh, no! No, no, that would not be good at all!" Suddenly, I was terrified of the idea of flying.

"Well, then," Waldhar said, turning to leave, "come on! I can make sure that doesn't happen!"

I rushed to follow him. He had a massive set of scales and instructed me to sit on one side. I did so, and he loaded stones onto the other side until the scales balanced out. He jotted down a number and told me I could hop up.

"There, I think that's all I need," he said. "You can go."

He said that last bit a little brusquely, but I knew my old friend wasn't being rude or dismissive. He was already so deep in thought and calculation that he probably barely realized he had said anything.

I headed back to my workbench, my trust in Waldhar unwavering. Despite my fear, I knew that if anyone could make this flight safe, it was him. Yet, the thought of testing this idea of flight still filled me with dread.

In the early days of October, as I was engrossed in my solitary task of crafting toys, a gentle knock interrupted my concentration. I rose from my workbench, crossed the room, and swung open the door to find Waldhar, Kylakki, and Nyllo standing there.

"It's time!" Kylakki said a huge grin on her face.

"The deer are ready to go!" Nyllo chimed in.

"And the sleigh is perfect," Waldhar added.

"That's wonderful," I said. "Thank you all. Now, if you'll excuse me, I have a lot of these tops to get to."

"Aren't you going to come out and give it a go?" Nyllo asked.

"Yeah, Nicholas, we can get the deer hitched right up!" Kylakki said.

"Oh, well, I, you see, I'm very busy," I gestured back at my workbench.

Waldhar hooked his arm around mine and dragged me out the door.

"Come on, Nicholas!" he said cheerily. "No time like the present!"

Grudgingly, I allowed myself to be led through the series of winding corridors to the barn (we had attached every building with hallways since it was usually too cold to go outside), where the new sleigh and the reindeer waited. Once there, I saw the new sleigh for the first time. It was a bit longer and narrower than the first one, but basically the same shape. It was also the same gorgeous green with golden accents.

"I kept the color scheme the same," Waldhar said when he saw me looking at it. "I just think it's an exquisite, elegant look."

"I agree," I said. But it looks mostly the same, aside from being a little longer and narrower."

"That allows it to cut through the air better," he replied excitedly. "You remember how I explained flight to you?"

"I remember you explaining it, yes. I also remember not entirely understanding it. But I trust you know what you've made here."

As we had this exchange, Kylakki and Nyllo were hitching the deer to the sleigh. They used the same order they had told me they would: Dasher and Dancer in front, followed by Prancer and Vixen, then Comet and Cupid, and finally Donder and Blitzen, closest to the sleigh. As they told me I would, I had learned to tell the difference between them all and now knew which was which.

Also, when I wasn't looking, we had been joined in the barn by Lisette, Adelgard, Odalric, Tuka, Erminlinda, Lars, and Snælaug, and a crowd was forming outside the large doors to the outdoors, which were wide open.

"Climb on in," Waldhar said, gesturing toward the sleigh. I eyed it nervously, then did so. Waldhar came to the side of the sleigh and secured a belt attached to the seat around my waist.

"What on Earth is this?" I asked him.

"Safety belt," he said, not meeting my eyes, "just in case."

"Just in case, what?" I asked with alarm.

"You know...just in case," he said, backing away.

"Oh no!" I cried, forgetting the belt and trying to stand up. Unable to, I started wrestling with the belt. "We're going to have to come up with something else!"

"Nicholas," Lisette said, coming to the sleigh and putting her hands on my arm, "it's going to be okay. How long have you known Waldhar? Think about it. He knows what he's doing."

I took a deep breath, my hands trembling. "I've seen them take off," I whispered to Lisette, my voice barely audible. "They go so high. I thought I was thrilled at the idea, but now I'm just scared."

"I understand," she said gently, "but you have to trust your friends. They put a lot of work into making sure this will go off without a hitch."

"Okay," I said, first under my breath, then louder, "Okay! Show me how to do this!"

Kylakki and Nyllo came over. Nyllo picked up the reins and put them in my hand.

"Give these a good shake up and down so they slap against the front of the sleigh there. Then yell out, 'Now Dasher, now Dancer, now Prancer and Vixen! On Comet, on Cupid, on Donder and Blitzen!'" Kylakki said quietly. "That is how they know to go."

"Once you're up there, it should be simple. Don't move the reins at all to go straight. Pull the left one to go left and the right one to go right. Slap them once against the sleigh to go up and twice to go down. Got it?" Nyllo asked.

"I sure hope so," I said.

"Here," Kylakki said and put a piece of parchment in my hand, "we wrote it down."

"Actually," Nyllo said, taking the parchment, "let's do this with it. Do you have any nails, Waldhar? A hammer?"

He reached into his apron, pulled out a few nails, and then pulled a hammer from a loop on his belt. Nyllo took them and nailed the little piece of parchment to the inside of the front of the sleigh, where I could see them.

"That's very helpful," I said. "Thank you."

"Well, then," Kylakki said, stepping back. Nyllo joined her. Lisette stayed by the sleigh.

"Good luck," she said. She kissed my cheek, then stepped back as well.

As instructed, I took another deep breath and slapped the reins against the front of the sleigh. The deer stood straight at attention, their muscles tensed.

"Now, Dasher!" I yelled. "Now Dancer! Now Prancer and Vixen!" The sleigh lurched, and the deer began moving forward before I even finished. We were out of the barn, faces passing quickly by all around me as the elves watched. I kept going. "On Comet! On Cupid! On Donder and Blitzen!"

The faces became blurs, and I felt the air rushing into my face so fast I could barely keep my eyes open. They watered so severely from the wind that tears streamed down my face and froze into my mustache and beard.

With a terrific lurch and a massive gust of air, I saw the lead two deer, then the next, and so on, rise into the air until finally, I looked, and I was in the air as well! We were still climbing, and the cheers below me grew faint as my friends grew tiny.

My stomach jumped into my throat, and, for an instant, I was frozen with terror, sure we would fall. I felt like I might be sick. But we stayed up there, the sleigh speeding straight ahead. I looked down and saw the snow below me, and then to the sides, I saw clouds racing by.

Then the thrill hit me—hard. I was flying! Soaring above the ground! The sinking, sick feeling I had moments before was replaced by a light, giddy feeling in my chest that bubbled up and could not be contained. I laughed—strong belly laughs of sheer delight—the type of laugh you probably associate with me all the time. Ho ho ho!

"Alright, girls," I called out to the sleigh team, "let's see what you can do! Hiya!"

I slapped the reins down once on the sleigh front, and the deer lifted their heads and pumped their legs. The team arced up! We climbed higher and higher, my laughing and whooping and the rush of the air the soundtrack to our flight. I slapped the reins twice against the sleigh, and the deer went into a smooth dive. The angle of descent made my stomach lurch up into my throat, and I was momentarily terrified again, but I pulled back on the reins, and we evened out. I pulled hard right, and we banked that way. Then I pulled the left rein, and the deer responded in kind.

"Good girls!" I cried. "Wonderful girls!"

I looked down and realized we were flying over the open ocean. We had flown so many miles in just seconds! It was incredible! This was going to change my entire mission!

I circled the team around and headed back to the village. At first, I wasn't sure how I would find it with the entire thing covered in a layer of snow and ice that matched the surrounding landscape. But, even though they had retreated into the sky and behaved like normal since we had finished the village, I once again saw the Northern Lights swirling and shining down onto the spot where we lived. I guided my team in, and the landing was bumpy. However, other than that, everything went exceedingly well!

All around me, the elves were cheering. Despite the frigid air, the entire village was out to greet me. I had barely gotten out of the sleigh when Lisette ran up, threw her arms around me, and kissed me. As soon as she let go, elves were all around, slapping me on the back, shaking my hands, and giving me hugs.

"Incredible!" Kylakki said above the noise.

"They were stupendous!" Nyllo added.

"And you weren't so bad as a pilot, old friend," Adelgard said.

"That was the most amazing thing that has ever happened in my life!" I cried. You won't believe how fast we made it to the ocean! We could have been to Europe in no time at all! I could go anywhere! I could go to places I've never been!"

"Oh, we are going to need so many more maps," Waldhar and Odalric said in almost perfect unison. They looked at each other and smiled.

I wasn't worried. I wasn't limited anymore, thanks to this new miracle of flight.

"Discovering" The Americas

So, over the next few decades, I flew. I mapped. I "discovered" new places (there were, of course, already people living in all those places. They were only new to me, Lisette, and the elves. Later, other people would claim to discover lands like they didn't arrive to huge, fascinating civilizations of people already there. However, that's something to learn about in history class, not here.). I tried to discover if Christmas was being celebrated wherever I went.

In those days, it certainly wasn't being celebrated in Southeast Asia. Oh, a few Christians had traveled to places like China and Japan to live and spread the word of their religion, and I visited them at Christmas, but they were outliers. The same with people celebrating Christmas on the African continent, which many Europeans sadly still thought of as a wild, savage place. I would, unfortunately, have many more years dealing with trying to bring some manner of comfort to mistreated Africans.

One thing I can say I discovered long before Europeans was the existence of the entire western hemisphere: the places that would later become North, Central, and South America. Of course, like I said, I didn't *actually* discover these places existed. The millions of people already living there knew about them thousands of years before I did. But no one in Europe yet knew they were there.

Because of this, when I visited these people, I found their cultures significantly different from any I had encountered before and was enamored with learning about them and their traditions. Since no Europeans knew about this place, I knew that there would not be Christmas here, but I was curious if there was another holiday I could visit on.

To my disappointment, as much as I loved these people and their cultures, there were a great many tribes across North, Central, and South America, and not only were they different from European cultures, but they differed from each other. I did not find any holiday shared by these people, or even in one tribe, that put importance on gift giving the way Christmas did, so I found no way I could naturally bring toys to their children. But, though I was disappointed, I was not sad. I didn't want to impose my way of thinking and doing on them.

One thing I found in the new lands I explored was tribes of elves. I was in the region that is now Massachusetts when I met up with the first group. They were pretty shocked to see me. And not happy, either.

They didn't call themselves elves. They went by the name that the Wampanoag, the native people of that land, called them: *Pukwudgie*. It was summer, and they wore light deer-skin pants and shirts. I was surprised when they sprang out of the woods at me and surrounded me, brandishing sticks. I had never met an aggressive elf before!

"Whoa!" I yelled, holding up my hands. "I'm friendly! I'm friendly!" I spoke to them in Elvish, and they scrunched their faces in confusion.

"No human is friendly to *Pukwudgie*!" One of them said, poking me in the leg and causing me to jump. Their Elvish sounded different but also similar to the Elvish I knew, like how Spanish and Italian sound similar and even share some words because they evolved from the same language, so I understood them well enough if not perfectly.

"How are you here, human?" barked another.

"Because I live among your kind in a different land," I replied.

"Among *Pukwudgie*?" asked the one who had poked me with a stick.

"Well, they don't call themselves that. They call themselves elves and *Huldufólk*, but, yes, they are like you. Hidden people."

They all exchanged looks and murmurs, and I waited to see what would happen. Finally, the one who had asked me how I was there spoke.

"What's your name, human?"

"I'm Nicholas."

"You know quite a bit, Nicholas," he replied. "Legend says our people came here to this land long ago when they left other tribes in a different land."

"Well, I know them," I replied.

"So it seems."

"You haven't told me your name, stranger," I replied.

"Tatasan," he said back.

"Pleasure to meet you."

"He's quite a kind human," said the one who poked me with a stick.

"Indeed," said Tatasan.

"And you are?" I asked the one who poked me.

"Winnupukutt."

"Pleasure," I said.

The group whispered to each other again, and then Tatasan said, "Follow us."

They turned and filed back into the brush from which they had come, and I followed. I was still confused but not afraid. Clearly, I was among elves who had a different culture and were not averse to physically attacking someone, but they didn't seem like bad people, just startled by my appearance among them.

Eventually, we reached a small encampment. The homes were made of wood and were circular, with domed roofs. I later learned they were made this way because it made them much easier to heat in the winter and keep cool in the summer.

Several others of the Pukwudgie gathered around doing chores, and they all turned to stare as a human was led into their camp,, I suppose, like a prisoner since a group carrying sharp sticks and clubs still surrounded me.

"Sit there by the fire," Winnupukutt said, gesturing with his stick.

I lowered myself to the ground and waited as a crowd gathered around me.

"Alright," Tatasan said, "tell us how you got here."

So I did. I told the whole tale of my life. Eventually, the *Pukwudgie* relaxed and became very interested in my story. When I finished my tale, there was a long silence before Winnupukutt spoke.

"Our people in other lands don't fight with humans?"

"No," I said, "they don't fight with anyone."

"And humans leave them alone?"

"Yes."

"Long ago," Tatasan said, "the *Pukwudgie* are supposed to have gotten along with the Wampanoag the way you say elves do. But something happened—a great divide. No one knows what it was. That is lost. But now, *Pukwudgie* and Wampanoag are enemies. We fear them, and they fear us."

"It doesn't have to be that way," I said. "You just said you don't even know why you are enemies! Don't you think that's silly?"

There were more murmurs in the crowd, and one woman said, "I do." The agreement went around the group.

"See?" I said, turning my head in a slight arc so I could look at them all as I spoke. "You all agree! There is no reason for you to keep up a feud so old that no one knows why it exists!"

"But how will we speak to the Wampanoag about it?" someone asked.

"Oh, I'm sure you could approach them in peace easily enough," I replied. "I've been to so many places in the world that I have learned something significant: humans are prone to get into fights and wars, yes, but they mostly do it because they are scared and think they have to. Very few people fight because they want to. Most humans don't want to fight. They want to live peacefully, just like you do."

There was another brief silence, and then Tatasan spoke.

"Thank you, Nicholas."

"For what?"

"For the gift of your kindness. And for your wisdom. We will consider what you have said."

"Oh, goodness, you don't have to thank me. I just helped you see what you already knew. I think you would have gotten there on your own."

"What if the Wampanoag don't want to listen?" someone asked.

"I'm sure they will," I replied. "Like I said, you just have to approach them in peace and friendship. Try doing what the *Huldufólk* were doing for humans when I met them. Take care of some of their chores for them in the night. Let them know you mean well. Helping them will show them you care."

"Truthfully, Nicholas, we are scared," Winnupukutt said.

"I'm sure you are. That's natural."

"We will discuss the matter," Tatasan said again.

"I know you will," I said, getting to my feet. "It really has been good to meet you all, but I must be going now. I have to get back home and back to work."

"Will we see you again?" Winnupukutt asked.

"Of course! I'll gladly come back any time!"

I visited the *Pukwudgie* many times after that. They took my advice about helping the Wampanoag people and eventually mended the relationship between the two groups.

Not long after they mended their relationship with the Wampanoag, Winnupukutt and Tatasan approached me on one of my visits to them. I had learned they were the most talkative of the bunch when it came to humans. The others spoke to me some but had not quite grown out of their shyness about humans.

"We wish to join you in *Alfheim*," Tatasan said.

"We want to help more humans," Winnupukutt added.

"You are certainly welcome to," I said, "but you understand our mission revolves around the Christmas holiday now and that the people here do not celebrate it?"

"We do," Tatasan confirmed.

"But we will still keep our relationship with these people," Winnupukutt said.

"In that case, welcome to the family!" I said and gave them each a hug.

And so the *Pukwudgie* came to join us in our mission. For many years after, they maintained a dual residence in our workshop home in the north and their native land. They would help us with toy making during the warmer months and then help the Wampanoag people through the harsh winter months. As history moved on, America, as you know, was colonized, and the Wampanoag territory became Massachusetts. With so many Europeans moving into the land and war breaking out between them and the Wampanoag at one point, the *Pukwudgie* moved permanently to the North Pole. They still visit their native land and the Wampanoag people, who are still there, occasionally. They have never let go of the friendship they worked so hard to rebuild all those years ago.

The Many Names of Nicholas

By the mid-1400s, my legend had spread far and wide. People across Europe were waking up on Christmas morning to find that gifts had been left for children at night.

After a while, and I am not sure how, my identity as St. Nicholas also became associated with Christmas gifts as well the gifts left on St. Nicholas Day. So, while some children got my gifts on December 6th and were happy St. Nicholas had visited them, others woke up on December 25th overjoyed to find that St. Nicholas had been there.

As you know, Christopher Columbus set sail from Spain in 1492 and eventually landed in the land that would come to be known as America. Once I learned that, I knew it was only a matter of time before Europeans moved there and that Christmas would accompany them.

However, beginning in the early-to-mid 1500s, Christmas was well on its way to getting more complicated. All across Europe, Christianity itself became more complex as more and more people became unhappy with the Catholic Church. People interpreted their religion differently and thought they would be better served by worshipping and living their lives in ways other than those prescribed by Catholicism. As such, they broke away in protest, earning any Christian doing so the title of Protestant. Eventually, there would be numerous branches of Protestantism, including the Puritans, who would play a significant role in Christmas history in England and America and my part in both places.

This period later became known as The Reformation. It began slowly in 1517 when a German priest named Martin Luther nailed a document to the door of a Catholic Church outlining how he felt people should worship. By 1529, Luther had formed a new branch of Christianity named after himself, Lutheranism. In this religion, people were not supposed to pray to saints or to believe that saints gave special favors to people. So, St. Nicholas was not to be welcomed into homes on St. Nicholas Day or Christmas. But, as just plain old Nicholas, I was not about to stop giving gifts, so I just kept making my Christmas Eve deliveries as usual.

A similar thing happened in England. In 1534, after the Pope refused a divorce from his wife, King Henry VIII left Catholicism and formed his own church, which he called the Church of England. This became the official religion of England for the rest of Henry's life. However, he mostly ran it like the Catholic Church, so St. Nicholas was still welcome. St. Nicholas continued to be welcome after Henry died in 1547, and his daughter, Mary, became queen and converted the country back to Catholicism.

However, when Mary died in 1558, her sister, Elizabeth, became queen. Elizabeth was a Protestant and declared that the entire country should convert again. Unlike when Henry VIII was in charge, Catholic saints were no longer welcome in England. But, just like in Germany, I kept visiting anyway.

This happened all across Europe as different places adopted different branches of Protestantism. Protestants believed in a more personal relationship with God and didn't want go-betweens like the Pope and Saints granting people special favors.

So, when their children kept getting Christmas gifts even though they were no longer Catholic and no longer prayed to saints, confusion arose over *who* was bringing these gifts if it wasn't St. Nicholas.

One of the more popular names that caught on after people saw me at my work was "Father Christmas." That was the name by which I was known in England. In France, I became *Père Noël*. In Italy, I became *Babbo Natale*. In Spain, they called me *Papá Noel*. In Scotland, to those who spoke Scottish Gaelic, I was *Bodach na Nollaig*, a variation of Father Christmas that means Christmas Old Man. In Germany, the Protestant people knew me as *Weihnachtsmann*. In my home country of Turkey, they called me *Noel Baba*.

Things got even more interesting in the areas that were still Catholic. In some of those places, children still expected me as St. Nicholas on December 6th and as a different gift bringer on Christmas. In many of these places, they believed Baby Jesus was bringing Christmas presents. So, in the Catholic parts of France, I was *Le Petit Jésus*. In the region that eventually became Hungary, they called me *Jézuska* or *Kis Jézus*, and in Italy, I became *Gesù Bambino*.

One of these names for Baby Jesus may seem familiar to you, and it came out of Germany, where much of this confusion had begun in earnest: *Christkind*. This name leaked into portions of France occupied by many German-speaking people and became *Le Christkindel*. This name may seem familiar because when Europeans began colonizing the Americas in large numbers, German-speaking people started living alongside English-speaking people. When the German-speaking children tried to tell the English-speaking people about the Christmas gifts they were going to receive from *Christkindel*, the English-speaking children would walk away not having entirely understood and believing they might get Christmas presents from "Kris Kringle," a nickname by which I am still known in America today.

Of course, I never cared what anyone called me. I was just happy to be giving gifts and spreading joy. If this meant having dozens of different names, that was perfectly fine by me! I got more wonderful names as Christmas spread worldwide to people speaking other languages. As Christmas traditions and beliefs changed, I also got more names.

The elves also loved that I collected so many names, and many of them grew fond of one particular name or another. I began getting called lots of things around the village.

Adelgard loved to call me *Père Noël*, and Erminlinda became partial to *Joulupukki*, the name they called me in our former home of Finland, which translates to "Yule Goat." Nyllo and Kylakki became attached to the name I was known by in Sweden, *Jultomten*, which means "Yule Gnome." Waldhar just called me *Baba* when he apparently found *Noel Baba* to be one word too many.

Lisette, however, continued to call me by my given name, Nicholas. However, as time passed, she shortened it to just Nick, and sometimes, when she was feeling playful, Nicky. Later on, another name would arise that she, and most of the elves, would call me, but we aren't at that part of the story yet.

Troublesome Chimneys and Stuffed Stockings

As I laid out in the last chapter, Christmas became more complicated in the 16th century, that is, between 1501 and 1600. This resulted from the changing religions and customs of the people I visited and the world's other changes.

No one locked their doors at night when I started my gift-giving mission. Sure, some would bar their doors, but no fancy locks existed. If a door was barred, I could simply enter a home through a window left open to let the smoke from the fire out of the house.

But, by the mid-1500s, doors began to have mechanical locks that required keys. They weren't widespread, but I had been around long enough to know this new technology would spread. Even at the homes that did not have these locks, I found more and more barred entries against nighttime intruders.

Of course, if I could have entered through the windows, this wouldn't have been a problem. But in these years, yet another technology was becoming increasingly widespread: chimneys.

Chimneys had been around for quite a long time. I had seen them even in the times of the Roman Empire, but they were not used in homes. They were typically found on things like bakeries. During the 12th and 13th centuries, I had seen them on castles. But now, in the 16th century, everyday people were putting them on their homes. It made sense to me, of course. The old way of opening a high window to let the smoke out was less than perfect. Many times, for example, a breeze would blow into the window, preventing smoke from leaving, and your home would fill with smoke, especially if you did not have a second window on the wall opposite the one the breeze was blowing in. Or, perhaps you had windows on two different walls, but no breeze would blow at all, and the smoke would rise and not be blown out the window, in which case your house would *still* be filled with smoke! A chimney allowed people to build a lovely fireplace with a smoke hood above it to catch the smoke and let it rise up and out of the house.

What this left me with, however, was a problem. Houses with barred doors and no open windows left me with no access to enter and leave my gifts! In the year 1560, I will never forget I returned home with gifts left undelivered because I could not enter so many homes!

I was devastated for days afterward. It broke my heart knowing that, on Christmas morning, children had awoken and rushed from their rooms to find that no presents had been delivered! This led to perhaps the worst part of my legend that persists today: the idea that I only give presents to *good* children! Oh, I can't tell you how upset that made me then and still makes me now! I knew that, since the early days of the St. Nicholas legend, I supposedly had kept track of which children were naughty and which were nice, an idea rooted in Catholic ideas of judgment. But all children had still received Christmas gifts, and the idea was primarily Catholic, anyway. When one Christmas morning came when some children did not get presents, frustrated parents were given a chance to say, "See? Because you behaved poorly, St. Nicholas (or whichever name the family called me by) did not bring you toys! You must do better next year!" This was never my intention. I believe that all children, regardless of their behavior, deserve love and kindness, and that's why I continue to deliver gifts to this day.

So, let me be clear on the subject before I continue my tale: all children are good children. Of course, they still misbehave occasionally, but this does not make them bad or undeserving of one of my gifts! Children's minds are not fully developed, so they sometimes act up! They will forget the rules. They will yell or break things or even sometimes strike another person. Even I, as a young boy, misbehaved from time to time. It's perfectly natural. What matters most is that their parent or another trusted adult does not teach them they are wrong. Children who are taught they are bad will often grow up to be bad adults. Not always, but often. Unlike children, there *are* bad adults, and bad adults add nothing meaningful to the world. Indeed, bad adults take joy from the world and try to harm others.

As long as a child is doing their best and learning and growing, they are a good child. Please let them know that. Yes, remind them there are rules when they act up and dole out some consequence for their behavior, but don't teach them I'm out there watching and judging and putting them on a list of naughty children who won't get a present. Show them that, as their parent or guardian, you love them despite their mistakes and want them to be their best selves, just like I do. In the long run, being kind, caring, loving, and generous to children creates more kind, caring, loving, and generous adults than does being hard and punishing to them.

Okay, now that I have addressed that, let's return to the matter of chimneys and undelivered gifts.

I was heartbroken. I sat in my den for days, not talking to anyone or making toys. I just tried to figure out how to get into every home with a child so I could leave a gift.

Finally, Lisette, who had only seen me for several days at bedtime and was then kept up by my tossing and turning, came into my den one day and sat in a chair across from me.

"Okay," she said, "time to stop sulking in here and get up and go ask your friends for help!"

"My dear, you know I am perfectly fine with asking for help when I need it," I replied.

"Normally, that's true, but you have taken this setback much harder than any of us expected, and outside that door, your friends and I are worried about you! Half the village is coming up with solutions! Meanwhile, you've been cooped up in here, only opening the door for meals to come and then leaving to come to bed!" Lisette's words struck a chord with me. She was right. I couldn't let this setback defeat me. I had a mission to fulfill, and I needed to find a way to overcome these new challenges.

I leaned across and put a hand on her knee. "As usual, my love, you are correct. I'm devastated, yes, but I can't keep sitting here wallowing in my sadness. I'm not coming up with any good solutions, anyway. The best I have come up with is to learn how to open locks without a key." I gestured at my private workbench, where lock materials were strewn across the surface.

"And have you?" she asked.

"Yes, but it's a slow process. Too slow. Oh, I've gotten the time it takes way down from when I started, but still, I would never make it into all the homes I need to."

"Well, come on out, have a meal in the dining hall, talk with your friends. I'm sure they have a better answer."

I stood from my chair, and so did Lisette. She took my hand, and we walked out of my den. I rejoined the rest of the village.

I talked to several elves who had excellent ideas, but when I spoke to Waldhar, who always had plenty of new and interesting ideas, he told me he hadn't even considered it yet.

"What?" I asked, completely surprised. "You don't have an idea?"

"I don't have all the information yet," he responded.

"Oh?"

"I haven't been out yet to look at the average home. In case you forgot, we've lived here one-hundred-fifty years. That's quite a while since I have not seen a human house. From what I gather, they've changed. Therefore, I can't determine the best way to enter one until I see one!"

"That makes sense," I mused, stroking my beard. "Care to take a little trip with me, my friend?"

A wide grin spread across his face. "*Baba*, nothing would please me more."

We struck out that evening for a small town in Germany that was one of the places where I had been barred entry from many homes. The reindeer were not used to going out so soon after Christmas. Usually, they rested and recovered from our long journey for at least a month afterward, so we had chosen to leave Dasher, Comet, and Blitzen behind since, as the three fastest, they used the most energy on our journey and did not recover as fast as the others.

We landed in Germany in the dark of night, right in the middle of the street, with no fear of being seen. Waldhar left the sleigh and stood in the street, turning in a slow circle and taking in the surrounding homes. He made little sounds to himself as he did this and talked to himself a bit.

"Hmmm...uh huh...interesting..." he said as he stopped turning and approached one house off to my left. I watched as he took the door handle in his hand and pulled. He nodded, then walked around the house, looking it up and down.

After he had completed three circles of the house, he craned his neck back and looked up at the roof, nodded to himself, walked back over to the sleigh, climbed in, and said, "Have the reindeer hop us up to the roof."

"The roof? It's a little steep for them!" I replied.

"After we're up there, they can hop back down or circle in the air," he said. Let's go."

I signaled the deer, and they leaped up and landed gently on the roof. We hopped out before they slid off again, and they jumped back down to the street.

"I don't feel particularly safe up here," I said to Waldhar as I wobbled to keep my balance on the roof's steep pitch.

"Have a quick seat," he said as he gently approached the chimney. "This won't take long."

So, I sat down in the cold snow atop the roof, and Waldhar had a look at the chimney. Again, he made his little sounds, then scurried to the top and peered into the opening on the top of the chimney.

"Yes," he said softly to himself, "yes, this will do nicely." And with that, he hopped into the chimney and was gone.

I got to my feet as quickly as I could and went to the chimney. It was slightly taller than I was, so I couldn't look down it, but I heard his voice come up the chimney in a cry of glee.

"*Baba*! This is the answer!"

"What?" I hollered back. I was about to say more when Waldhar's head popped out of the chimney, followed by the rest of him as he pulled himself out, swung his legs over the edge, and dropped back onto the roof.

"I said this is the answer! This is how you get into the homes! Through the chimneys!"

"Be serious!" I replied, thinking he must be joking.

"I *am* serious," he said.

"Waldhar, that chimney is barely big enough for *you* to fit down, and I don't know if you noticed, but I'm quite a bit larger than you.

"You'll fit," he said, a twinkle in his eye. He got down on his hands and knees, peered over the roof's edge, and made a clicking sound to call the reindeer up to us. They leaped to the roof again, landed for a few seconds as we climbed in, then jumped back to the street.

"Listen, *Baba*," he said, turning to me, "this will work. Here's what we're going to do: we're going to have the reindeer take off, fly up to that chimney, and we are going to swing ourselves out of the sleigh and drop down it."

"Waldhar!" I cried, exasperated. "I'm *not* going to fit!"

"If you were attempting it in the human realm, no, you would not. But this is the elf realm. Just because you have lived here for almost twelve hundred years doesn't mean you know all about this place," he said with a smirk.

I stared at him, completely gobsmacked for a moment or two, trying to think of how to respond. Finally, I said, "You've all been keeping things from me?"

"Not exactly," he replied a little guiltily. "It just never came up. But, Nicholas, think about it for a minute. The *Hylgan Rikalt* has powers. We move faster than humans can perceive. We barely age. At *Alfheim*, the aurora borealis literally guides us home. And, if need be, we can squeeze in places that are quite small. Please don't ask me how. I don't know. It just happens."

I took a deep breath, then placed my hand on my friend's shoulder. "I trust you. Let's do this." He smiled at me, then took up the reins himself and gave them a sharp crack.

We flew up beside the chimney in a way that allowed me to swing my legs around and place my feet right in the opening. For a brief second, I was again positive I wouldn't get much more than my lower legs in there, but I reminded myself that I trusted my friend and took him at his word, and without another thought, I pushed out of the sleigh and into the chimney.

There was a very brief feeling of tight compression, but not in an uncomfortable way. I felt almost like I had been wrapped tightly in a heavy blanket. There was a flash of darkness, and then I stood on the fireplace floor. I looked down and saw that I was standing in a pile of glowing embers, which should have been hot enough to burn through my boots, but I could not feel a thing. I dropped quickly to my knees, crawled out of the fireplace, then stood and looked around me.

"Amazing," I said to myself, completely in awe. It had worked! I was actually inside the home! This was going to change everything!

I heard a noise from the fireplace and turned around to see Waldhar exiting it. I rushed to him and lifted him from his feet in a big hug. He laughed, and when I set him back on his feet, he looked up at me and said, "Told you!"

"Yes, you did. I'm sorry I ever doubted you."

"Eh," he said, shrugging, "if I were a human like you, I wouldn't have believed me, either. Some things they just don't teach to non-elves." He winked mischievously at me, and I laughed.

"Okay, so we're in here," I said. "But how do we get back out? I'm not much of a climber."

"I know how I did it, but how to explain it…?" He stroked his beard and thought about that. "The best way I can tell you is that once you're in the fireplace, turn sideways so your back is against a chimney wall and push off with your feet. Once you're in the chimney proper, place your feet on the other wall and do a kind of scoot motion. You'll be up before you know it."

"That sounds a lot like climbing," I said glumly.

"I know it does, but you have to trust me again. Just remember, once you're at the top, grab the lip of the chimney, or you'll fall back down again."

So, once again trusting he knew what he was talking about, I crawled into the fireplace, stood, turned my back to one wall, and pushed off with my feet. For just a moment, I was lighter than air, floating just above the ground, then I pressed my feet against the opposite wall and scooted with my feet. The tight feeling was there again, but also a feeling that I was very light and rising like a wisp of smoke. The brief flash of darkness of being inside the chimney was there again, and then my head was poking out the top. I quickly grabbed hold with both hands and pulled myself out. I dropped to the roof, slipped in the snow, and almost slid off the edge, but managed to wrap my arm around the chimney and save myself.

A moment later, Waldhar exited the chimney and got down beside me. He looked at me and how tightly I was clutching the chimney.

"You alright?" he asked.

"I almost fell off," I said, my heart still pounding.

"Hmm…we're going to have to train the reindeer to circle while you're down there and be ready to swoop in with the sleigh when you come up," he replied.

"That would be good," I said. Then I called for the reindeer, and they flew back up from the street. We climbed into the sleigh and took off for home.

Thanks to Waldhar and the discovery that I could enter and exit homes through the chimney, Christmas 1561 went perfectly. I had spent a long time practicing going up and down a chimney with a large sack full of toys in one hand, and Kylakki and Nyllo had trained the reindeer to drop me off and pick me up. We were all pros by the time we left that Christmas Eve. On top of that, it was the year another Christmas tradition began.

Early in my journey that Christmas Eve, I went into a home in Norway via the chimney and, as I exited the fireplace, found I had to push past socks hanging from the mantle. I stood, turned back, and looked at the socks. They were good, heavy winter stockings that were quite tall to keep the legs warm. Either it had been wash day in this family, or they had been out in the snow, and their stockings had gotten wet. Either way, here they hung from the mantle to dry overnight.

My mind journeyed back to the first gifts of gold coins I left for Deniz's daughters' doweries. On that magical night, I had stumbled upon stockings hanging by the fire and left the coins in the girls' stockings for them to discover in the morning. I had also filled stockings on my very first Christmas Eve in Iceland. Recalling those moments filled me with a warm, nostalgic smile and sparked a brilliant idea. I had done very little stocking stuffing since that first Christmas Eve. Because I mostly entered through doors or windows up to that point, I hadn't encountered many stockings and either left toys by a child's bedside or piled them there in the living room. But now, I took one of the child's stockings down, filled it with a few toys, and hung it back on the mantle. The joy that surged through me was indescribable as I ducked back into the fireplace and ascended the chimney.

From that moment on, wherever I found stockings drying by the fire, I filled those of children with toys. In a few short years, the news had spread far and wide that the Christmas gift giver, by whatever name he was known, had a fondness for leaving gifts in stockings. And soon, wherever I journeyed, I discovered children had hung stockings for me to fill.

When Christmas Was Illegal

From the time that Columbus landed in the "New World," known as The Americas, in 1492, through the following hundred or so years, Christmas traditions from Europe did not make it to America. While I was discovering I could slide down chimneys, explorers in those lands were busy trying to survive harsh weather and battles with native peoples and establish colonies that people from Europe could move into to help expand the wealth and resources of whatever land they hailed from.

However, by the early 1600s, many colonies began celebrating Christmas as they had in Europe; it was a glorious patchwork of traditions. In New York, Dutch and English traditions were practiced. Scandinavian traditions took hold in New Jersey, Delaware, Minnesota, and Wisconsin. Meanwhile, German traditions gave me the name Kris Kringle in Pennsylvania and Maryland. These traditions all blended over the next couple hundred years and eventually led to the Christmas in America you now know. But we aren't at that part of the story yet.

No, this is the part of the story where Christmas, and my part in it, came very close to being wiped out in entire parts of the world. I could probably write a whole separate book on the subject. But since this is a book about my entire story, not just this part of it, I'll try my best to keep this part brief.

The trouble began in 1620. In September of that year, a group of people from a growing religion known as Puritanism set sail from

England to escape what they viewed as persecution in their homeland. These people called themselves "The Saints," and they brought with them a group of people who were not Puritans but skilled artisans who could help them build a life in the New World. History remembers The Saints by another name, one you probably know well: The Pilgrims. The Pilgrims and the craft workers, one hundred and two people total, set sail on a boat named *The Mayflower,* hoping to land in the city of Jamestown in the colony of Virginia. They got pretty lost, however, and landed in Massachusetts in December. No one else was there then, and they were forced to set up an encampment to survive the harsh winter. They faced bitter cold, poor, drafty shelter, and barely had enough to eat.

At first, those who were not Saints were too busy rushing to survive the winter to think about Christmas. But they started looking forward to it when they made it through the winter, and it became clear they would make it in their new home for Christmas time of 1621.

However, The Saints, led by a man named William Bradford, had other ideas. In December 1621, Bradford announced that there would be no celebration of Christmas in the Massachusetts Bay Colony. The Puritans viewed Christmas as pagan and, to their minds, even worse, Catholic. Because no one knew precisely on what day Jesus had been born and because it was making another day as holy as the Sabbath, Bradford said Christmas was sinful. Further, he said, it encouraged drunkenness and excessive eating, also sins. So Christmas was declared illegal, even for those who still wished to celebrate.

It made me sad I wouldn't be able to visit that part of the American colonies, but I could still go to other parts of the Americas and all across Europe, so I looked on the bright side. I had been around long enough at that point to know that things change and that Christmas would probably eventually come to Massachusetts.

What I did not expect, however, was that other places would take Christmas away!

One day in 1642, I was sitting in my cheerily lit study, reviewing a list of supplies we would need to restock on, checking to ensure I hadn't forgotten anything. The smell of old books and the crackling of the fireplace filled the room. I was just wrapping up this chore and thinking about heading to the dining hall for a snack when my door creaked open. Lisette came in and then shut the heavy oak door behind her.

"Hello there, my love," I said to her, my voice filled with warmth and affection. Then I noticed the serious look on her face and my heart skipped a beat. "What's the matter?" I asked, my voice tinged with concern.

She sat in the chair on the opposite side of my desk and looked across at me. "There's some trouble brewing in England," she said gravely, "trouble that will probably affect us and our mission."

I leaned forward, elbows on the desk, hands steepled together, and asked, "What kind of trouble?"

"Apparently, people are becoming upset with King Charles. He does not listen to the elected officials of Parliament and does whatever he pleases. Of course, people are mad about that. They want to be represented in their government, which is why they send people to Parliament in the first place. Now, it seems, members of Parliament are prepared to start a civil war against Charles and his supporters to abolish the monarchy."

"War is always terrible," I replied, "but I don't see what that has to do with Christmas."

"Because the people leading the charge are Puritans," Lisette replied glumly. "If they overthrow the government and put a Puritan-led government in place, they are going to outlaw Christmas in England the same way they did in Massachusetts."

"Oh, come now," I said, "you just said this whole thing is starting over the fact that the people in England want to be heard by their government! But most people in England are not Puritans! Even if the high-ranking officials in Parliament *are* Puritans, they must know they will have to listen to the people or end up having a war waged against *them*! Why lead a revolution otherwise?"

"I don't think it's that simple. I think this is their excuse to do as *they* want, just like Charles does. Other people in England do, too. The Puritans watch and judge them for how they live, worship, and celebrate holidays. The English people are pretty worried that if the Puritans take out Charles, they'll impose their beliefs on everyone else. Which will, of course, mean outlawing Christmas."

"But the people of England *love* Christmas," I protested, my voice filled with disbelief. "I just don't see them allowing it to be taken away!"

Lisette shook her head, her eyes filled with sadness. "I don't think they will have a choice," she said.

I sat back in my chair, rubbed my hands over my face, and thought for a moment. Finally, I sighed and said, "There isn't much we can do except keep doing our job and see what happens."

And that is what I did. Over the next five years, I watched, a growing lump of despair forming in my stomach, as, little by little, Puritan influence grew stronger and stronger in England. Though they did not yet have the power to outlaw Christmas altogether, they made it clear that they probably would when they had the power. Puritan-owned businesses would not close for Christmas and would force their employees who were not Puritans to come to work or lose their jobs. They commented to those who celebrated about how they were sinners and other hurtful things. English citizens, who had once celebrated Christmas with grand feasts and public festivities, began to celebrate Christmas more quietly and privately as it became more apparent that the Puritans were winning their battle against King Charles.

In 1647, the Puritans captured Charles and abolished the monarchy. They then won total control of Parliament and, just as Lisette had said they would, made the celebration of Christmas illegal in England and Scotland.

"I'm not sure what to do about my deliveries in England and Scotland," I admitted to Adelgard as Christmas 1647 approached. Or in the

Puritan colonies in America, either." We were in the dining hall, having peppermint tea together at one end of one of the long oak tables where we ate. It wasn't mealtime, so the large hall was deserted.

"Well, with no Christmas," he replied, "you can't deliver Christmas gifts."

"I know that, but the children expect it!"

"I know, I know," he said, patting my arm comfortingly, "but if Christmas is not being celebrated, that means you are no longer welcome. Plus, you would make those families criminals! You don't want to do that!"

"Goodness, no!" I cried. Then I heaved a heavy sigh and said, "You're right, of course. I just have to accept that, like in lands where the people are Jewish or Muslim or Buddhist or any other religion, the Puritans don't want Christmas. I think it's so horrid of them to *outlaw* Christmas when so many of their fellow citizens still want it! They are making it criminal to celebrate and be happy!"

Adelgard took a long sip of his tea. Then he set his cup down and gazed into it for a few moments. Finally, he spoke.

"From what I gather of these Puritans, they aren't particularly happy folks. You've been around long enough now to notice that unhappy people tend to want to make others as miserable as they are."

I sipped my tea and then stroked my beard, thinking about that. "Yes, that's true. But I also notice that keeping the human spirit down is hard. You know, my friend, I have just become hopeful again. Christmas may be illegal in several places right now, but I don't think it will be forever. I think if we wait a few years, people will rise against these Puritans and demand Christmas back!"

He smiled and raised his teacup in a toasting gesture. "I think you're right."

Christmas remained illegal in England for another thirteen years. Yet, as I had foreseen that day in the dining hall, the people of England, with their unwavering spirit, put up a mighty fight to reclaim their beloved Christmas.

On Christmas Day 1647, the first year Christmas was illegal, riots broke out in the English town of Canterbury. History calls them "The Plum Pudding Riots."

On that fateful day, the Lord Mayor of London made a visit to Canterbury to enforce the new law that outlawed Christmas. The Mayor, accompanied by his guard, marched through the streets, compelling shopkeepers to open their establishments and demanding the removal of any festive decorations.

However, the more forceful he was, the more the people of Canterbury began to grumble and complain, then shout insults at the Mayor. The tension escalated rapidly, and soon, the disgruntled crowd began looting the open shops, hurling goods about, and trampling them into the muddy street. One defiant shopkeeper stood outside his closed shop, refusing to comply with the Mayor's demands. This act of resistance further inflamed the crowd, and they surged towards the Mayor. In a matter of moments, he was overpowered, thrown to the ground, and trampled on. His guard was also under attack.

Somehow, the Mayor got back to his feet and screamed that this all must stop immediately and the people must disperse and go home. At first, he thought it worked. People quieted down and began to leave.

But then, to the Mayor's disappointment, two inflated pig's bladders rolled into sight, followed by people rushing in to kick them around. A couple of games of football (soccer to my American friends) had broken out.

Soon, people were again rushing around. The football games continued, and other people began hanging the holly and garlands back up. People broke out in song. The crowd was so unruly that the Mayor and his guard were forced to retreat.

In the spring of 1648, many of the people named as leaders of the riot in Canterbury were jailed, but more riots broke out over this, and the jailed people were set free. Within weeks, thousands of people signed a petition saying they wanted a king again.

England remained in a civil war until 1660. That year, the Puritan government was overthrown by pro-monarchy forces, and Charles II was crowned King of England. His first act as king was to restore Christmas officially. He also commanded Josiah Winslow, governor of Massachusetts, still an English colony, to restore Christmas there. Winslow refused, and Christmas was not legal there until he died in 1681.

Unfortunately, in England, even after Charles II made Christmas legal again, many people feared the Puritans would regain power and so didn't celebrate Christmas. Many business owners took advantage of this and stayed open on Christmas Day, forcing their employees to come to work. It would be a long time before Christmas came back to England.

But, as I said before, Christmas wasn't illegal everywhere, and in America, while all this was happening, a big part of my story was about to be born.

"A Visit From St. Nicholas"

I don't think the story of my life would be complete without telling you how the poem, *A Visit From St. Nicholas,* or, as you probably know it, *The Night Before Christmas,* came to be written.

It was Christmas Eve in the year 1821. I was making my rounds in Manhattan. I landed on the roof of a large house that had a name: Chelsea. Back then, Manhattan did not have nearly the number of buildings it does now, so Chelsea sat on a large property called an estate. Today, the entire neighborhood that sits on the land that was that estate is still called Chelsea. I could land on Chelsea's roof because, unlike many other houses, it didn't have a steep angle. It actually had some flat places.

I was at Chelsea to visit the Moore children. There were six of them: Margaret, Charity, Benjamin, Mary, Clement, and Emily, who had just been born that year.

I slid down the chimney, and just as I opened my bag to get the Moore children's presents, I heard a cough from out in the hall. I had slipped into the human realm without realizing it. Actually, I had realized it as I had landed on the roof but had entered the elf realm again to get down the chimney. Apparently, I slid back to the human realm at the bottom without noticing. As I've said, this happens occasionally, but every time it happens, it surprises me, and I lose precious time.

I looked up, and there, just outside the family room, was Mr. Moore, whose full name was Clement Clarke Moore. I remembered him from when he was a child.

Later, on another visit to the Moore household, I learned how it came to be that Clement was standing there watching me. Back then, before the invention of the whole-house furnace, it was common for people to have small wood stoves in their bedrooms so they would be warm while they slept. That Christmas Eve, Clement's wife told him she felt colder than normal before bed. So, being a thoughtful husband, Clement threw a few extra logs on the fire than usual. What happened because of this, though, was that while Mrs. Moore fell asleep just fine and comfy, Clement was a little too hot and couldn't sleep. When he climbed out of bed to crack the bedroom window to let some cool air in, he heard the famous "clatter" described in the poem, which was me flying in for a landing on his house. Shocked that he was seeing my visit, he ran downstairs, which is when I heard him cough because, as he told me later, he disturbed some dust as he rushed and got some in his throat.

As I spotted him in the hall, I knew I had little time to spare. But I wanted him to know that his presence was not unwelcome. So, just as the poem describes, I offered him a warm smile, a playful wink, and a subtle nod. Clement returned the smile, and I continued with my task, his quiet presence comforting company.

Before I was about to head back to the sleigh, Clement said, "St. Nicholas, wait!"

I turned to him and said, "Yes, Clement?"

"I think," he said, then paused, took a deep breath, and started again, "I think I would like to write about this incident. If you don't mind, that is. I think a poem."

"I would like to read that poem, Clement," I replied, then slipped back into the elf realm and went back up the chimney.

Two years later, on December 23rd, just as I was helping load all the gifts to prepare for my journey the next night, Tatasan, who acted as head of the department that kept track of important information from the United States, rushed in, waving a newspaper above his head.

"Kris!" he shouted, using the name most popular in The States. "Kris, you have to see this!"

I turned to him, thinking something was wrong. "Whatever is the matter, Tatasan?"

"Nothing! Nothing! The opposite of wrong! This is fantastic!"

He thrust the paper into my hand, and I looked down at it. It was that day's copy of the newspaper *The Troy Sentinel*. He pointed where I was supposed to read, and there I saw, written by editor Orville L. Holley, the following:

We know not to whom we are indebted for the following description of that unwearied patron of children—that homely, but delightful personification of parental kindness—Sante Claus, his costume and his equipage, as he goes about visiting the fire-sides of this happy land, laden with Christmas bounties; but, from whomsoever it may have come, we give thanks for it. There is, to our apprehension, a spirit of cordial goodness in it, a playfulness of fancy, and a benevolent alacrity to enter into the feelings and promote the simple pleasures of children, which are altogether charming. We hope our little patrons, both lads and lasses, will accept it as proof of our unfeigned good will toward them—as a token of our warmest wish that they may have many a merry Christmas; that they may long retain their beautiful relish for those unbought, home-bred joys, which derive their flavor from filial piety and fraternal love, and which they may be assured are the least alloyed that time can furnish them; and that they may never part with that simplicity of character, which is their own fairest ornament, and for the sake of which they have been pronounced, by authority which none can gainsay, the types of such as shall inherit the kingdom of heaven.

Below this introduction by Mr. Holley were the fifty-six lines that have become, perhaps, the most famous poem ever written by an American. I enjoyed reading the account and realized at once, although it had been given to the paper anonymously, that this was the poem Clement Moore had told me he wished to write.

Then I read lines forty-one and forty-two, which claimed, "The stump of a pipe he held tight in his teeth, and the smoke it encircled his head like a wreath."

"I don't smoke a pipe!" I cried. "Why would he put that in there?"

"Pipe smoking is very common," Tatasan replied. "Lots of fine gentlemen use tobacco now and smoke it from a pipe. He must view you as a very fine gentleman!"

"While I appreciate him thinking of me so kindly," I said, "and I understand artists should be free to use their imaginations, I'm not so fond of this depiction of me with a pipe. It might give children bad ideas."

I should mention that, back then, the terrible health effects of tobacco were not known. In fact, the opposite was thought to be true, that tobacco was good for health. Tatasan was right—a considerable number of men smoked in many forms: cigarettes, cigars, and pipes. But I never understood why anyone would willingly breathe that foul-smelling smoke into their lungs. It never seemed like a good idea to me, regardless of its supposedly medicinal properties. I had breathed in enough wood smoke in my life to have an idea that any smoke entering the body was probably not a good thing. I was uncomfortable being depicted doing something I felt was terrible that children might emulate.

"I understand, Kris," Tatasan said, "but so many people smoke already. I don't know if this will change much."

I sighed. "Maybe. I just hope they pay less attention to that part than the rest of the poem."

"You'll also notice he spelled Donder and Blitzen in the Dutch spellings *Dunder* and *Blixem,*" Tatasan pointed out, probably trying to change the subject.

"That's fairly minor. I suppose, since he also refers to me as St. Nicholas, he is probably a scholar of Dutch traditions. But I do have a question. It's about Mr. Holley's introduction. What is this name, 'Sante Claus'? I don't remember seeing that before."

"A small number of children and adults in America call you Santa Claus now," Tatasan replied. "I think that is just a misspelling. But I don't know as it's a name that will catch on."

"Interesting," I said.

"But it's a good poem, though, right?" Tatasan asked.

"Yes," I agreed, "it's fabulous. I hope lots of people read this paper. This poem deserves an audience!"

Of course, I had no idea how famous the poem would become or how many millions of people over two hundred years and counting would read it. All these years later, it's still my favorite poem.

Oh, and Clement apologized for including the part about the pipe the next (and last) time I saw him. He said he was looking for something that made me "more familiar and relatable" and the pipe did that, and the wording fit the rhyme scheme and rhythm of the poem. I, of course, forgave him.

Santa Claus

Although Christmas had been declared illegal in the colonies that made up the portion of America known as New England, in other colonies, known as The Middle Colonies, it was celebrated as joyously as it was in Europe. As I mentioned in the last chapter, Dutch, German, and Scandinavian colonists populated the areas of New York, New Jersey, Maryland, Pennsylvania, and Delaware. These people brought with them all the Christmas traditions of their homelands and shared them with their neighbors from different places. America became a patchwork of Christmas traditions blending to make one big, happy holiday.

Germans, for example, kept up the tradition of bringing evergreen trees into their homes and decorating them with pretty ornaments and candles. It would be many years before this caught on with other groups of people, but there it was in America in its very early days, just the same. And, of course, I already mentioned how they also brought the gift-givers Pelznickle and Christkindl with them, names which eventually evolved into Belsnickle and Kris Kringle.

Moravian immigrants, who were some of the first Protestants to flee what they viewed as religious persecution in Europe, settled in Pennsylvania and North Carolina and brought with them the traditions of paper stars to hang on Christmas trees and something they called a *putz*, an elaborate Nativity scene to be placed underneath the Christmas tree. Their contributions, along with those of the Dutch, German, Scandinavian, and English settlers, played a significant role in shaping the diverse and rich Christmas traditions we see in America today.

In addition, English settlers living in Virginia and the southern colonies never gave up Christmas like the English Puritans of New England had. These settlers celebrated Christmas by ringing bells, burning Yule logs, singing carols, feasting, dancing, playing games, and exchanging gifts. This festive atmosphere, combined with the traditions brought by other groups, created a unique and diverse Christmas culture in America.

However, the most significant part of my story was a blending of all these cultures into one new thing that became a huge influence not only on Christmas in America but also on Christmas the world over.

This new tradition begins with the Dutch colonists. The Dutch initially settled in Fort Orange in what is now New York state. Eventually, they moved south and purchased the island of Manhattan from the Native Americans in 1625. They named their new city New Amsterdam, after the capital of their homeland. The Dutch gift giver was Sinterklaas. However, Dutch children expected me as Sinterklaas for St. Nicholas Day, not Christmas.

Despite this, the story goes like this: England got into a war with Holland soon after King Charles II took power at the end of the English Civil War. Eventually, England won that war, and in 1664, Holland had to surrender Fort Orange and New Amsterdam to England. Fort Orange was renamed Albany, and New Amsterdam was renamed New York.

Soon after, settlers began arriving in both places from England. English children who had never celebrated Christmas mingled with Dutch children who knew all about Christmas and told the English children about Sinterklaas. However, because the Dutch children did not speak English very well, the English children walked away thinking they would be brought gifts by *Santa Claus.*

The problem is that the Dutch children would not have told English children they would get *Christmas* gifts from Sinterklaas. Also, once

England took control of the Dutch colonies, Dutch people stopped moving to those places, and those who were already there moved away or died, so there wouldn't be too many Dutch children left to spread the story of Sinterklaas. Still, the name Santa Claus came to be, however it was created, stuck, and became attached to older legends of Father Christmas that had survived the outlawing of Christmas in England. Eventually, many children believed Santa Claus brought their Christmas gifts.

At first, we didn't even know the name existed in the village. We tend to pay attention to things like that, but for a long time, the name that seemed to be winning as my official name in America was Kris Kringle, so the name Santa Claus slipped by us. I had seen the name when I first read "A Visit From Saint Nicholas" in the Troy Sentinal in 1823 but hadn't seen or heard it since. When we read American media, we saw the name Kris Kringle (early on, the first name was usually spelled "Kriss," but eventually the second "s" went away). And though I am very fond of my given name and all the other wonderful names I am known by, I often thought of myself as Kris Kringle during that time rather than Nicholas.

Santa Claus was a name spread by word of mouth, but Kris Kringle was being spread in print, so more people assumed it was the name of the gift giver. Three children's books were printed that used that name: *Kriss Kringle's Book* in 1842, *Kriss Kringle's Christmas Tree* in 1845, and *Kriss Kringle's Raree Show For Good Boys and Girls* in 1847.

Even more interestingly, the first time someone played me in a store was under the name Kriss Kringle. A man in Philadelphia, Pennsylvania, named J.W. Parkinson, had a department store, and in 1841, he had a man dress as me and greet children there. By 1846, he declared the store "Kriss Kringle Headquarters" and advertised it as such. No one would portray Santa Claus in a store until 1896, when the Boston Store in Brockton, Massachusetts, had someone play me there.

The second time I remember noticing the name Santa Claus was in 1853. That year, an English newspaper printed an article about Christmas in America, naming the gift giver Kris Kringle in Pennsylvania and St. Nicholas or Santa Claus in New York.

I read this and went to find Lars. I, as usual, found him with Lisette. The two were always near to each other since they were constantly bouncing around new ideas about ways to make everything run smoother and faster. I am forever grateful for how efficient they both are and how their fabulous planning and time management skills make our mission possible. I couldn't have hoped to have married a better woman for a partner or made a friend so incredible.

"Have you seen this?" I said, opening the paper and pointing to the name in the article.

"Santa Claus," Lisette said quietly. "I haven't seen that for about thirty years.

"Neither have I," said Lars, "but I like it!"

"So do I, actually," Lisette replied.

I looked at the name again and repeated it in my head a couple of times, then nodded, "Yes, so do I. It looks like I am going to be Santa Claus in some parts of the United States now!"

So, I was Kriss Kringle and Santa Claus for a little while in the United States. Slowly but surely, however, by word of mouth and, eventually, print, the name Santa Claus spread and took more and more hold. I am sad to say that what eventually cemented the name Santa Claus was the American Civil War.

During that war, a cartoonist named Thomas Nast drew pictures of me for a magazine called *Harper's Weekly*. In these cartoons, Nast took Clement Moore's "jolly old elf" line literally and drew me just about the size of my elf friends! And though I am unsure how he knew it, Nast accurately depicted me as living at the North Pole! I never met him, unfortunately, so I never got to ask him how he learned we lived there. Since he was imaginative, I suspect he didn't know we lived there; he just imagined it was a whimsical, faraway place to show me living. But, by showing me living there, it brought the idea to the people, so my home at the North Pole became common knowledge and was set into Christmas traditions forever. Nast drew thirty-three illustrations of me for *Harper's Weekly* between 1863 and 1886. They all made it clear they showed Santa Claus, not Kris Kringle, and they were all *very* popular.

One thing I didn't like about Nast's drawings is that they showed me favoring people from the Union side of the war. In one of the first two drawings to appear in 1863, I am shown wearing the stars and stripes of the American flag as a suit and handing out gifts to Union soldiers. While I appreciated that Mr. Nast was against the horrible practice of slavery that the Confederacy wanted to hang on to, I certainly didn't love the people of the Union more. I still visited the children of Confederate families at Christmas and the children of their slaves who had adopted the holiday. I hoped to teach them that there was no difference between them and hoped that when the children of the slave owners saw that, they would learn that what was being done to enslaved people was wrong and that one human should never own another.

With the end of the Civil War, Christmas had firmly established itself in America, with Santa Claus playing a significant role. This role would only grow in the years to come, eventually spreading beyond America and becoming a cherished part of Christmas celebrations worldwide.

The Bottomless Bag

Boy, I sure have told you a lot about history in the last few chapters, haven't I? I hope it has interested you because it's definitely been an important part of my story. But I understand how sometimes learning about names and dates can seem dull and dry. I've tried my best (and so has my wonderful collaborator) to make it captivating for you rather than boring.

But let's be done with history for a bit and talk about more magic! In the midst of the American Civil War, a time of great turmoil and conflict, and as Santa Claus was growing in popularity, one of the most important and helpful magical things to ever happen to me took place.

In April 1864, we were building an expansion to the village. We needed extra toy storage space, so a warehouse was being built. I was at the base of the warehouse, along with Tuka, Lars, and Adelgard, shoveling snow into buckets attached to ropes that would be hauled up to the roof of the building to finish covering it in snow as part of the insulation.

We had been shoveling for quite some time, and I needed a break to stretch my back and limbs. Ever since becoming a permanent resident of the Hidden Realm, I haven't gotten exhausted and have required little rest, but doing old-fashioned, hard, repetitive work for a long time still can give me muscle aches, and I need to stretch out. So I stood up, leaned backward to give my back a good stretch, and leaned my shovel against a large piece of ice jutting out of the ground. The polar ice cap floats on the ocean and moves around, and sometimes, this movement causes large chunks of ice to break and move and poke up, forming ice pillars, mountains, and hills. This frequently happened all *around* our village but never within its borders. We seemed to be safe from random breaks in the ice destroying our home unexpectedly.

Anyway, I turned to this ice pillar and leaned my shovel against it. The moment the handle touched the piece of ice, the surface shimmered like a pool of water, and the whole shovel disappeared into the pillar.

"Whoa!" I cried, drawing the attention of my friends. They turned to me, their eyes wide with surprise and concern.

"What happened?" Tuka asked.

"My shovel! I leaned it against this ice pillar, and it just disappeared!" I exclaimed, my voice filled with a mix of surprise and disbelief.

"Really?" Adelgard asked as they gathered around. He looked at the pillar momentarily and walked around the entire thing.

"Yes, I wanted to set it aside to stretch, and I leaned it right there, and the whole pillar shimmered, and my shovel was gone!" I explained, my voice filled with a mix of surprise and concern.

The three elves exchanged glances, and Lars asked, "Are we all thinking the same thing?"

"Fairy door," Tuka said.

"Definitely," Adelgard agreed.

"Yup," Lars said, "we're all in agreement."

"Fairy door?" I asked, confused.

Adelgard shook his head. "You know, Père Noël, you should eventually read *The Great Tomes*. I've only been telling you that since we met."

The Great Tomes were the official history of the elves, a collection of several large volumes of books that contained all of their history and knowledge. The original group of elves I met had their own, as did every group of elves we had met since. They had all combined them into one giant library. I had meant to go through them at some point, but there were just so many books with so many pages, and I had so much work to do all the time that I had never gotten around to it.

"Okay, that's true," I said, "but since I haven't, could one of you please explain what a fairy door is?"

"It's a gateway," Tuka said. "It connects two places. A fairy door can be in anything: trees, rocks, walls, pillars of ice, apparently, anywhere."

"But how do they get there?" I asked.

The three of them looked at each other, exchanging confused looks, and then Lars said, "Fairies put them there, of course."

"Hold on," I said, holding both my hands up in front of me, "fairies? No one has said anything about fairies."

"We don't really interact with them," Adelgard said, taking his shovel and drawing three slightly overlapping circles in the snow. "See, the human realm is here in this circle in the middle. We're here in this circle on the left, and the fairies are here on the right. We all meet in the middle, in the human realm, but notice how the elf and fairy circles barely touch."

"So we hardly see them," Tuka said. "We don't like to, either. Fairies are mean little creatures. They play a lot of nasty tricks. From what we can tell, the fairy doors are one of those tricks. A human will be out somewhere hiking or hunting or whatever, fall into a fairy door, and end up somewhere far from home, with no idea how they got there, probably lost forever."

"So, where does this one go?" I asked.

"No idea," Lars replied, his voice tinged with excitement. "It could go anywhere. Only one way to find out, I suppose." He took a step toward the pillar, his eyes gleaming with anticipation.

"Wait!" I cried. He stopped. "Is it safe?"

He looked at the other two, and they shrugged in response.

"It should be," he finally said.

"I don't think I like the sound of that," I replied.

"Hey, I'm not worried," he said with a smile, then stepped directly into the ice pillar and vanished. I gasped and held my breath, hoping it would be okay. A moment later, he stepped back out of the pillar, laughing.

"That was neat!" He cried.

"What was it like?" Adelgard asked.

"Where did you go?" I wondered.

"It was a jungle somewhere," Lars said. "I stepped out of a large tree. It was quite an experience! It didn't feel like anything, just like passing through a door. But as I stepped into the ice pillar, there was a long, shimmering white tunnel in front of me that, just as I walked into it ready to take a long walk, turned into a short, dark brown tunnel, and then I was coming out of the tree in the jungle. The whole thing took no longer than it would to walk through a door into a house."

"Incredible!" Adelgard said.

Tuka, though, said nothing. He had a thoughtful look on his face.

"What's on your mind, my friend?" I asked him.

"I think we can use this," he replied. "Wait here."

He came back a little while later with Erminlinda in tow. She was carrying one of the large volumes of *The Great Tomes*. This ancient book had maple wood planks carved with depictions of flowers and animals as covers.

"Okay," Tuka said, "over the years, I've talked a great deal with Erminlinda about elf history, lore, and magic. We've worked a lot together to combine all the different elf histories. That's why I brought her. She's got probably the best memory of lore ever, and I knew she'd know what I was thinking of. Erminlinda, the floor is yours."

She stepped forward and opened the large book to a page she had marked with her finger. "Tuka told me you found this fairy door and that he had an idea of how to use it, but he didn't know if it would work," she began. "But, according to this," she tapped the book page with her finger, "it definitely will!"

"Does either of you care to explain what you're talking about?" I asked.

"We can redirect the door!" Tuka exclaimed, his voice filled with the excitement of a breakthrough.

"Okay," I said, still not understanding. "So you do that, and then what? How do we use it?"

"Santa," Tuka said, using the new American name for me that was becoming popular among the elves, "how many trips do you make back here to the village to reload the sleigh each Christmas Eve?"

"Ten or twelve."

"Right. There are more and more children all the time! You're wasting valuable time coming back here to reload repeatedly, and it's also a lot of work for the reindeer to haul so much weight. If we redirect this fairy door, we will *never* have to load the sleigh!"

My jaw dropped in awe. The idea was so ingenious it was hard to fathom!

"We can use one of your sacks as the new end of this door," Erminlinda explained. "Elves have redirected fairy doors before to use them for their own reasons, and this explains how it was accomplished right here in this book! You can build the whole warehouse around this one fairy door, and then all the gifts can be arranged in delivery order and fed through the door directly into your bag all night long!"

"You can really do this?" I asked.

"Absolutely!" she replied.

"Well, then! Let's get to it! We've got a whole warehouse to remodel!"

It took another week, but we tore down part of the warehouse we had just built and made it large enough to enclose the pillar of ice that was the fairy door. We then built a long track lined with wheels right up to the door and set items onto it to test with.

Erminlinda, meanwhile, redirected the exit of the fairy door to the bottom of one of my many toy bags. It was a beautiful pine-green canvas with a gold drawstring. She explained that we could repeat this process whenever we wanted if I felt like carrying a different bag.

When it was all done, a crowd gathered in the warehouse to watch the first test. Elves lined the track to push items forward into the door, and I stood beside it with my bag ready.

"Okay," I said, reaching into the bag, "here's hoping!"

I reached deep into the bag and, incredibly, saw my hand poke through the ice pillar! I watched and felt as Tuka pressed a doll into my hand, and then I pulled back and drew the doll right out of the bag!

The crowd of elves cheered and clapped. The elves lined along the track pushed the gifts forward, and I reached in again, producing a rocking horse, a ball, and more and more gifts.

"It works!" Tuka yelled with a laugh. "This is great!"

"Yes!" I replied. "This is fantastic! Tuka, Erminlinda, you two have made our jobs better forever!"

Erminlinda clapped and bounced, her red hair flying about as she did so. Tuka came over to me and shook my hand.

The number of children in the world has grown since then, but no matter how many there are or how various the sizes and shapes of gifts they all want, I never have to worry because I can pull them out of my fabulous bottomless bag.

The Famous Red Suit and The Coca-Cola Myth

Nowadays, everyone has pretty much the same idea of what I look like: white hair and beard, red coats and pants with white fur, and a long hat. But that wasn't always the case. For many years, I wore various outfits when I made my Christmas Eve rounds.

You'll recall that, way back when I first met the elves and went on my first gift-giving trip after that, Erminlinda made me a beautiful green robe with brown fur. I wore that for a long time and other ones like it. But she also made me robes, coats, pants, and hats in all colors and styles! I had white outfits, green outfits, purple outfits, red ones, yellow ones, blue ones, and even some brown ones! She used fur from whatever animal she could find that had died of natural causes to line and accent the outfits, so some had gray fur, some had brown, some had white, some had white fur tipped in gray, and so on.

Because of this, when people would catch me at my work at different times, they would see me dressed in something different. So, if you look up older paintings of me, you'll see me dressed in various colors and styles throughout the years. But something happened in 1905 that set in motion a change that would be in store for Christmas tradition and me.

Christmas Eve, 1905, I was visiting the Sundblom home in Muskegon, Michigan, when, without knowing it, I slid back into the human realm. I was pulling a gift from the bag to put under the Christmas tree when my elbow bumped into a chair and knocked it over with a crash.

Thinking that I had plenty of time to set the chair back up, leave the gifts, and go up the chimney, I turned and lifted the chair back to its feet. Then I turned back to my work. That's when I heard a child's voice say, "Santa Claus!"

It wasn't the first time it had happened, and it wasn't the last, but it surprised me every time. I stood and turned, and there, in the living room, was little Haddon Sundblom, who was six.

"Haddon," I whispered to him, "it's good to see you."

He stared at me wide-eyed, his mouth agape. I chuckled and put a comforting hand on his shoulder, radiating warmth and love.

"What are you doing out of bed?" I asked.

"I heard a bang!" He said.

"Sorry. That was me. I knocked that chair over," I replied, pointing at the chair. "But it's very late, and I have a lot of other children to bring presents to tonight. Plus, it would be best if you had your sleep so you can wake up feeling good to celebrate Christmas with your family tomorrow. Why don't you head back to bed?"

"I left you cookies," he said, pointing at the plate.

This tradition started several years before when European children began leaving me various sweets and snacks as a thank-you gift. I still remember the first home I entered and found a plate of food by the fireplace. It was in Iceland, where they had long had a tradition of feeding elves. I entered the home, and there, on a little table, I found a slice of *jólakaka,* or Christmas cake, which is a delicious pound cake with raisins and hints of cardamom and lemon. Next to it was a little note saying it was for me as a thank-you for gifts. I was so touched I left a few extra special gifts in that home that year. After that, word must have spread because soon I found treats everywhere. In America, the traditional treat had become cookies.

"I see that! Thank you. I am in a bit of a hurry, so I can't eat them now, but I have some parchment paper in my bag. I will wrap them up and take them on the sleigh with me."

"Can I watch you go up the chimney?"

I smiled at him. "Of course you can. But it's going to happen quickly, so don't blink." I stepped back from him, hoisted my bag over my shoulder, and said, "Merry Christmas, Haddon!" With that, I slid back into the elf realm and up the chimney. To Haddon, I probably looked like a blur of color that disappeared as quickly as a blink.

Of course, Haddon Sundblom remembered that Christmas Eve forever. Years later, in 1931, the Coca-Cola Company was looking to run a printed Christmas ad to sell its beverage and hired Haddon, who had grown up to be an artist, to paint the ad.

Haddon recalled the Christmas Eve when he caught me at my work and decided he wanted to feature me with Coca-Cola in the company's ads. He got his friend, Lou Prentice, who did indeed look an awful lot like me, to be his model for the ads. Later on, Haddon would say that he got his inspiration from the now beloved poem "A Visit From St. Nicholas," but I knew it came from his actual meeting with me.

When Haddon pictured meeting me in his mind, he saw me in the outfit I had worn that night. For Christmas Eve, 1905, Erminlinda had sewn a beautiful scarlet coat, pants, and hat for me. The coat had gorgeous white fur around the sleeve cuffs and along the bottom edge, and the hat had a fur bottom to keep my head and ears warm in colder climates. The end of the hat had a little brass bell, and the coat buttoned up the front with several large, shiny brass buttons. I also wore a large brown belt with a glossy, rectangular brass buckle and brown boots that year. (Fun fact: that belt is not just decorative! You may have looked at images of me and wondered why I wear a large belt over a coat. Well, it actually helps me a lot! I do a lot of bending, lifting, and climbing on Christmas Eve, and the belt allows me to keep my back straight so I get less tired and sore!)

So, when Haddon did his paintings of me, that's precisely the outfit he painted me in. Coca-Cola's executives were thrilled because their logo was also red and white! This led later on to the myth that Coca-Cola *created* the modern look of Santa Claus. But that is not true. There are other paintings of me wearing red and white before Haddon's paintings because I had worn red and white outfits before, and people had seen me in them. What the ads did, though, is make this image of me *extremely* popular. The ads were so well painted, fun, warm, and lifelike that people across America quickly became positive that this was how I looked.

Sundblom painted me for Coca-Cola for 33 years. The paintings were so famous and beloved that Coke still uses some of those originals in ads and still features me in its Christmas marketing. In those 33 years, this image of Santa Claus became ingrained in American culture. People who dressed up like me wore that same red and white suit. I appeared that way in movies and TV shows. Other artists began to draw and paint me that way.

"As much as I love Haddon Sundblom's paintings of me," I said to Lisette in 1960, "and I am glad they are so popular, I do sort of miss wearing other outfits on Christmas Eve."

Since Haddon's paintings of me had made the red-and-white coat, pants, and hat so famous, I hadn't worn any other outfits since they debuted. I didn't want anyone who might see me at work on Christmas Eve to be disappointed or, even worse, think some imposter with bad intentions had broken into their house! I wanted everyone to know it was just me, friendly, jolly ol' St. Nick, bringing Christmas joy.

"Well," she said without even looking up from the map she was marking up with a new delivery plan, "you said you want to make sure everyone who might catch you at your work is happy, and they all expect Santa in red with white fur. It's too late to change that now."

"Yes," I said, "I suppose it is."

At least, that's what I thought then. One of my favorite developments in more modern times is that people who dress up like me are changing that expectation. Santa portrayers everywhere are rediscovering those old paintings of me in different colors and styles of outfits and thinking to themselves, "Oh! I want to wear that!" They then find fantastic tailors and seamstresses to recreate the outfits from those old paintings and wear them for families they see!

So, some Christmas Eve soon, if you wake up and find me leaving presents in your home, don't be surprised if maybe I am wearing purple or green or blue or even all white. I promise it's still me.

A Final Very Brief History of Christmas: Russian New Year and the Santa-fication of Europe

As I creep up on the end of my story (so far), I want to tell you about a couple of things that changed Christmas and my part in it that happened in relatively modern times.

In 1917, there was a revolution in Russia where the Communist Party gained control of the country. Communist ideas didn't allow religion, so they sought to wipe out Christianity. Eventually, Communism and Russia took over a huge chunk of Eastern Europe and formed the Union of Soviet Socialist Republics or U.S.S.R. In the U.S.S.R., there was no religion or Christmas, at least officially. The leader of the U.S.S.R., Vladimir Lenin, tried very hard to stomp it out. But, as I have learned throughout history, people love Christmas and want to keep it around. So, in the U.S.S.R., people celebrated it illegally.

In 1924, a new leader, Joseph Stalin, assumed control of the Soviet government. His regime was even more oppressive towards Christmas celebrations, banning the figure of *Ded Moroz* (my name in Russian) and the display of fir trees. Despite my sadness at not being able to visit Russia, I did not wish to make any families there criminals by bringing their children gifts.

In the mid-1930s, for reasons that aren't entirely clear, Stalin changed his mind and decided to take a less harsh approach to Christmas festivities. In December 1935, the Soviet government declared that New Year's Day would be The Festival of Winter, a non-religious holiday, and people could once again display fir trees (with a red Communist star on the top) and get visits from Ded Moroz, who they declared was Russian, not some outsider. And, of course, the people could feast and drink and celebrate.

This spread to all the nations that were part of the U.S.S.R.. In each country, Grandfather Frost, however it was said in the native language, would visit for New Year. I did not want to let any of the children down, so I began making an extra gift run specifically to those countries on New Year's Eve.

In 1991, the U.S.S.R. dissolved, and all the nations that were once a part of it returned to independence. However, many kept the old Communist tradition of the Winter Festival rather than Christmas. So even today in Russia and several other countries, I am expected on New Year's Eve rather than Christmas Eve. Interestingly, I am also still expected on the night of January 6th in some parts of Russia where people still practice the Russian Orthodox religion, which follows an older calendar and celebrates Christmas on January 7th rather than December 25th.

Throughout Europe in the 20th century, more and more local Christmas gift-givers began to resemble me. Of course, they had always been me but had not always been depicted as such.

But America's biggest export to the rest of the world is and has been its media and entertainment for many years. During both World Wars, soldiers from America brought ideas of Santa Claus with them to Europe. They got Christmas cards featuring me and, during World War II, probably got magazines from the U.S. with Coca-Cola ads with my picture. I'm sure Coca-Cola also sent ads featuring me to Europe, hoping to sell more of their drink in foreign markets.

People in Europe watched American television and movies, and there Santa Claus was every December. Soon, Father Christmas in England was less like a traditional English Father Christmas and more like the American Santa Claus. People in England even used Santa and Father Christmas interchangeably.

In France, where the most traditional gift-givers had been St. Nicholas and Le Petit Jesus (the Baby Jesus), Père Noël gained more traction and overtook them as the main gift-givers. He, of course, looked pretty much just like Santa Claus.

It happened over and over until, finally, most of the world, who had once not known or agreed upon what the mysterious gift-giver who came in the night at Christmas looked like, all agreed that he looked a lot like me.

Only a few places are left where I am not expected to fly in on a sleigh with reindeer wearing red and white on Christmas Eve. The Netherlands still expects, on the night of December 5th, Sinterklaas in his bishop's robes on his white horse, the only country that remembers my old friend Wulfgang. As mentioned, Russia and many former Soviet nations expect Ded Moroz on New Year's Eve or Orthodox Christmas. And, in Italy, for January 6th, a religious holiday called Epiphany, children expect *La Befana*, a kindly old witch who rides around the night of the 5th on a broomstick, leaving gifts for them.

I do my very best to keep up with all these changing names and traditions, of course. I don't want anyone to be disappointed!

The Mission Goes On

So there it is—my whole life story—well, most of it, at least so far. There is so much more I could have told you, but those are the significant bits of it. And it's not over yet! I have no idea how long I will be around (but I know it will still be a long time) and have no intention of stopping while I am here!

I have had to adapt because Christmas has changed a lot over the years. More and more children were born all the time, and cities grew larger and larger. At some point, chimneys mostly disappeared when furnaces were invented!

That's an interesting story I should tell you before I'm done. One Christmas Eve came where, once again, I could not get into every home where I was expected. Another sad Christmas where children worldwide thought they had been naughty and Santa had not come because of it.

"Waldhar," I said that December the 26th, "I've *got* to learn to pick locks!"

So, we set to it. I got very good at it, too. But the following Christmas, I still wasn't fast enough at it. I ended up leaving my last present just as the family in that house was waking up for the day! I could see the sun! I barely got out before they came to the living room!

That December 26th, I was sitting in my study, pondering how I would get into these homes faster, when there was a loud bang outside, and the walls rattled. I jumped from my chair like I was launched by a spring and rushed outside, along with just about everyone else in the village.

In a large crater in the ice and snow, there was a piece of rock and metal that had fallen from the sky. A meteor!

"Just a few feet in either direction, and that would have caved a roof in!" Adelgard said.

"Indeed," I replied. "We're all lucky we're alright!"

Waldhar, always the most curious of us all, walked right up and crouched to look at it. He made a little hmm sound and said, "Very interesting."

"What's interesting?" I asked, walking up beside him, but I saw almost as soon as I asked. Like the Northern Lights, the rock and metal were swirling with colors!

Waldhar looked up at me and cocked an eyebrow. "You don't suppose it picked up any sort of...properties as it passed through the lights, do you?" he asked.

"I'm not sure I know what you mean," I replied.

"Like how the lights guided us here the first time we found this place or how they ensure you get home every year."

"Oh, well, I guess I have no way of knowing," I said.

Waldhar heaved the chunk of debris out of the hole (it was almost as big as him!) and began to walk it back to his workshop. "Guess we'll find out," he said as he walked off.

He played with that rock for weeks. Then, one day, with barely a knock, he burst into Lisette and me's house and yelled, "This solves everything!"

"Waldhar!" Lisette said to him, perhaps more sharply than she intended. "Manners!"

He looked down, shuffled his feet, and muttered, "Sorry."

"It's okay, my friend," I said, crossing to him. "Now come sit and tell us what solves what."

Perched at the edge of a chair across from where Lisette and I sat on a couch, Waldhar brandished a gold key in our faces that swirled faintly with other colors.

"This," he said, "solves the lock problem!"

"It's a beautiful key," Lisette said, "but surely it can't fit into every different lock in the world."

"It doesn't have to!" he said, then reached into the bag he had slung across his body and brought out a miniature model of a door with a knob that locked. "Watch."

He showed us that the door was locked tight, then took the gold key and tapped it on the handle. There was a soft *click*, and he turned the knob and opened the door!

"How did it do that?" I cried.

"I don't know! It did it on its own. I had been working with the meteor for a while, hoping to figure out if it did anything since it passed through the aurora, but I set it aside to figure out if we could pick locks faster. I was putting this model on the bench to get to work when I bumped the handle into the meteor, and the lock just opened! Just like that!"

It wasn't the first time that something magical had happened to us at a time when we needed it. We found our home that way, but I was still amazed.

"So, I got an idea and just chipped the rock away to get at the metal in it. It's real gold, by the way."

"Gold from space?" Lisette asked.

"Gold is one of the natural elements," Waldhar said. "I'm sure lots of gold is out in rocks in space. Anyway, I got it all out, melted it down, and cast it into this key! It doesn't have to be in the shape of a key, of course, but it's fun and appropriate that it is, don't you think?"

"I do," I said and thanked my old friend profusely. I still use that key to get into homes today.

The key made it much easier to deal with skyscrapers and apartment buildings when those became normal in every major city on Earth. These huge structures full of so many families certainly made my job harder, but I learned pretty quickly the trick of how to deliver in cities.

When I enter a large city, I land on the top of the first building I plan to deliver to and enter it from the roof. I then deliver from the top down. While I am inside, the reindeer leap to the next building. When I reach the street, I walk to the next building and deliver from the bottom up, then come out on the roof, hop in the sleigh, go to the next building, and do the whole thing over again until I've delivered to every highrise in the city!

Toys, too, have gotten more complicated. Video games baffled us initially, and I had to send a whole crew of elves out to learn how to make them. Now, we have an entire building full of elves who know how to code, animate games, and build consoles! It's a vast, high-tech hall full of computers, TV screens, and electronic parts. It looks a lot to me like being on the starship Enterprise! We mostly stick to making and distributing simple gifts like sporting items, dolls, action figures, and plush toys, and I'll tell you why.

Over the years, as times grew better for people worldwide, parents saw fit to give their children gifts as well. Where once upon a time, one or two small gifts from me would be all a child would get, eventually, the gifts from me would be one or two of several! One thing parents did that eventually became a bit of a problem was write "from Santa" on a few extra gifts that really came from them, happy and unselfish enough to let someone else take the credit for their children's happiness. Imagine the joy in their eyes as they unwrapped each surprise, believing it was from me.

The problem, of course, is that not all families can afford all gifts. So, if one family has a lot of money and I bring, say, a basketball and a doll, they will also give the child a lot of other presents. Some, like video game consoles, are very expensive, and they will say they are also from me.

Meanwhile, a child from a poorer family will only get the basketball and the doll from me, and their parents may give them some new clothes they desperately need. That child may also have wanted a video game console and is left wondering why Santa doesn't love them as much as the child who got one.

I have been wrestling with this problem for years. I'd love to provide every child with everything they want. But even with all my magic speed and the speed of the elves, we can't make and deliver every child's every wish, especially since fancier gifts often take more time to make. Even magic, it turns out, has limits.

Sticking to simpler gifts rather than fancy ones allows me to spread love more equally. No one anywhere will feel left out if Santa brings them all balls and dolls and trucks and bears and action figures. But, if we make as many video games as we can in a year, we likely still won't have enough for every child who wants one, so some will feel left out and less loved, especially if their family cannot afford to provide one and give me credit for it. It's a delicate balance, ensuring every child feels equally loved and cherished.

So, if you are a family that can afford to add some gifts to what I bring and you choose to put my name on them, please look at that expensive gift and reconsider. If you feel like sharing credit with me, by all means, put "from Santa" on one or two extra, simpler items like a Barbie doll or a Batman figure. But I would appreciate it if you let your child know the expensive gift came from you. Also, it gives you a chance to teach your child that your family is more fortunate than some others, and they should be humble about it around their peers to avoid making them feel bad. Plus, this way, it's easier for all children to understand I love them equally. It's these lessons of humility and gratitude that will shape them into compassionate individuals.

Goodness, I sure let myself get a little preachy there, didn't I? Please forgive me. It's something I feel strongly about.

Right at the end here, let me say this: in this modern age of science and cynicism, in an age where a child can easily Google me and perhaps see a lot of stuff about how I don't exist and can't exist, know that I'm here. Maybe science can't currently explain how or why I exist and do what I do, but you're right to believe in me.

I know eventually, children grow out of belief. It's a part of life. They eventually succumb to their rational adult thoughts and decide I am more of a beautiful idea than a real person. That's okay because they then teach their children about me, and their children believe in me for a while. It's a perfect cycle of belief that not only brings joy but also teaches children about the profound joy of love and giving.

Even when you reach the age where you no longer believe in me, I keep believing in you. I have been around long enough to know that, no matter how hard times get, people generally stay good, kind, and helpful, and humans can solve any problem. I've seen it happen repeatedly. You may feel like the news is constantly feeding you the end of the world, but I promise you that people are inherently good. And, once a year, at Christmas, I keep doing my mission to show you that.

My sincerest hope, my Christmas wish, is that once Christmas passes, you keep that feeling of love and generosity to all and carry it with you throughout the year; you use that feeling to improve the world a little every day. If you all do that, then, one Christmas Day, we can all wake up to the best Christmas gift ever: peace on Earth and goodwill to all.

Merry Christmas!

—Santa Claus

The North Pole

August 13, 2023

Acknowledgements

Writing a book is something that is done in private, with no one else around. Sometimes just getting that work done is tough to do without some cheering on. But, once that book is written, it takes a lot of people to get it to the point where it's ready to be in the hands of readers. Both Santa and Matt would like to extend their thanks to the following people:

Brendan Low, Anthony Caruso, Nick Casey, Pat Spaulding, and Carol Nickles for reading the earliest draft of this book and providing input. Nothing comes out exactly right on the first try and early feedback is essential.

Jenny Robinson for providing the wonderful cover art. She was the first and only pick for the job.

Paul Sating for all the inspiration to get the work done. There's this belief that every artist getting a later-in-life start has that it's just too late to make it. Paul is a shining example that's just not true. If you enjoy horror or fantasy, give Paul's work a read.

Also, a big thank you to Cortney Lofton, Melissa Rickard, Charlie Johnson, Dan Pless, Todd Bristow, Bruce Kotowich, Jeff Harris, Chris and Kim Terry, Bob Smith, Madalyn Tanner, Rich Lange, and Robert "True" Seutter for their support. This book came along a lot quicker because of you!